ENCOUNTER WITH AN
ANGRY GUARDIAN . . .

Suddenly—and without explanation—the front of the ancient capsule began to open. No one in the underground chamber dared breathe. All eyes were riveted on the slow motion unfolding in front of them.

When the cover had moved back some 120 degrees, they could see a padded interior. A rainbow of wires, pads and things with unknown and unimaginable functions enclosed and criss-crossed the inert body of the alien.

One of the technicians screamed.

Another fainted.

All four of the alien's four eyes opened slowly, all at once.

Then they all heard the voice at the same time.

It was similar to the voices heard in dreams: Precise, sharp, but very far away.

"I am . . . *the* Guardian!"

Also by Alan Dean Foster
available now from Ballantine Books:

MIDWORLD

ICERIGGER

DARK STAR

THE TAR-AIYM KRANG

ORPHAN STAR

STAR TREK LOGS 1–9

BLOODHYPE

Alan Dean Foster

A Del Rey Book

BALLANTINE BOOKS • NEW YORK

For
Lynette Harrington
who lives around the corner

A Del Rey Book
Published by Ballantine Books

ISBN 0-345-25845-2-150

Manufactured in the United States of America

First Edition: March 1973
Second Printing: June 1977

Cover art by Darrell Sweet

I eat, therefore I am.

Such was the extent of the Vom's consciousness.

This had not always been so, but at the moment there was no way the Vom could become aware of it. The mechanical process of remembering required energy the Vom did not have to spare. All of the tiny amount of radiant energy from the system's sun that the Vom could convert was needed to preserve the life-sense.

To do this the Vom had assumed a special configuration. At present it varied in thickness from a few millimeters to several microns. It had done this out of necessity, millennia ago. How many millennia? The Vom did not know or remember.

It couldn't spare the energy.

The system hadn't always been dead. At one time this planet had harbored a modestly successful ecosystem: plants and animals from the one-celled to the very complex; vertebrates, invertebrates, things warm- and cold-blooded, gymnosperms, fungi, lichens, fliers, burrowers, crawlers, runners and swimmers. It was ruled by an undistinguished if moderately intelligent race. It had begun to die when the Vom arrived.

As to the method of arrival, the Vom could recall neither when nor how. Dimly it could remember a state of former greatness, of which its present self was less than a shadow. In that state it had dominated a thousand systems.

Arriving in this one, it had toyed with the local dominants. Its persistent and strenuous attempts at achieving

1

mental assimilation with another life-form failed, as it had failed a hundred thousand times before. That didn't keep the Vom from trying.

The race resisted with violence. It was consumed. The planet was rich in life-force of more primitive kind. Having absorbed that of the most intelligent beings, the Vom began on those less so. It worked its voracious way slowly through the ecosystem, down through the simple plants and fungi and even to the bacteria and viroids. The Vom was frighteningly efficient. It ate until the globe was scoured clean, clean. Then nothing moved on its surface or in its seas except wind, water, and the Vom.

Sated, the Vom rested for a long time. Then, using its always successful ploy of contacting another intelligent race and taking control of the curious vessels that would come to investigate, it broadcast into the space around it. Once carried by unwilling servitors to a new planet, it would begin the cycle of feeding anew.

But this time the Vom had waited too long. The race it contacted came, but they were strong—stronger than any the Vom had ever encountered. Its mental control wavered. For the first time in its well-ordered existence, the Vom panicked. It destroyed all aboard the approaching ships. A fatal error. The race was made aware of the true nature of the horror that had contacted it. The next time, it sent robot warships with a single prepared Guardian. One of their most powerful and capable minds, the Guardian was not understood even by its own kind. The Vom now tried to attract the ships of another species, but space-going races were scarce in this section of the galaxy. Those few who did send ships were warned away or destroyed by the robot watchers. As its stored energy was drained by these efforts the Vom grew progressively weaker, shrinking in power and ability. No longer necessary, many of the robot warships were recalled by their builders. There was a great war with another race tormenting the center of the galaxy.

Almost, the Vom escaped. A wild photonic storm tore

through that section of space. The few remaining robot controls were incapacitated. Even the Guardian itself was weakened. The Vom drew some strength from the strange life-forms that rode the storm, but. . . . not enough. In utter terror the Vom discovered that every space-going race within its reduced sphere of influence had died off or perished in the storm. Its mental collapse was hastened by hopelessness.

Now the Vom had plenty of time to reflect on its mistakes. It had used the planet too thoroughly, scoured it too clean of life. The system had been overemployed. Enough should have been left to reproduce and maintain a reasonable ecosystem, for just such an emergency. But the Vom had glutted itself thoroughly. Not a living cell had existed on the planet for a thousand years. Great as it was, it could not create life.

So, one by one, the higher functions were shut down, lost, as the great organic factory that was the Vom ran down, until only the barest flicker of life remained.

One day—the Vom knew it was day because of the presence of solar energy—a ship came down. It was not a large ship, being midway between courier and destroyer classification. But it was quite well armed and very functional, as were all the ships of the AAnn.

By rights the reptiles had no business in this part of space, on the fringes of the Humanx Commonwealth. The immensity of nothingness, however, made an excellent hiding place. Occasionally, daring scouts penetrated the humanx patrol cordon in search of unexplored systems possessed of exploitable resources—and sometimes on even less savory missions.

They nosed around, nowtimes finding something, now-times running afoul of a Church patrol (and then there would be empty places in many nests), rarely discovering something. All traveled without Empire sanction. Since by treaty with the Commonwealth this was prohibited, all such activities were of course quite illegal. However, since goods not traded for on a legal footing were exempt from taxation, the rewards for the AAnn businessman who backed a successful incursion were often enormous. In this respect the Emperor indirectly condoned such actions.

Rockets flared at the base of the small vessel. Being a scout, it was expected to have to land on planets not equipped with shuttle facilities. This was as expensive as it was necessary. Naturally, it could not land on interstellar drive (the AAnn equivalent of the advanced humanx KK drive propulsive system). The gigantic artificial mass generated by a KK or similar drive system could not impinge on the real mass of a planetary surface without something giving. Matter caught in such a manner invariably reacted. Violently. So ships used advanced shuttle-vessels to transfer passengers and goods from the surface to orbiting ships. A scout could, in effect, become its own shuttle.

The vessel set down close by the southern edge of the Vom. That section of the creature reveled in the sudden, unexpected surge of radiant energy. Within the metal capsule that rode the column of energy it sensed far stronger forces in the form of clean life-force. Almost, it reached out for them. Then a feeble spark of thought overrode primal instincts.

Not yet! Not yet! Patience! Besides, there was a more urgent need for the surprise gift of energy.

The Vom began to wake itself up.

Navigator-First Paayton RPHGLM was chewing reflectively on his tail, staring out the port of the captain's cabin. He spoke without turning.

"Well, Exalted Captain, *I* have surely never seen anything like it!" The bright red pupils were unblinking.

Exalted Captain Laccota SJFD scratched his belly where two of his ventral plates joined and turned to his principal scientific advisor. "Well, Carmot, this is where you start earning the credits Lord Ilogia—his scales be thrice-blessed!—has been paying you. You've sat on your tail for four time-lengths while we've sweated dodging humanx sting-ships."

Carmot MMYM was shorter than the other two. In fact, he was the shortest lizard on the ship. Externally he was rather a foppish specimen, addicted to brightly-colored body harness and (to the captain's mind) the decadent habit of dyeing his incisors pink. A million years ago he would have been a quick meal for an attacking tribe. Today, however, intelligence counted for more than fang and claw. He possessed a sharp mind, excellent recall, and was as devious as anyone else on board. Personally, Exalted Captain Laccota disliked him. Professionally, he held him in high esteem.

"I don't like it," said the Observer-First finally.

"You are not paid to like or dislike anything," offered Laccota patiently. "With the best will in the world, I remind you that you are paid only to estimate any potential profit in whatever we may turn up. We have definitely turned up something, here in this egg-forsaken system."

"I reiterate; I don't like it! I don't understand this at all, and I don't like what I can't understand."

"An attitude shared by many," said Laccota. "Tell us what we have here, Observer-most-competent-and-over-paid, and I will like it or dislike it for you."

"Very well, Exalted-flier-of-ships-by-the-tip-of-his-tail." Carmot nibbled idly on a claw. "When Observer-Fifth Plowlok first brought it to my attention, as we proceeded with our standard survey orbit, my initial reaction was the mental composition of a severe reprimand. Being young, Observer-Fifth Plowlok SFDVJUTVB has the usual tendency of young explorers to draw fanciful rather than objective readings from strictly prosaic instrumentation. This time, however, he was full accurate."

Carmot stopped chewing and waved in the direction of the glassalloy port. "We have out there, gentlesirs, an organic impossibility. An area of total living blackness that follows the contours of the land, every dip and rise, at a paper-thinness for several thousand square *cluvits*. Absurd, of course. There is nothing else like it anywhere on the planet. Nor, I venture to hypothesize, in this system. It is unique. It is utterly remarkable. It is impossible . . .

"Properties, gentlesirs, properties! It is not harmed or visibly affected by any kind of radiation we can generate. Possibly more sophisticated devices will be able to—I don't know. Nor is the energy so directed reflected. It simply disappears, as measurements of the underlying basalt seem to indicate. Somehow, in the space of a mere *section* or two of itself, it absorbs all radiation or otherwise removes it from the understandable physical universe . . .

"Two days ago, First-Geologist Onidd CRCRS and I left the ship to perform what we innocently believed would be the simple task of removing a few samples of the thing for analytical purposes."

"Didn't have much luck, did you?" murmured Navigator Paayton, still chewing on his tail and staring out the port.

"Hardly," said Carmot drily. "When I first attempted to touch it, it drew away from my fingers. I believe my sense of surprise was rather peremptorily expressed over the communit."

"Your command of the invective was something of a surprise," admitted Laccota.

"Um. Yes. After several similar attempts at different spots along its border failed, I walked off and took a long run at the thing. The lower gravity made such an idea seem feasible. It retreated completely, with incredible swiftness, just before my boots made contact with its surface . . .

"Geologist Onidd observed that it was noticeably thicker around its new edge. Therefore we established that it was folding back on itself and not performing some mystifying vanishing act. Onidd then removed his beamer and attempted to cut a piece from the main body. The results were enlightening . . .

"While it had retreated precipitately from physical contact, it made no effort to dodge the lethal beamer. Onidd concentrated his beam on one thin spot for several timeparts. No effect was observed. The thing did not cut, burn, smoke, or otherwise take notice of a sharp-focus beamer that can cut through most metals and heat armor-plate red-hot. I then joined the efforts of my own beamer to Onidd's. We might as well have been beaming at the sun . . .

"Now, as to the problem of its aliveness, about which there has been some question. If it is alive, it is a totally alien sort of aliveness that permits itself to be energy-beamed at close range yet refuses to allow a mere touch from a living being."

"Your conclusions," prompted Laccota impatiently.

"Even so, I believe it lives. It may draw sustenance from the sun, although I find no evidence of a photo-synthesis-type reaction, and certainly no sign of chloro-phyll. I do not see how else it can draw food. The basalt revealed when it drew back from us has been minutely examined. It exhibits no abnormalities and is in no way different from untouched samples taken elsewhere. I still will not attempt to say whether it is more animal than vegetable. It may, indeed, be neither."

"And your recommendations?" Laccota asked.

Carmot stood quietly for a long moment. "Raise ship and traverse parsecs as fast as this antiquated tub will go."

The captain's transparent nictitating eye membranes flickered. Even Paayton was sufficiently stimulated to turn from his extended contemplation of the outside.

"Indeed," murmured the captain. "And your reason-ing?"

Carmot said simply, "I have a feeling."

"Really! You have a feeling. My, my. Shell of females, an interesting entry to make in the log. Lord Ilogia will be most understanding and sympathetic. You 'have a feeling.' Rejected. First alternate proposal?"

Carmot sighed—a long, hissing sound, like a steam en-gine running down. "Tie into the nearest intersystem re-lay. Use long band. Break in if you have to. Contact the nearest planet where we have landing privileges—it will be humanx controlled, of course. . . ."

Laccota looked to the navigator. "Is there an appropriate place?"

Paayton's computer-trap mind turned businesslike. "Umm. The humanx outpost colony world of Repler might be . . . yes, I foresee no problems. A sparsely populated world, much of it still in the wild state, with a largely urban population and a considerable tourist trade. The largest shuttle station is very modern, but not equipped to handle much in the way of a naval force. No orbiting naval station. We have a fair-sized diplomatic mission there, with plenty of privacy and room. The weather is miserable, but most of the station is underground, naturally. It should be adequate."

"Contact them," continued Carmot. "Tell them we want the biggest freighter in the sector, along with five or six of the largest shuttles, two of which must be max-class, and about twenty miles of flexible harmony plating, with plenty of tow cable. Operators for all, of course. Also, at least one large, high-intensity beamer—it needn't be military; industrial strength should do fine. One that can provide a steady output without burning out every other time-length. Tell them to bring replacement parts, just in case."

"You plan to transport the thing, then?"

"If we can induce it to assume manageable proportions, yes. From hindsight-clever Paayton's description of the station we have at this Repler place, we should have facilities which can at least be expanded to provide a place where this thing can be properly handled and analyzed."

"Won't that be rather risky?" put in Paayton. "Attempting to work in secret right under the sensors of the humans and thranx?"

"Quite likely," replied Carmot. "However, until we know a great deal more about it, I do not wish this thing trans-shipped to a nesting planet. It is an unknown quantity of awesome possibilities."

"Another feeling?" said Laccota.

"That as well. I am suspicious of anything that can

survive on several thousand *cluvits* of bare rock, on a planet on which nothing else lives, yet clearly could support other life. I'm suspicious of anything organic that's thinner in places than my claw-tips, yet can take the continuous application of high-intensity beaming. Yes, another feeling."

"Your imaginings begin to approach those you ascribe to your fifth-grade assistants, Observer. Still, I see no reason to deny any of your requests. I'll leave that to higher authority."

"I think that's very just of you, Exalted Captain. And very wise."

The Vom had restored facilities sufficient to assess the beings who had happened upon it. The minds were simple, yet far from primitive. In its weakened state the Vom doubted its ability to control even a single one of the species, let alone the shipful. Now was the time to move, oh, so very carefully!

P-a-t-i-e-n-c-e. It had waited half a million years now, give or take a few millennia. It was aware of itself, and that gave it strength.

It could wait a few days more.

Russ Kingsley was in the mood for it.

And when Russ Kingsley was in the mood for it, he usually made out quite well. First off, he was almost classically handsome. He knew he was. It said so on his guarantee from the cosmeticians. They'd done an excellent job. It was one that few folk could afford. Kingsley's father, who was one of the five richest men on Repler, had given Russ the new face for his eighteenth birthday.

He was satisfied with his present 180 cms., although he wished the surgeons could have added another 10 or so. Still, no need to be greedy. The face was perfectly proportioned—inclined plane of a jaw, no-nonsense nose, sensuous thin lips, red hair with just the right amount of casual wave. He cut an exotic figure in sea-green foxfire fur vest over matching turquoise silks. His appearance was as good as money could buy. As good, he reflected, as any tridee star.

Honed in Repler's most exclusive gyms, the body was muscular without running to extremes. Though his appetite for gourmet meals kept the physiological techs at constant war with an incipient pot.

A pity they hadn't been able to do anything with his personality.

At the moment he was lolling in the main debarkation lounge of Replerport, eyeing the recent off-planet arrivals. A ventilator pulled the smoke from the Jimson Kelp in his pipe roofward.

Kingsley was a chap who liked variety. He'd already gone through most of the country beauties in Repler City. Some willingly, when his looks and money served; some unwillingly, where his father's name served.

The back-country types held little attraction for him. Too much trouble attendant to bouncing from small town to small town. And the food! Ghastly! Besides, the back-woodsmen were too remote to be impressed by the Kingsley name. They were apt to shoot despite thundering threats of retribution.

The passengers off the first ship had been disappointing. Thus far, the second hadn't provided anything better, with the possible exception of that blonde stew. Well, better than nothing. He felt in his jacket pocket to make sure the slip of paper with the number on it was still there.

A flash of color near the end of the first-class line caught his eye. He straightened, smiling. Well now, this was more like it!

The girl had paused at the gate to talk to the debarkation officer. That's why he hadn't spotted her till now. An off-planet citizen, obviously. Even better.

She was dressed in a bright yellow jumpsuit that clung to her like lemon icing. A simple band of some silvery metal on one wrist was the only jewelry. Not that a ring would have made a difference to Kingsley, but he preferred things simple to complex. A dun-colored bag was fabricatched to her right thigh. Jet-black hair was gathered together by a yellow band. It fell in a single thick braid to just above her waist, where it was held in place by another band and knotted. Kingsley pursed his lips disapprovingly. Minoan had gone out months ago.

Eyes deep blue, complexion deep tan, little makeup. The eyes were sharply slanted, cheekbones high and prominent. At least half chinee or mongolian ancestry, he thought. What he could see of the body was exquisitely proportioned, if not voluptuous. It deviated from the perpendicular in all the appropriate places.

The only thing that made him a little uncomfortable was that she appeared to stand a good five centimeters taller than he. He left the counter and moved to intercept her as she headed for the public transport park.

Subtlety was not Kingsley's forte. He grinned his best grin, every bicuspid and molar perfect (he had guarantees for that, too), and said, "Hello, stranger!"

The gaze she offered in return was faintly amused, otherwise noncommittal.

"Hello yourself, native." The voice was a husky soprano, with just a trace of terran accent.

Better and better! Everyone knew about terran girls, didn't they?

"Russell Kingsley, but you can call me Russ. Can I give you a lift? My rates are reasonable."

"Kitten Kai-sung. Sure. Are you passing anywhere near the . . ." she paused, "the Green Island Hostelry?"

"Green Island." (Not filthy rich, but well-off—not that it mattered much.) "I am now. Got any luggage?"

"It's being delivered."

"Well, then. Come along!" He tried to put an arm across her shoulders. She shrugged it off.

Uppity bitch, he thought. He'd change that quickly enough, as soon as he got her back to the Tower.

His hoveraft was a Phaeton Mark IV, the latest. He

was just a bit put off when she didn't acknowledge the gleaming hunk of machinery. Not even a little oooh! or aaah! Let her play it cool, then. He'd change that, too.

As soon as he was sure all doors were secure, he gunned the powerful engine and blasted away from the station, scattering grit and sand over several pedestrians.

The cloud cover was still fairly heavy, the air typically warm and damp. Now and then a light mist would not so much fall as simply appear in the air. Wood was utilized to a great extent on Repler, not only because the planet was blessed with tremendous softwood jungles, but because wood had a natural advantage over many metals. It wouldn't rust.

"You plan to be with us long?"

"Depends. My time is flexible."

"Business?"

"Very little. Vacation, mostly."

"Wise decision. Pleasure before business, I always say." He made a hard left and swung out of the downtown section, heading towards the harbor.

She didn't say anything for several minutes, but did take a long look out the back of the plastic bubble cabin. Getting a little worried, luv?

"The Tower's only an hour off," he said easily. "We've got our own island. Not so extraordinary when you consider that Repler is mostly islands, with very few open oceans; but Wetplace is unusual."

"Tower? Wetplace? We're supposed to be going to the Green Island Hostelry."

"Only theoretically, luv. Take my word for it, you'll prefer the Tower. It's got some interesting extras that would startle the management of a common tourist trap like the Green Island. Magnificent view from the top, and the privacy can't be beat. Can't even be broken, in fact." He giggled (that was one thing the cosmeticians hadn't been able to correct). "Oh, *everyone* who visits the Tower enjoys it!"

"I'm sure," she said drily.

"Especially some of the interesting devices I've had installed in my own quarters. Many of them custom-built, you know."

"I can imagine." There was a pause. "You don't intend to turn around, I take it?" she said finally.

He sniggered. "Not while I'm still vertical, sister!" He kicked over the autopilot and reached out. Not voluptuous, no, but the breast that filled his left hand was more than satisfying. Expecting at least a mild protest, he was surprised (and a bit disappointed) when she continued to allow him to fondle her.

"All right. That little island coming up on our left . . . the one with the climax vegetation."

"Clever, too," he grinned. Inwardly he was upset. Sine needles and bugs! Oh well, if she wanted to start that way . . .

"Your wish is my command." He drew away and swung the hoveraft in a tight arc, slowing.

"Your snappy repartee stuns me," she said, but he chose to ignore the sarcasm. Plenty of time to wipe that out.

He pulled into a small cove, dodging one floating log, and cut the engine at the proper moment. The Phaeton sank gently into the sand. He released the doors, letting her exit first so he could watch the tight suit tauten over her perfect backside as she stepped out. He followed.

Passing her, he unlocked a side storage compartment in the lee of the ship, started to pull out a large package.

"I think you'll find that for an inflatable setup this is rather exotic, including as it does a—"

"Don't bother."

He paused in his unwrapping, looked up at her. She was grinning right back.

"I hope you'll understand, but while you're not bad looking, something about obvious cosmetic jobs puts me off my tick. More importantly, initial psycho-emotional analysis indicates mental discrepancies confluent with your successive immature oeillades."

"Huh?"

"To summarize, you don't turn me on, buster. And besides," she said as she turned to re-enter the cab of the raft, "it's way past my check-in time."

"Just a second, pretty bitch. You know what this is?" All pretense at politeness had been dropped. A small object sat in his palm. She glanced down at it.

"It appears to be a Secun vibraknife, battery powered. Very efficient. It will cut many metals, most plastics, but not ceramic alloy and a few other things. Do I pass?" She was facing him now, hands on hips.

"Oh you are funny. But we'll change that. Since your face is not composed of ceramic alloy, or 'a few other things,' this toy is sufficient to make a very unpretty mess of it. I'd rather do this nicely, but if you'd rather be persuaded—"

"Okay, okay. I was only kidding, luv! I'm convinced." She came towards him, biting her lower lip uncertainly, and put both hands around his neck. Trembling, her lips moved towards his.

Kingsley was puzzled. He couldn't remember lying down. That blueness above him was unquestionably the sky, so he knew he was lying down. Yes, it was very blue and had fluffy white clouds in it.

The back of his neck hurt.

He sat up and rubbed it. The Phaeton floated a few meters offshore. The tall girl was leaning out of the cabin, staring back at him.

"Sorry, Mr. Kingsley! The tag next to the ignition here lists several private comm numbers. I'll see that someone comes out to pick you up before it gets too cold!"

Maybe he could make it to the craft before she could swing away. He got to his feet and started a mad dash for the beach. He got four steps before an excruciating twinge at the back of his neck crumpled him to the sand.

"Goddamn you!" he moaned. "What did you do to me?"

"Cooled your ardor!" she yelled back over the dull

whine of the idling fans. "Nothing permanent. Ask next time before you reach!" She closed the door and pivoted the ship expertly, flinging small wavelets onto the beach.

He sat staring after her long after the hoveraft had disappeared over the horizon. Curses did equal time with moans.

His sea-green foxfire vest was full of sand.

"Miss Kitten Kai-sung?" The clerk tried hard to keep from goggling at her. She nodded. The gangling adolescent was trying to shift his eyes from the computerized registry to her face without lingering on any of the intervening territory. He was failing miserably. Eighteen, maybe nineteen. Only a few years younger than she. But the way he was staring at her you'd think he'd never *seen . . . !*

She sighed. She ought to be used to this by now. The smile she gave him was seductive.

"And you say the room has a *nice* view?"

"Oh yes, ma'm! Best in the hotel! You can see most of the harbor. It's nice here. You're away from the noise of the shuttleport and docks." He hesitated, stared statue-like at the register. "Uh, if there's anything, uh, you need, Miss Kai-sung . . . ask for Roy. That's I. Me." He didn't have enough room in the tiny clerk's cubby for an honest swagger, but he tried.

She reached out and touched the tip of his nose with a finger, dropping her voice another octave.

"I *shall* keep that in mind . . . Roy." She turned to leave.

"Oh, Miss Kai-sung!"

"Call me Kitten, Roy."

The youth grew ten centimeters. Hate yourself, hussy, half of her thought! Love it, came the other half's reply!

"There's someone been waiting up for you in your room. He has diplomatic credentials, so I couldn't keep him out. Says he's an old friend. He's not human."

"That's all right. I'm expecting him. His name's Porsupah, isn't it?"

"Yes," the boy said in surprise. "You know him, then?"

"I've been his mistress for five years. Those Tolians . . ."
She rolled her eyes as the door to the lift closed, leaving
a fish-eyed clerk below. Somehow she contained her
laughter. By eventide 90 percent of the hotel staff would
know about the "stranger" in room 36.

Her apartments were at the end of the hallway. She
inserted her right thumb into the small recess at the left
of the room number. The door registered her with the
central computer and it slid back with the slightest hiss
from the pneumatic guiderail.

She had a small suite. It was tastefully decorated, just
extravagant enough to be in keeping with her supposed
income. A well-stuffed conversation round was at one end
of the greeting room, facing a broad ocean-view window. The being perched on it was the only thing out of
place in the room.

That worthy stared back at her evenly. It . . . he . . .
was just over a meter and a third in height. He looked
remarkably like an oversized, portly raccoon. The major
differences from the tiny terran mammal consisted of six
long, dexterous fingers, more massive forearms, and a
high, intelligent brow. There was no mask, the ears were
sharply pointed and proportionately larger than the terran look-alike, and the rear feet were webbed.

It also possessed a biting tenor voice. This it used at
her entrance, with practiced effect.

"Where the conceptualized clam excrement have you
BEEN?"

Kitten tossed her thighbag on a small table holding
local magazines and a vase of dampish green flowers.

"Conceptualized clam excrement . . . I like that one,
Pors. Your knowledge of arcane invective is always stim-
ulating." She walked across the room to the bedroom
portal and peeked in. "I see, wonder of wonders, that
my luggage arrived reasonably intact and together. Did
you overtip the bellhop again?"

"I was not here at the time they were deposited.
Doubtless they were transported by a mechanism."

"On this planet, in this metropolis? Don't bet on it." She began undoing the long braid. "This place has all the feel of a world that could still make a profit on slave labor. Oh, stop trying to burn holes in me! I was late because one of the local playboys, convinced of his masculine irresistibility, attempted to abduct me. He had visions of performing odd things on my precious body." The last gold band slid off and she shook her head, generating an obsidian waterfall at her back.

Porsupah said nothing, continued to stare at her. She reached over suddenly and tickled his nose. "Now, wouldn't that have upset you?"

Porsupah sneezed, attempted to slap her hand, but she drew back too quickly. "I begin to think not." She moved close again and tried to cuddle, stroking the fur on his spine.

Lieutenant Porsupah was tolerant, but being regarded as cuddlesome was one thing he couldn't quite put up with.

"Have you no shame, woman! We're not even of the same species!"

She ruffled his fur again. "You'd have a hard time, by now, convincing the hotel staff of that. Besides, you're as mammalian as I."

He couldn't help a slight smile. "Not by several points."

"Anyhow," she whispered huskily, "we could manage a little something, you know . . ."

Porsupah gave a loud screech and scrambled behind the circular couch. "Kai-sung, you are irrevocably, utterly, spiritually indecent!"

"That's the nicest thing anyone's said to me in four days."

The Tolian recited several rapid and extremely potent native curses under his breath before he tried again.

"Major Orvenalix had to cancel a scheduled meeting between the three of us and Governor Washburn. At last word he was waiting in his office, steaming at the joints. I strongly suggest haste to arrange yourself properly so

that we may be off before he sends the local constabulary
to fetch us!"

"Oh, pooh!" She tumbled off the couch, thumbed a
drink from the portabar. "I can handle the Major. Want
something?"

"As you are well aware, none of the effects alcohol has
on the Tolian system are in the least pleasurable. Fermented *Ropus* lymph, now—"

"Okay, have some of that, disgusting as it sounds."

"I will not imbibe when late for assignment."

"Foo. You're worse than impossible. And stop worry-
ing about Orvy-Dorvy. We're old friends."

"That may well be. The Major has an eye for a well-
turned ovipositor. However, if I may so delicately point
out, you are decidedly deficient in that area, however well
compensated you may be in others. And I want to hear
you call him 'Orvy-Dorvy'."

"Thanks . . . I think." She sipped the pink and yellow
liquid the machine had prepared. "Still, there's a way
of caressing the soft spot where thorax and b-thorax
meet that—"

"Aghhhh!" The Tolian covered his eyes. "Disgusting,
obscene, profane! No morals. No morality at all! If it
were possible you would consider intercourse with a
rock!"

"All right, all right, calm down! Listen, Pors, I've seen
you with a few under your pouch, you sly tail-tickler,
and you—"

"No more! Desist! Cease!"

"And stop throwing your fuzzy carcass all over the
furniture or you'll build up a charge that'll shock the
first diplomat you shake hands with two meters sunward!
If you insist on throwing a fit, throw a stationary one."

Porsupah tried a new tack. He ignored her while he
rehearsed the explanation he would have to present to the
Major. Ideas did not come rapidly to mind.

He was finally making some progress when his thoughts
were scattered by a shrill, protesting voice from the nether
depths of the bathroom.

"And I do *so* have morals!"

Outwardly a quiet, intense person, Major Orvenalix, the commander of Repler's tiny military force, was capable of violent displays of emotion. These he kept private. It wouldn't do for the members of Repler's governing council to know to what extremes their stubbornness could push him. They also did not know that the peaceful commandant held an equal and much more impressive rank in the intelligence arm of the United Church.

Repler warranted an intelligence operative of Orvenalix's stature because of the AAnn Imperial Enclave, several hundred kilometers to the south across open seas. The Enclave was the vestigial remnant of early altercations between the Commonwealth and the Empire over planetary claims. The AAnn hadn't really wanted Repler, but it was a matter of self-respect that they dispute all territorial claims by other races.

Johann Repler's claim eventually proved the strongest. The AAnn demanded, however, and were granted sovereignty over, a small area south of the eventual capital. This was done to speed colonization and to promote a harmonious settlement. Actually, the Commonwealth had argued against the idea, the Church had been noncommittal, and the humans and thranx already settled positively blasé. After all, the great majority of the planet was unexplored, and the AAnn could probably have established a secret station anyway. Why not be generous and give them one?

When the AAnn found out that they wouldn't be allowed to use the interspace facilities at Repler City and that the largest island in their Enclave was insufficiently bedrocked to support a shuttle station of any size, they almost gave up the Enclave idea in disgust. But to refuse after having won the concession would have been twice as bad. It would have made the AAnn diplomats who had arranged the treaty look ridiculous. This would be fatal to certain parties. Those same parties made sure that an elaborate facility was constructed on the main land mass. At least the oceanologists, a group that most AAnn considered congenital idiots, were happy. The AAnn home world and most of its colonies were desert-type planets. Those assigned to the Repler station were, with the exception of the scientists, very unhappy reptiles.

Major Orvenalix sat in his thimble-shaped chair and stared across at Kitten and Porsupah. At the moment the Major was employing his mid-pair of limbs as a second set of hands. In imitation of a human habit, the thranx was tapping all four sets of claws on the table in front of him. The twelve digits made a considerable racket.

The Major was about average height for a mature male thranx, standing about midway between Kitten's and Porsupah's. His thorax was unusually broad and powerful. The black and silver harness reflected his occupation rather than personal tastes, which were less conservative. Also the result of his occupation was a premature purpling of the chiton, although his antennae were straight and strong. And the great compound eyes sparkled as brightly as those of any youth.

The tapping stopped. The resultant silence was louder. Orvenalix spoke quietly.

"Well! The magnificent, munificent Lieutenant Kai-sung has deigned to grace Operations with her presence!" The Major bowed ironically. That is, he inclined his head and b-thorax. Encased in bodies of unyielding armor, no thranx could manage a really smooth bow.

"Burn it, Orvy!"

"You will address me as becomes my rank, Lieutenant!" he roared, smacking the table hard with one truhand.

"Yes sir," she replied in mock-military tones. "Major . . . Orvy."

"YOU WILL . . . !" Orvenalix sighed and relaxed in his seat. "Never mind. I can see you haven't changed one micron."

"You're the second person today who's said that. Seriously, sir, what exactly is the situation? I haven't seen you in over a year, but when you were lecturing at the

Academy you were nowhere near this tense. You can't tell me a year's hitch on a backwater planet has gotten to you that much!"

"You leave out many ramifications of which you remain uninformed, Kitten. However, before we go into *my* problems, consider this. You were ordered here for an assignment which required that you remain mildly active and controversial. *Mildly.* A moderately wealthy young lady, independent, spoiled, and apt to stick her nose into anything hinting of new thrills. Here to enjoy the delightful sun, fun, boating, fishing, and cheap souvenirs of exotic Repler."

"You sound like a travel brochure, Major."

"In my public capacity such banalities are occasionally called for. My nest-mother would be ashamed, but fortunately Eurmet is many parsecs away . . .

"Instead of making a nice, smooth arrival, you forthwith take off, in full sight of a busy shuttleport crowd, with the most notorious, spoiled young human this backwater capital has to offer. He may not be in the same class with his counterparts on Armela, Trix, or Perth, but around here he is noticed. You next turn up at the family estate-lodge in the most exclusive section of the capital and turn over the keys of this young man's expensive hoveraft to the chap's valet—his talkative valet. You order a public transule and take leave of this bemused servitor, off-handedly mentioning that his master may be found languishing by his lonesome on an island at such and such coordinates. Whereupon you return to the city and breeze into your hotel, blissfully certain, I suppose, that you have performed all this while leaving the general population in total ignorance."

Kitten appeared genuinely contrite. "I apologize, sir. How would I know the valet would spread it all over town? I didn't even realize who he was until the conversation had passed the point of no return. I'd planned to slip the keys under the door with a note explaining that . . ."

She broke off. Orvenalix shook his head in disgust.

"It all would have been so much simpler—not to mention better for your cover—if you'd merely gone along with the gentleman, performed the simple act of non-reproductive copulation with him, and allowed him to escort you back to the hotel."

"It is stated categorically," said Kitten, "that the Egg which gorges itself too early will deny its offspring."

"You are being impertinent, but if he was *that* bad . . . You always were up on your Saduriquil, soft-angles."

"Why Orvy! You still remember my pet name! Now that you've gotten all that off your thorax, why not relax and tell us why we've been pulled off our post-graduate work and plunked down here in the midst of savage pisces and piscean savages?"

"The good Governor would not care-for-that-tone," Orvenalix grinned.

"Say, how did you know I was doing post-grad work?" yelped Porsupah.

"I picked your pocket back at the hotel. Before I went in to change. Your school relief notice was in there, along with relevant material. Hardly consistent with *your* cover, Pors! Tch!"

"Not only morals!" said the seething Tolian. "No scruples, either!"

"That's an insult! I put the wallet back, didn't I?"

There was a long silence. Finally, unable to stand the suspense, Porsupah put a paw into the pouch under his belt to make sure. . . .

Orvenalix put a truhand over his mouth to cover the slight fluttering of mandibles that signified laughter among the thranx.

"All right," the intelligence officer said. "Let us observe. Repler is backward in many ways, sure. It has a limited population, true. But its shuttle and spacecom facilities are modern and well-manned—very true. Major industries are tourism and exotic woods, but the main income is derived from Repler City's use as a busy transfer point for interstellar shipping. It's the only habitable planet between Fluva and Praxiteles as you drive down the Arm. And it's still fairly close to the center-ward systems."

"A good place to trade around," agreed Porsupah.

"While also avoiding major tariffs on planets of desti-nation. True. Nothing like the business Terra, Hivehom, or Drallar do, of course. But the merchants here make a good living, and business is growing steadily if not spectacularly."

"I've read the manual," Kitten said drily.

"Fine! Good!" Orvenalix reached into a drawer and removed a small vial of glass . . . no, quartz . . . with a pressure lock twice as big as the container, and a small bit of black board. Kitten and Porsupah slid their chairs closer.

Orvenalix keyed the lock and sprinkled, very carefully, a few grains of white crystal onto the board.

"Since you've both, presumably, 'read the manual,' per-haps you can tell me what this is?" Both junior officers leaned forward.

The Tolian sniffed once, gently. "Odorless. Clear, rhombohedric crystals with a glassy luster." The Tolian crushed one of the largest pieces to powder in a sharp, trimmed claw. He sniffed again, careful not to inhale the dust. "Concoidal fracture, no odor released on pulverizing . . . yes, I think I know what it is, Major." He turned and looked at Kitten. "The lines of fracture turn blue, they turn blue."

Her eyes widened, and she couldn't help but whisper when she spoke to Orvenalix. "Bloodhype. Very high grade, too, if the fracture line turns that dark."

The antennae dipped slightly. "Almost pure. Also known as jaster, brain-up, phinto, silly-salt, and many other names the mere mention of which are sufficient to inspire thoughts of regurgitation among intelligent, feeling beings."

"I thought I read that the Hyperion forests on Annubis were sterilized and wiped out ten years ago," Kitten said.

"As indeed they were," the intelligence officer con-tinued. "Naturally, that was the first place the Service checked. We found nothing to indicate that any of the plants had survived the holocaust. At that time it was believed that the Hyperion plant could grow only on Annubis. Transplanting was attempted for scientific purposes, but the seedlings and mature plants died rapidly as soon as they were removed from the planet. Fertilized seeds likewise transshipped did not sprout. In wiping out the supply it turned out that the species had been effectively exterminated for *all* purposes!"

"I wouldn't imagine anyone raising a fuss over *that*," said Porsupah.

"Other than a few masochistic botanists, no one did."

"It seems, though, that someone, somewhere, has gotten hold of some seeds and found a way to make them sprout, and worse, reproduce."

"What sort of . . . of creature, would want to restart the traffic in bloodhype?" said Kitten, shuddering.

"Soft-angles, I remember you to be a brilliant student. Someday I hope you will make an even better agent, but in many ways you are still an immature grub. The galaxy contains a high volume of pure loathsomeness. Of which I have seen far more than is good for one's sleep. There are plenty of beings nominally labeled 'intelligent' who would sell their own eggs, and worse, for a few credits. The thing here that makes me marvel is not the perpetrators, but their science.

"I don't have to tell you what bloodhype addiction does. These new users display the same symptoms and reactions as those of over a decade ago. Which means that this new strain is at least as powerful as the original. It affects any living creature with a complex neural system and circulating liquid in its body. This includes every known intelligence, with the exception of a few silicon-based primitives on restricted planets. Direct injection is the most common method of application, but inhaling the drug in sufficient quantities is also effective.

"Concentrating on the neurons, the drug produces an extremely pleasurable sensation. The thing about blood-hype is that most drugs work only on the mind, by distorting and affecting the images it creates and the information it receives. Bloodhype, on the other hand, is more in the nature of direct neural stimulation. In other words, instead of producing distortions in the information-interpreter (the brain), the original information is distorted right at the beginning, at the original nerve pickups in hands, feet, liver—everywhere the blood can carry it. The effect has been described many ways. One addict said it was like being the highest-pitched wire on a stringed instrument. It's many, many times more powerful than anything that works just on the mind, acting as it does directly on the nerve cells rather than the brain. A moderate dose produces a 'fire-fit', an intense burning sensation that seems to add to the overall pleasure.

"Withdrawal symptoms commence anywhere from 60hh or 72 t-standard hours after the last injection. Coordination begins to go, accompanied by a speed-up in involuntary muscular reactions. Breathing can speed up or slow, as can the heart and other self-regulating muscles. The senses are badly confused and feed false reports to the brain, which is itself undergoing severe emotional changes, from depression to exaltation and so forth. The body goes downhill like an unhatched egg with insufficient yolk. It's possible to be in excellent physical shape and be dying—until the final moment, when everything seems to jump on you at once.

"You go slowly insane, aware of what's taking place all the time. 'Dying by inches,' I believe a terran author called something far less extreme. The only way an addict can survive, once hooked, is if the medics can get to him fast. A lot of very complicated and expensive equipment supports the being's nervous system until the drug has burned itself out. Very painful and not always successful. If the brain itself has been too badly damaged, nothing can be done. In such cases, mercy killings are not unknown.

"If 120hh or 144 t-standard hours have passed, there is a ninety-eight and something percent chance of an excruciatingly painful death occurring. In such cases even the best of medical treatment is useless. There is, of course, nothing like a simple antidote."

"And the shipments are coming through Repler?" said Kitten.

"It is thought to be so. We intercepted one, just one, by accident. No persons were taken. The best evidence we have is that every planet where new addicts have appeared was visited shortly before by a vessel that stopped to change or exchange cargo on Repler. There are a few suspects here, whom we're being very careful not to warn off. And this is not the only planet that's being carefully checked out. But at this stage it seems like Repler is the best of several thin possibilities—Everything about the operation suggests professional planning with plenty of brains behind it. There's a lot of experience behind this setup."

"I don't wish to minimize our abilities, sir," interrupted Kitten, "but if all this is true, why send for two fairly inexperienced agent-students instead of a hundred pros?"

"One, your very inexperience is your best asset. You will be equally unknown to the runners. The one thing we fear more than anything else is that they might become aware that we suspect their operations here. And with something of this magnitude running smoothly, it's a likely bet that the pros handling things would stay quiet and shut down until they could shift their base elsewhere. We don't want to start over again somewhere a hundred parsecs down the Arm. We might not be fortunate enough to intercept another shipment. And the traffic hasn't assumed the proportions . . . yet . . . where an investment of that kind would justify the risk. A large sweep would be likely to catch up a lot of the small fry. The moguls usually manage to slip away and start raising hell somewhere else. You two stand a chance of cutting through a lot of opaque membrane and latching onto them before they have a chance to get suspicious. At least, that's the theory. If you're caught, the worst that can happen is we lose two agents."

"You frame things so delicately," murmured Porsupah.

"The covers we've prepared for you don't require a lot of effort to maintain. Barring," he said, staring hard at Kitten, "unforseen complications! Lieutenant Porsupah is listed as a wealthy tree-farmer's nephew from Tolus Prime. Your covers provide you with a number of common interests. A shared interest in mildly dangerous sports, for one thing. It means you have reasons for wanting to jet all over the place—and incidentally, for carrying sidearms. Sport pistols. Licenses will be issued to the both of you on your way out. Your 'sporting weapons' each pack a much greater wallop than their appearance will suggest. So for Hive's sake, be circumspect with them—Look around, take your time, and honestly try to have fun. I don't believe in miracles, but 'erecting the proper superstructure facilitates acquiring interior trappings.' "

"Mathewson, twenty-third edict, section four," said Kitten.

" 'Accidents and miracles will happen if you can find the proper place in space'; yes, you're right, my dear," replied Orvenalix. "I never knew theology interested you."

"Only the juicy parts. For example . . ."

Porsupah elected to chew the upholstery.

Malcolm Hammurabi was counting his money. The awkward fact that he didn't have it yet failed to interrupt the pleasure he took in the mathematics.

It had been the kind of trip that ship-masters drink over: no muss, no fuss, and plenty of profits. Even the drive had been trouble-free. Who'd have thought that those attenuated seals on Largess would be crazy for imported *alva*—let alone Replerian *alva*. Granted, though, the stuff was tasty enough. Even if Rodriguez wouldn't program the stuff for the galley. Mal's share of the profits would be, well, healthy. Might even be enough to refinish that verdammt upper right quarter of the *Umbra's* KK drive projector screen. Not that it was an essential job. . . not yet. But it would boost her favorable energy conversion ratio by a good thirty percent. That would convert to a savings of, oh, so and so much in ignition radioactives. Not to mention reducing wear and increasing efficiency in the engine systems.

He'd been told, often, that his habit of making a personal, solitary survey of ship's cargo the night after it had been shuttled down was just a little peculiar. The excuse he offered in return was that he wanted to be certain of the cargo's proper alignment for redistribution, etc., etc., right up to the moment of transfer.

In actuality, the fascination of standing alone with tons and tons of goods from the far reaches of the galaxy, piled high in rainbow-hued plastic and metal containers, was one he had carried from childhood. Then he used to wander through similar warehouses (which towered so much greater in his childhood memories) and dream of the days he might visit planets with magic names like Terra, Hivehom, Almaggee, Long Tunnel, Horseye and Entebbe.

He'd had little idea that one day he'd be transporting similar goods himself. Too often the planets had proven dull and unattractive. But there was enough spice in the life to make things interesting. (Besides, you crazy hypocrite, you hated pro ball. Being the best goalie who ever maintained parallax with a ball was hardly fit epitaph for a man.)

Anyhow, it was important that the luxury goods be easily accessible for tomorrow, in case that old pirate Chatham and the others wanted an early look.

A good percentage of the cases were emblazoned with the CK crest of arms, customs stamps, impression of destination and planet of origin. A few were consigned to small dealers on Repler, some to members of the crew, and a number were sealed in the aquamarine of the Commonwealth. There was even one small crimson case of holy goods for the Church. Mostly biochemical and oceanographic instrument parts, plus a few specimens of Largessian life.

Another section of the gigantic warehouse was filled with a massive shipment headed off-planet. Idly, he wondered who'd pulled off that job.

Old Chatham's success had been due in large part to his policy of hiring free-lance cargo vessels or those of small companies to transport his goods, rather than acquiring his own fleet. It was a risky way to do business, since he was entirely dependent on the will of men who were not beholden to anyone. Cargos could disappear with sobering swiftness on short or nonexistent notice. And a merchant or trader who operated in such fashion built nothing in the way of transportation equity.

At the same time, the system offered unequaled flexibility without fear of loss in manpower or ships. Some few men could make a success of the arrangement, while those with a huge investment in ships and men might go broke in spectacularly short periods of time. Chatham was one who'd spent a lifetime mastering the first system.

The huge outgoing shipment sat there, its noble immobility staring back at him. Maybe Scottsdale had landed the job. Or crazy Alapka N'jema. He'd heard rumors that Al's ship, the *Simba,* had been operating this far out. Although the last he'd seen of her she'd been headed Centerward. There was always the possibility that the merchant or merchants involved hadn't contracted with anyone yet.

And the possibility that they had their own ship, idiot.

Still, it was an appealing thought. If the cargo were available and he could sign it, maybe they'd give him an advance on estimated profit. That, coupled with what he would make off the Largess expedition, ought to provide enough to refinish the entire screen. Plus getting an ultrawave booster for Ben, the *Umbra's* comm operator. Ben would give his left arm and part of his soul for even a pre-war booster. For a new one from, say, GC, his shouts of pleasure would be heard all the way to Alpha C.

The silver plastic of an especially bright casing caught his eye. He saw himself reflected in the moulding and smiled, running the revised balance for the ship over again in his mind.

Reflected in the plastic, Mal Hammurabi was a big man. Not particularly tall, he was structured much like a number twelve symbo-speech printed dictionary—unabridged. Or a collection of children's blocks, tossed together in a haphazard rectangular shape and dipped in half-wet glue. Sandy-brown hair was cut square in back and receded slightly from the high forehead, which overshadowed deep-set amber eyes. The remainder of that face was an insane collection of rough angles, juts and points. The only honest curve in the whole assemblage was the thick walrus mustache which drooped from beneath the nose. Combined with a rather remarkable build, the ship-master looked like a surreal cross between a land-tank and a basset hound.

Equally incongruous was the group of peppermint sticks which protruded from the left pocket of his leather jacket. Hammurabi neither smoked nor flashed. His vices were confined to milder liquors such as ale, fine ones like brandy, and sweets . . . not all of them peppermint, nor in stick form.

There was a lot of cargo; the lanes of crates and casings were long, high, and shadowed. So he didn't notice the thieves until he was right on top of them.

There were two, totally absorbed in rifling the contents of a yellow-orange plastic case bound with metal strips. The container was the size and shape of a coffin, which it wasn't. Mal would remember loading a stiff. Melted plastic showed at one end where the seal had been burnt away.

Mal could have done several things. He might have taken another two steps forward and inquired in his most sepulchral ship-master's tones as to the object of the gentlemen's intrusion. He could have walked over and offered casual, even flippant commentary. He could have slipped quietly away and buzzed for the port police.

However, men who spend their lives riding the saddle

of an artificial field with the mass of a sun (a) know when men will and when they will not react favorably to orders, (b) are aware that the derring-do of tri-dee heroes, when attempted in real life, seduces suicide, and (c) do not run for help.

So what Hammurabi did was put his hundred and twenty-five kilos under a crate not quite as big as himself and heave it in the direction of the two preoccupied paracreds. This by way of getting them off-balance.

Unfortunately, the ship-master once again misjudged his own strength. The crate was intercepted by the skull of the nearest man, who had chosen that moment to sense Hammurabi's presence and whirl, gun in hand. It was an unequal contest, which the man lost. Both crashed to the floor.

The other intruder made a dive for the dropped laser and reached it just as Mal landed on his back. The thief gained the weapon and lost his breath simultaneously. He squirmed.

Mal got the arm with the vicious-looking little gun in a modified arm-bar, one knee planted firmly at the shoulder joint. He raised the arm a little, up and back. The man screamed shrilly and dropped the pistol.

Leaning carefully forward, Mal reached down and gathered in the gun. The stock was still warm. Obviously it had been used recently. He hoped it had only been used on the crate.

The thief was fifteen cms shorter and a good sixty kilos lighter than the ship-master. He looked around wildly, as much as his awkward position permitted, and moaned. Apparently he'd caught sight of his companion. Mercifully, the box hid most of the other, but it didn't hide the large pool of red that stained the ferroconcrete to one side. Mal noticed the small man's glance.

"I didn't mean to be so messy with your friend. Nor fatal. But there were two of you and I like odds in my favor. Don't worry, I'll be much neater with you." He placed the muzzle of the pistol behind the man's right ear.

"Now, you've got just thirty seconds to come up with a real good reason why I shouldn't send you hustling after your partner . . . spiritually speaking, of course."

The man moaned again, his voice tight from the pain in his arm. "Go ahead! You're going to kill me anyway!"

"Nonsense! Don't be any dumber than you are. If I wanted you dead I'd have killed you, oh, minutes ago. I'd just as soon see you alive. I didn't mean to pass your friend on to the supervision of the Church, either, but I'm not fond of thieves. See, I was stolen myself once. No. . . tell you what. You cheerfully tell me what you were hunting for—and don't tell me this was a general expedition; you pulled that crate out of a hundred tons of similar ones—that, and who sent you for it, and maybe I'll let you depart rare instead of well-done." He pressed the pistol a little harder into the man's neck. "I suspect you'll have enough trouble avoiding the attentions of your employer, who will doubtless send you greetings when he finds out how sadly you've bungled."

The thief said nothing.

"Or," Mal continued conversationally, increasing his pressure on the spindly arm, "we could make this even more interesting and do it by pieces. I think this arm would be a good place to start. Then, if I lower the power on this toy and turn it in a little instead of down (he did so), I can start on one side of your head and fry you slowly to the other, maybe spiraling around. Sort of artistic like, you know?"

"All right!" the man screamed. "All right!" Mal let up slightly on the arm. "Rose."

"What? Stop whimpering, man, and speak up."

"Rose. He's the one sent me and Wladislaw."

"Dominic Rose? The drugger?"

The man nodded, slightly.

"How very interesting. You're working for an especially disgusting employer, did you know that? What did the dyspeptic slug want with my cargo?"

The man was gasping painfully. Mal let the arm drop and the thief immediately clutched it protectively.

"There was something about a mixup in ship transfer. That's all I know, God's truth!"

"Your piety rings as truthful as your kind intentions. This supposedly misshipped shipment originated on Largess?"

"Yes. No. Maybe, I don't know. Believe me, I don't!"

"Stop whining. I'm not going to hit you. Yes. No. Maybe. I believe you. You don't strike me as a policy maker."

"Let me go," the man begged. "Rose'll have me killed if I'm caught in the capitol."

"Patience. I'm here and he's not. And if you don't stop stalling and tell me what you were sent for, I *will* kill you!"

"We were supposed to find a small blue container, uncrested and umarked. That's all the information I was given, I swear!"

Mal got off the thief's back. He moved back slowly, keeping the gun trained on the back of the man's neck.

"Okay, you've got thirty minutes to get wherever it is you'd best like to get to. After that I give your description and my charges to Port Authority. I'm finished with you. You'd better start thinking about Rose and his delightful associates. But Repler's a pretty empty planet. With luck you might . . ."

But the man was already running full speed for the main entrance, apparently uncaring of being seen by Port guards. His right arm swayed limply at his side. Damn, Hammurabi, when will you learn to watch yourself! If you'd broken the arm any worse the man might have fainted on you. Then you'd be stuck trying to revive him before a patrol arrived.

He turned back to the vandalized crate. Except for the unpleasant problem of disposing of the remaining body, things had been pretty much cleared up. He was curious to know what a slimeworm like Rose might have transshipped from a place as dull and straitlaced as Largess. Dull enough, obviously, to cause him to send two men to break into a government-owned warehouse and crack a private shipment to find.

He had an uncomfortable moment as he bent to look into the opened casing. Suppose the small paracred had pulled one on him and the crate was full of nothing but small blue boxes? He could have saved the worry. There was only one blue container in sight. As the man had described, it was unmarked and small. About 10 cms by 20 by 20, with a slightly concave top. It was packed solidly among other containers of myriad shapes, sizes, and colors. He vaguely remembered the crate as being full of class-C luxury goods. A diverse collection.

The small case was half out of its assigned spot, indicating that the would-be thieves had discovered it just as he'd arrived. He entertained brief thoughts of leaving it untouched. Mal had had occasional dealings with Rose in the past. The old man had accrued a certain amount of power. Although on a major planet he would have to strive to be noticed, on Repler he could wield a definite amount of heft. He stayed just the right side of legal, meaning he paid taxes.

Mal was a little surprised when the small box opened with the merest touch of the laser. It might be a trick. One device many people used to protect valuables was not to protect them at all but to give the impression of their not being valuable. Once the initial cut was made, the plastic rolled back easily enough. A sturdy case of some silvery metal was revealed beneath. He lifted it out of its plastic casing and held it up to the dim warehouse lighting. It was attractively engraved, although clearly machine-cut. The decorative etchings cut into the metal were recognizably Largessian. A modest thing, certainly. Hardly worth the expensive and highly illegal efforts of two men to recover secretly.

There was a simple combination lock and snaplatch on the box. He could have used the laser, but if it proved necessary to repair the box, a simple break would be easier to explain than a meltcut. The latch snapped on the third tug, just as he was beginning to fear that it was stronger than it looked and that he might have to use the pistol after all.

The cover sprang back to reveal ten bottles of a slightly greenish cast. Each bottle of cut crystal was filled with a different colored powder. On the inside of the box cover was a printed key. It located the bottles below and gave their contents in thranx, terranglo, symbospeech, and formal largo:

These special spices have been carefully selected by the professional staff of Sirial Foods, Inc., to add exotic and tasteful seasoning to any organic vegetable dish with a cellulose content of at least 90%. Exceptions and/or maximum recommended servings for . . .

There followed a comprehensive list of races and species, with specialized information for each spice printed inside a small booklet resting on top of the bottles. This went into detail on which being could consume what spice and in what quantity, with effects varying from unappetizing and mildly corrosive at worst to aphrodisiacal at best. The multi-lingual instructions indicated that the contents were marketed over a wide section of the Commonwealth and perhaps even outside it. If the machined box was any indication, the spices were a highvolume item. But that didn't jibe with its being shipped as a luxury good. Still, maybe the old man was primates for Largessian spices and wanted to insure their arrival.

He tasted the contents of the first jar, after first consulting the book to make sure it contained nothing likely to take his feet off. The dark-maroon granules had a sweet-sharp tang, an intriguing cross between ground black pepper and white mint.

Mal considered what to do. Obviously he could sit and taste spice all night. That led nowhere. One thing he was still certain of: Neither of the two men he'd surprised was a mad gourmet chef out for condiments, which would be the case if the green bottles contained nothing but spices. While attractive, the metal case was clearly in no way valuable—although alloys *could* be deceiving. Still, it was likely that whatever Rose was so desperately concerned with was tied in with those spices. If there were drugs present, he'd do well to stop tasting.

There was another possibility. The "key" might contain some sort of coded message. Well, Rose could cry for that. Mal tucked the box under his arm. He'd give the stuff to Japurovac and see what she could come up with.

He took a step to his left and several square meters of floor nearby exploded in haze and superheated dust. He dove behind the nearest stack of containers, rolled, and came up running. He dodged down canyons of mining machinery, around monoliths of fresh fruit, ziggurats of preserved fish. He knew what had happened. Clearly, the two thieves hadn't been alone. The sore-armed escapee had returned with friends. No wonder he'd been willing to talk! Now he was out to see that his garrulity was rectified. Mal didn't think he'd find the little man especially forgiving.

Pity you're such a peaceable chap, old man, or you'd be carrying a decent gun of your own. Still, the laser he'd borrowed was nasty enough at close range. He paused abruptly behind a far corner and waited. A dim figure came tearing blindly around the bulky equipment, gun at the ready. Mal hastily remembered to readjust the pistol for a killing beam, took careful aim, and fired. The red light cut through the man at waist level as though he was a cartoon drawing and continued past to sear a black spot on the plastic cases behind him. The figure looked down at itself for several seconds, dumbfounded, and pitched forward onto the ferroconcrete floor. Mal looked at the tool in his hand with more respect. It was a good deal more powerful than its size hinted at.

Two more figures poured around the corner. They spotted the body and reversed their direction with admirable rapidity. They would move after him much more cautiously now.

He ran again. Another pile of crates went up in crackling smoke far to his left. He had them shooting at shadows now. Sooner or later, however, someone would slip behind him and fire at a shadow that wouldn't be so insubstantial. It was up to him to put that meeting off permanently, if possible.

His knowledge of the floor plan of the great building was superficial at best. Ship-masters didn't stoop to supervising storing procedure first hand. He knew that there should be several small personnel entrances spotted around the enormous expanse of metal and plastic, however. Warehousing permitted little flexibility in construction; they rarely varied except in size from port to port. The same lack of variance also told him that none of the personnel entrances would be left unlocked at night unless operations were proceeding. It happened that tonight the nearest new cargo was light-minutes off. He doubted that his pursuers would be so stupid as to permit him to slip unnoticed out the main entrance.

Zig-zagging constantly, laser at the ready, he made his way unevenly to the closest section of wall. There was a door there, all right. It was locked, all right.

He turned the laser to pencil thinness and began cutting around the circular automatic lock. If nothing else, that ought to alert the port police to the presence of intruders. Obviously the watchman had been taken care of. There was the chance that this alarm was tied in to the one at the main entrance, in which case it would have been rendered useless when the thieves cut the main one. Not that the police would arrive in time to save his own skin, whatever the case.

It was slow work, damnably slow! The high-intensity pistol was built to cut packing plastic and maybe people, both of which were considerably softer than bomb-proof plating. The metal glowed, began to drip lazily down the side of the door. Much too slow. Tridee stars smashed in such doors with the same ease that they dispatched assassins via clever verbiage. Hammurabi was considerably stronger than any tridee star and valued the bones in his shoulder. Doors were usually as unyielding as certain women.

He wasn't going to cut through in time.

As a last resort, he would put the pistol to the open

case and threaten to melt its inexplicably valuable contents to an aromatic puddle.

They continued to fire wildly and often, behind him. Maybe he'd gotten them so confused that they thought he'd slipped behind them and had started shooting at each other. That thought gave him enough respite to relax slightly.

Three men appeared in the shadow of a towering processing tank, newly arrived from Wolophon III. The lock was barely a quarter burnt through. He pressed his back to the door and shoved the muzzle of the warm pistol into the case, thumbing the beam to wide fan. The gun was hot from continuous use.

The men came closer, stopped. One detached himself from the group and walked up to Hammurabi.

"The locals won't like it if you go around burning holes in their government-issue buildings, Cap'n, you shouldn't mind my saying so."

Hammurabi flicked the pistol to Safety, stuck it in his pants pocket.

"You're a fine First Mate, Maijib Takaharu, but how the Devil did you happen to come looking for me?"

Takaharu made a gesture to his two companions. They moved off silently among the stacked crates, presumably to insure that if any of the intruders remained, they would not be in shape to offer argument.

The First Mate looked up from his full meter and two thirds. He carried a slim Hornet-VI needle thrower.

"Why, don't you remember, Cap'n? Since that night four months ago on Foran III, when you put six of the local finest into the native version of a hospital with assorted contusions, broken limbs and other souvenirs, defamed the statue of a local hero, and otherwise did not endear yourself to the local populace, you gave me a standard order to follow. The local magistrate fined you—"

"Don't remind me." Hammurabi winced. His rare drunks were difficult times for him. He couldn't understand why the crew persisted in bragging about them at every planetfall. It was getting so he couldn't walk into a bar before the owner or tender called frantically for the cops. Doc Japurovac, with fine insect logic (also, she was a little romantic), labeled them heroic. Mal thought they were merely embarrassing.

"You told me that if you didn't check in with Ben or myself by midnight local time, I was to grab a few of the boys and come hunting for you. Knowing your habits, it wasn't hard to trace you, sir. Also, strangers find you easy to remember. A number of them recalled seeing you enter the port grounds."

"I think I'd have preferred to have gone bar-hopping, this time. One more question, First."

"Sir?"

Hammurabi rubbed the side of his jaw where a flying splinter of molten plastic had struck him. He held out the open spice case.

"What do you know about cooking, Maijib?"

Circuits were enclosed in metal which was embedded in ceramic which was enclosed by the metal-that-was-not-cold which floated near something at the edge of emptiness.

The Machine was old, but purpose was retained. For the first time in eons it had cause to shift electrons with reason. The computer, which was so far in advance of what then were called computers that it deserved another name (but we will call it computer), began making decisions as though today were yesterday's yesterday. It was designed and equipped to handle only one Problem. To that end it was capable of making several billions of individual decisions in order to arrive at one solution.

None of them covered the present difficulties.

The Machine finally was able to resolve the multitude into Two Actions. First, it began to follow the Problem, which was moving away, and it began to search out a way to awaken the Guardian.

It was all a question of stimuli.

"Well, little Japurovac, what do you find?" Hammurabi asked the ship's thranx physician.

The diminutive female insectoid looked up at the Captain, her usually pretty face a red moon nightmare. The ferocious aspect was caused by the special goggles she wore. They included built-in analytical equipment and sensors, not to mention special magnifying lenses for compound eyes. Japur cocked her head to one side, curious.

"Tell me, dear Captain. If you are so keen to have these substances analyzed, why do you not convey them to the customs offices in Repler City? The facilities there are far in advance of what I have to work with here."

"I hope the answers you give me show more insight than that question, Doctor. You're too shrewd a gal to miss something so obvious."

"I did talk to Takaharu, in fact, but I wanted some confirmation from you. Keep your carapace on! I've done what you requested. Not at all surprised someone tried to kill you for these bottles."

"Several someones. At least one man has died because of them already. Have you really turned something up? Or are you just putting me off because you couldn't find anything?"

Japurovac drew herself up to her full meter and a third, truhands and hand-feet assuming a posture of mild outrage. Whether insult or flattery, Japur was more susceptible than most to either.

"I shall choose to ignore that. Of course, if you don't wish the efforts of my poor labor . . ."

"Okay, I give up. Don't get your ovipositors in an uproar. You know the entire ship would go to pieces without you."

She relaxed somewhat. "That's better. And watch the dirty language. I *am* a lady, you know! Now, the analysis of the materials in question was simple enough. The process of gravity separation was purely mechanical. To be certain I reran the time-consuming procedure several times. I wanted to be sure all questionable particles had been separated out. The reason for this will be self-defining when you see the results. Even so, I doubt that you will honestly appreciate my efforts, but no matter."

Hammurabi looked ceilingward for solace. Why, Malcolm, do you inflict a petulant, spoiled female physician on yourself and your ship? Why?

Because she's too damn good to get rid of, that's why.

The doctor continued. "There are measurable quantities of the drugs tween, mithrah, pollus, felturney and felturney-B mixed in with the spices. Some of the latter are quite tasty, I might add."

"I'm sure. What else?"

"There are also considerable amounts of two more potent narcotics, aelo and mak, each in its own spice jar. On the current market they ought to bring about 5000 credits."

"Those are both artificially produced drugs, aren't they?"

"Just so. To produce either in quantities pure enough to be useful or deadly, depending on which end of the injector you're on, considerable production facilities are required. Also a good deal of chemical know-how. Why? What difference does it make which Hell they originate from?"

"It's just that I rather liked our seal friends on Largess. Honest, friendly businessbeings, they seemed to me. They're not noted for their skill as chemists. Of course, that doesn't rule out any of a hundred other possibilities. They might have hired off-worlders to produce the stuff locally, or may just be serving as transfer agents. Go on."

"A jar full of very high grade heroin—for traditionalists, I suppose. And scattered throughout several jars, I am mottled and shattered to say, a probably priceless quantity of a foul substance that cannot be anything but bloodhype."

That set Hammurabi back a bit. They'd all heard rumors that the jaster traffic had been resumed. But to be confronted with the stuff in person! He thought again of his friends among the seal-beings. They'd be equally susceptible to the stuff. The fact that the drug operated on such a tremendous range of sentients greatly enhanced its value, since it could be marketed practically anyplace.

And he'd been selected to play delivery boy! He thought of the fellow who would be expected to find the blue box on another ship and his frantic efforts to locate it when he found it had been shipped to the wrong freighter.

"You separated all of it out, then, Doc?"

Japurovac gave the thranx equivalent of a mild shrug. "As I said, and with extreme care. Lucky you didn't taste one of *those* bottles. And I wish you would address me as 'Ship-healer,' as is my right, and not as a 'Doc.' "

"Sorry, D . . . Ship-healer. Didn't you know when you signed on that humans are notorious for an addiction to nicknames and abbreviations?"

"Please, Captain. No talk of 'addictions' now. My insides are queased enough from handling this stuff. It is dangerously potent if taken orally, and since my olfactory organs are located on my hand-feet, extreme delicacy in handling was required to insure safety. Injection works a lot faster, but is no more deadly."

She turned and grasped a labeled, covered vial with a truhand, switched it to the less delicate but stronger grip of a hand-foot. It contained a small quantity of a plain white powder. A thousand kilos of poisonous projector polish was less dangerous.

"That *is* all of it?"

"Well, perhaps I have been too positive. However, after separating out all I could, I placed the metal box and the twelve crystal jars in the sterilizer. The resultant slag was reduced to powder, remelted, and ejected out of the gravitational field of the planet via courier drone. After which I let the sterilizer bake itself for several hours, then sprayed the entire dispensary with a disinfectant designed to break down any unsealed organics. Cost me a good leather neck-strap I forgot to seal, too."

Hammurabi took the vial gingerly. "I'll buy you a new one, Japur. With perfume striping."

The vial, Mal noticed, was quartzine, thick and solid. He held it up to the brilliant surgical lighting and the creamy crystals within sparkled. If a gram of the stuff was powdered and released into the ship's ventilating system, everyone on board would be dead in a week. The unbreakable permalloy silicon dioxide vial was pressure sealed. It would take an hour's soaking in strong acid to dissolve the bonding resins.

"You seem to be up on the value of these goodies, Japur. What do you guess the value of this little jar at?"

"It's the business of a healer to know the cost of his tools and related materials," she said. She was intent on the interior of a half-filled beaker. "An aelo-vyacine combination, for example, can slow a thranx heartbeat to near nothing without ill effects, and without the use of a Dancer, or any other drugs. It makes open surgery practical to us, with our open circulatory systems. Otherwise many would bleed to death rapidly. I mention this by way of indicating relativity."

She looked back at him. "To me, that vial is worth nothing. To you, nothing. To an addict—anything short of his life. Any sentient in the galaxy 'took' on bloodhype would gladly trade you all his worldly possessions, his offspring, his mate, parents, and all his limbs save the minimum needed to inject the drug, in return for the hollow splinter of glass you hold in your hand. *'Ex pui restact al phempt,'*" she added in pure High thranx.

"Pardon?" Hammurabi asked. His schooling had neglected the formal dialects in favor of practical semantics.

"I couldst in my shell-of-shells vomit," the dainty healer replied. She turned back to her examination of the beaker, added something from another.

The ship-master considered the vial a moment longer, then laid it gently on the workbench. "I think maybe you ought to take charge of this, Japur. Myself, I'm going to try and arrange a chat with a certain old man."

The AAnn soldier approached the small group. It sheathed its claws and bowed slightly in salute, turning slightly to expose the jugular as a sign of respect.

"Most Exalted Commander, the place for the monster is completed."

"Thank you, Engineer," the tallest of the three intoned.

Parquit RAM, Supreme Commander of His Imperial Majesty's Grand Territory and Colony Station on Repler, turned from his two companions and made a gesture of politeness in the direction the engineer had come from.

"My compliments, Engineer Sixth . . . Waya SCXNMSS, I believe . . ."

"My ancestors are honored at your remembrance, Excellency!"

"Convey to Engineer First Vynaar my personal congratulations on a complex task efficiently done. The same to your associates. Even though," the Commander spared a glance for his thumb chronometer, "they pared things very close to our deadlines. Your speed will be mentioned in my official log of this project. I should hope to obtain more suitable compensation for the entire engineering staff from Imperial Sector Headquarters."

"A thousand thousand days of sun on all your progeny, Excellency!" said the engineer, bowing and turning every few steps.

Parquit gestured irritably at the younger nye. "And stop bowing so much! You'll acquire a crick in your neck."

The junior engineer turned hurriedly and scooted out of sight.

"Now then, gentlemen, my apologies for the interruption. Carmot MMYM, be known to Arris CDC, senior Xenobiologist First. Arris has been elevated to the position of nominal head of our scientific station here, for the duration of the project. We didn't bother with such plebeian formalities before—on a world like this, the nye will barely tolerate normal routine—but ever since Sectorcav have gotten their official tails in a frenzy on this thing . . ."

"Our First Psychostamin, Beirje, would have been a more appropriate choice," said Arris jovially. "All that fresh meat strolling around in the person of solitary hunters and tourists that the nye aren't allowed to touch— that inhibiting of their natural instincts, plus the amount of sickening free water present on this planet—"

"Please," interrupted Carmot. "I know. One look from the shuttle coming in was sufficient. I am not a strong nye. I confess to having become ill. I extend sympathy to my colleague."

"A more apropos greeting you couldn't give," replied the xenobiologist. The two scientists performed the AAnn ritual greeting, clasping each other's throat with claws retracted.

"I know your reputation, CDC. I am honored to meet so venerable a superior."

"What compliments you to me even more than your judicious and professional flattery, Observer First, is the relief from boredom that your discovery has brought to this Sector. I have never seen requests for supplies and scientific personnel filled so rapidly! While I dislike being exiled to this hell, I confess I'm enjoying the unusual cooperation from those pause-thinkers at headquarters."

"Again, sympathy. How do you stand the dampness?"

"The machinery does its best. But you should see some of the nye who are forced to run outside patrol." Arris shuddered.

"It's a choice slice of purgatory, Observor," Arris added. "Yet I believe, too, that your discovery may prove justification for the Corps false pride in maintaining this station."

"Your pardon, gentlenye," Commander Parquit interrupted. "Since Engineering has completed the last of the facilities, should we not hasten to observe the transfer of the thing? It is due shortly."

"Surely, surely!" said the xenobiologist. He led the way down the hall.

"I might hope even that the efforts expended in this project might yield, yea, a small advantage to the Empire for the next conflict with the humanx underbeings."

"You anticipate war, then, Commander?" asked Carmot.

"One can anticipate without predicting. When the predictors feel it worthwhile, we will engage again. Meanwhile we must curb ourselves. Each must make his sacrifice. When I am required in the City, for example, I find myself considering the well-fleshed human governor from a culinary rather than diplomatic stance. Restraint is the marker of confidence."

"Well said," huffed Arris as they turned yet another corner.

For a time now the Vom had perceived atmosphere around itself. At least its senses had improved to that point, however little. Otherwise it was aware only of being suspended in a strong metallic container between two pulsing energy sources. These it correctly interpreted as sources of motive power for its "cage." The gravity field of the planet beneath had been felt long ago. The Vom was still terribly, terribly weak. Its awareness of that weakness made it cautious.

For example, even though it had now regained enough strength to break free, it did not long consider the idea. It knew that it could spread its organic envelope thin enough to float gently to the surface below, or compact itself and drop to safety deep in rock.

Wait and observe, counseled one neural nexus. Pause and see, concurred a thousand others.

Commander Parquit and the two scientists entered the hastily constructed central control area. All observation and experiments to be performed on the creature would be supervised from this room. The center was buried even deeper than most of the AAnn station. A good nine or so fathoms beneath the low-tide point, it rested in water a deep blue. Tridee after tridee gave views of the interior of the special holding room, the halcyon surface, and a respectable portion of gray sky. Just now the center was a hive of frenzied activity. Technicians and mechanics predominated, making last-minute inspections, wirings, installation, and equipment checks. Engineers and an occasional scientist argued quietly over the performance or placement of various bits of exposed instrumentation.

The xenobiologist gestured towards one of the larger screens. It displayed a view of what seemed to be a large rectangular hole in the sea, surrounded by *pecces,* the Replerian coral-equivalent. Most of the small reef was the metal and plastic product of AAnn camouflage experts.

"The cage is located at the bottom of that shaft," Arris informed Carmot. "It rests at the same level as this control center and is actually only *verrs* away, beyond this very wall. The paneling is undergoing final wiring, so I can't pull them off the glass yet. When that is done we shall be able to observe directly everything the creature does. Or that we do to the creature. There will be no temperature or pressure difficulties, I am assured. The sides of that 'hole' are quite strong. They are also easily removed, as is the 'reef.' The walls of the shaft will be towed away as soon as the creature is safely ensconced in its new home. If the thing accepts water as a barrier, it will be barred from the surface by a good forty *teverrs* of ocean. And the restraining walls, of course.

"The most difficult problem was one that you and the spatial corps solved for us. Whether or not we would be forced to maintain an artificial atmosphere similar to the one of the planet from which the creature was removed. Fortunately, the thing appears extremely adaptable."

"Insofar as our very cursory testings indicated," Carmot reminded.

"True. A fortunate bit of luck for us, since our experimenters and handlers will be able to operate without the bother of special equipment and protective suits. Its sole requirement seems to be a certain minimal amount of oxygen. From tests it appears that the creature can break down any of a great number of substances and remove the required element. If nothing else, it proves itself a remarkably efficient combustion engine."

"Perhaps a noteworthy fact already," said Parquit. "Ah, here they come now." He indicated a smaller console screen, and the two scientists moved closer for a better look.

Three rapidly moving blips, set close together, showed on the screen. As they descended further, they gradually resolved into two *Aphon* shuttles sandwiched around a massive, featureless ellipsoid.

"Compliments to the Emperor's pilots, Commander," said Carmot honestly. "Some remarkable maneuvering, there."

"Proper balancing of forces for such a task, on descent . . . yes, very well managed," said Parquit, adding, "I'm certain Sectorcav supplied the best nye available."

"I can guess the need for such a complex arrangement," said Carmot.

Parquit spoke without taking his eyes from the screen.

"Yes. There are no shuttles this side of the Homeworld capable of handling that much bulk. Not only would it take too long to transfer one, but the humanx would be certain to inquire into the need for shuttles of that size. *Aphon*-class occasionally operate out of the capitol. We manage things too openly for my taste as it is."

The two shuttles slowed and maneuvered from side to side; a little lower and they were positioned directly over the shaft. A lift pressor at the bottom of the shaft gently locked in and the two shuttles released their hold. A tricky operation. The idea was that the two shuttles would release their hold at the same moment the main pressor took over. Unless timing and power were precisely matched, a catastrophic misalignment of forces could occur.

The two shuttles pulled away, one to the left, one right, and boosted heavenward to rejoin the mother ship somewhere in orbit. If the timing had been exact all around, none of the operation should have been observable from Repler City's beacons hundreds of kilometers to the north.

Not that the humanx could do anything about it even if they were to detect the movements. The AAnn rights were unassailable where practically everything was concerned. But it was better not to have nosy bureaucrats poking around until many answers had been obtained. So the only humanx within detector range were a few improperly equipped hunters and fishers.

Gently, Engineering lowered the massive container to the bottom of the shaft. A basso grinding from the big room heralded touchdown. Relays snapped and sliding panels formed a new, permanent roof to the great cage. Outside, automatic work-tugs set about the task of dismantling the camouflaged shaft. Parquit did not permit himself to relax until all four panels of the structure and the accompanying artificial reef had been removed and stored. An unbroken sea flowed over the now-sealed subterranean structure. He smoothed his tail absently.

"Over and done and buried. So. Now the besotten freefliers may flit overhead to their heart's content!"

"The structure, then, is completely invisible from the air?" asked Carmot.

"Like the rest of our undersea facilities, the containment area appears as normal seabottom when viewed from a height, complete with *Pecces* and an artificial piscean breeding ground." The Commander leaned over the railing of the upper observation ramp and yelled into the big room. "Communications!"

From within a maze of screens and dials a slim technic looked up alertly.

"Radar and audor report all negative, Commander."

"Good!" He turned back to the two scientists. "It only remains to release the creature from its life-support container. Then, Arris, you and your eager subordinates may proceed with the first of your experiments." He turned to Carmot and began easily. "As a military man, I am of course particularly interested to see for myself proof of your claims as to the thing's ability to resist powerful laser and other heat. . . ."

Within the shell the Vom rested quietly. It allowed its perceptions to roam freely through the thick metal and plastine and ferroconcrete walls. Still unbearably weak, it could nonetheless differentiate between the atmosphere within its container and that outside a yet larger cell. There the atmosphere became liquid. It was pleasingly high in oxygen content and well-mixed with hydrogen. A short distance above this area the atmosphere turned gaseous once again. An ocean or sea, then.

The Vom detected a host of small intelligences performing typical heat-generating tasks in the liquid around it. Others lay dormant and unmoving. Extending further, it made a tremendous discovery. This liquid atmosphere was violently alive with organisms! The sheer bulk staggered the Vom. It had been so long since lifeforce had been present nearby in any quantity that the Vom was stunned by the sheer fertility. True, the intelligence of all was low, low, carrying a proportionately smaller amount of life-energy. The volume, however, would come near to making up for that. There was no question as to pure numbers.

For one moment the Vom bravely extended its perceptions to the utmost. At the furthest limit of its terribly fatigued senses was at least one, possibly two large concentrations of high-quality life-force.

The Vom debated. It was still difficult to think clearly. How much longer could it wait before a real feeding was necessary to insure expansion? In order to energize the higher functions, it was life-energy and not bulk protein that was needed. Especially intelligent life-energy.

A small number of AAnn technicians floated in little work-cars above the metal ellipsoid, equipped with strip saws. They positioned themselves preparatory to cutting the shell from the creature. From there it was presumed the being would move about on its own to relax in the cell. There was no reason to think it would behave otherwise.

The Vom considered.

It was hungry *now*.

Tortured metal screamed. The ellipsoid tore like paper in half a dozen, two dozen places. Long pseudopods black as the Pit extruded from the cracks and snatched the scooter-mounted techs like a frog catching flies. A few barely had enough time to scream. Metal and nye alike were absorbed into that black ichor. The Vom flowed out rapidly in all directions, examining every section of the vault.

Two biologists who had been taking notes nearby the single massive door turned and ran for their souls. They barely beat that flowing black hell. It slammed up against the water-tight barrier like a wave of ink seconds after they'd slipped through to safety. Sensing intelligent construct, the Vom began to analyze the barrier separating it from its food. A moderately complex duralloy construct, the metals yielded to rapid identification. Their tolerances were judged, gauged. A small section of the Vom began to produce heat, focused it on the door.

The duralloy turned red-hot, then white-hot. It began to flow like soapy water.

Parquit reacted first. The mental blast that had been the Vom's first free-emoting thought—that of a cosmic hunger—had momentarily paralyzed everyone. "Close all doors in that tubeway access! Also all doors in sections six, seven and nine!"

Suddenly the room was a frenzy of activity. Parquit's commands galvanized the technicians into action.

The first doorway melted through, giving access to the first section of tubeway. The ravenous intelligence consumed the envelopes and life-energy of two more nye. The two scientists had narrowly made the tube before the first door slammed shut behind them. They hadn't made the second ahead of Parquit's orders. The life energy the Vom received, however, was less than it might have been, since the minute the monster had breached the first door and flowed for them, one biologist shot his companion and then turned the little needle-ray on himself. They perished differently from the scooter-techs in that they didn't have time to scream.

Parquit strode up and down the railing, bawling orders at every section.

"Power nexus!" he roared.

Engineer-Physicist Pyorn looked up helplessly from his control desk. "Commander! Consider, the final linkage has never been tested! The possible effects remain theoretical at this point and—"

Parquit looked hard at the Engineer. "To the Dead Star with your linkages, nye! A good time to test them, vya-nar? And if your effects prove theoretical, our deaths will not. Full power! And hold!"

"Exalted commands," Pyorn muttered faintly. He broke back two plated switches, one yellow, the other brown. Pressing both in sequence, he uttered a quiet prayer to the dust demons to hold the newly installed systematization together.

The Vom recoiled in terrible pain. The entire vault, excepting a large section of the center flooring, had suddenly and unexpectedly come alive with several million volts. The access tunnel was similarly charged. In its weakened condition, the powerful overload was more than its unprepared cells could distribute. It shrank back on itself towards the one section of the vault that was uncharged. All movement was agony. Misjudged, misjudgment! it cried. One by one centers shut down to avoid being burned out forever. Those which tried to distribute the charge had some success before failing. Those on the organic periphery went first.

Unfortunately, very unfortunately, it did not quite die.

"Full off, back down slowly," Parquit ordered after several minutes had elapsed. The Vom had long since ceased all movement of any kind, but the Commander was not about to be undercautious. Obediently, Pyorn

closed down the system. The Engineer examined dials
and meters intently.

"All sections holding, Commander." There was a hint
of pride in the voice, which Parquit, under the circumstances, did not reprimand.

"Compliments," he said curtly. To the two scientists,
"Follow me, please, sanderings." They descended to the
floor of the great control center. Parquit singled out an
elderly AAnn seated alone amid thousands of tiny glass
cages with captive dials.

"Well, Amostom, is it ruled a final dueling?"

"I cannot say yet, Commander. According to life-support monitor . . ." he gestured at the meters and such,
" . . . the thing still lives."

"Impossible," Arris said quietly.

"Strange words to come from a xenobiologist," replied
the Commander.

"Exalted, there isn't a living creature that can take
half the voltage that was poured into that vault for more
than a few milliseconds. Even then, the aquatic being
in question has all its higher neurological functions
crisped. The thing must at least be paralyzed beyond
possibility of recovery, a point where 'death' becomes an
exercise in convenient semantics."

"Well," Parquit said grimly, "you may be right, there.
If not, your scheme of tolerance will be forced to revise
itself to include a variable." He turned to stare at the
monitors which relayed images from the vault.

"If it is still alive, it shows no sign of it. All visible
motion has halted."

"I beg to question, Commander, but there is no 'if'
involved," interrupted Amostom from his seat. The elderly nye made a sweeping motion with hands and tail. "The
readings are plain for those who have the openness to
read them. The thing lives. Weakened, granted, but it
lives."

"How 'weakened'?" asked Parquit.

Amostom performed the AAnn shrug-equivalent. "By
any reasonable standards, I should guess near to death.

Indeed, it may, as the good Arris observes, never recover. But then, little of it observes normal or reasonable standards. By its own—who knows?"

The Commander grunted and turned back to the largest tridee monitor. It remained focused on the quiescent black mass.

"Well, we shall have to find out. A good external stimulus ought to be the best way. And we have one that has proven itself effective." He gestured to Carmot and Arris to follow.

"Your pardon, Commander," said the Observer-First, "but where are we going?"

Parquit looked back over a mailed shoulder. "Inside the vault, of course. What kind of stimuli did you think I had in mind?"

Carmot had not moved. "I hardly think that is wise, Commander."

"Perhaps. But useful, certainly." Parquit looked the small scientist over carefully. "Is it possible the nye have a coward in their midst?"

Carmot flushed. "A heightened instinct for preservation in the face of death is not cowardice."

"Very facile. I will not force you."

"Then of course I must come," said Carmot.

The clumsy armored suits held their speed to a crawl. Designed for use in the weightless vacuum of space, they were terribly awkward on land. In ordering the use of the bulky suits, Parquit privately doubted that they would afford much in the way of protection should the creature decide to go on another rampage. If it was capable of further rampaging, he reminded himself. Amostom's analysis left an uncomfortably large amount of room for disarming speculation.

Psychologically, however, the armor was valuable for such as the Observer-First. For a race of reptiles equipped with their own body armor by nature, armor of all types exerted an almost religious appeal.

Within the vault, the restored lighting (cut out when

the emergency power was cut on) was sharp. Colors, shadows, even the walls showed grayish in the even lighting. The jagged debris of the creature's interspace ellipsoid lay strewn about the room, twisted and torn like so much parchment.

The enigma *in vivo* rested in the center of the room. A huge, silent mountain of ebony opalescence and awesome power. It represented a universe of unanswered questions.

Together with a heavily armed escort, which was present primarily for psychological effect, a small group of volunteer scientists accompanied the three.

A single soldier preceded the small party. He walked slowly up to the unmoving hulk. A few nye held their breath. The soldier walked slowly around the base of the creature, tapping it at various points with the stock of his powerifle. After several minutes of this he flicked his tail at the waiting party.

A low sussuration, part relief and part burgeoning curiosity, began to emanate from the group of scientists as they spread through the vault. The atmosphere seemed to grow ten degrees warmer. Two were already deep in a heated discussion by the base of the melted watertight door.

Others were soon plying about the edge of the monster. Still others were pouring over the shredded remnants of the transportation ellipsoid that lay scattered about the vault.

Parquit still found it difficult to think of the mountain-quiet mass as alive in any sense of the word. Its one brief display of insensate violence and explosive motion had taken on the aspect of a bad dream, was receding into memory.

He passed one elderly observer calmly dictating notes into his belt recorder. The oldster was examining a fused lump of metal which lay close to the base of the creature. It was easy enough to identify—a partially digested arm and part of a shoulder protruded from the metal. The lump was the remains of one of the little inspection-

repair scooters that had carried the nye who were to release the creature from its metal shell—and the remains
of the scooter operator.

The Commander spotted Arris studying the point where
the black hill touched the floor. He strolled over and the
xenobiologist waved in greeting.

"Initial deductions?" Parquit asked smoothly.

"I am still trying to adjust to the fact that this is
indeed a living thing and not a mountain of inorganic
sludge, Commander." The scientist tapped the black substance with a clawed foot. "I find it difficult to relate to
something so enormous on any kind of personal level."

"A feeling we all share. Still, I could do with some
first impressions."

"Well, if Amostom's instruments *are* correct, then we
can assume the thing capable of unknown actions at any
time. Yet I would tend to believe we may have pulled
its spines. Its intelligence remains an unknown—the most
important one, I should think."

"You believe it is of a high enough order to learn
from its experience, then?"

"Its present lack of action might be read as such. But
I hesitate to ascribe intelligence to an action which
may be dictated solely by bodily demands and be thereby
entirely involuntary. I don't think in any case that it will
risk another encounter with Pyorn's electric charges. Not
when it has been so obviously damaged by the first."
The xenobiologist scratched his leathery hide with one
claw. "With your permission, Commander, I'd like to be
about our schedule of experimentation. Suitable precautions will be observed."

"I should expect so. Yes, certainly. Begin at once."
Parquit caught sight of Carmot standing off to one side
and walked over. The Observer was careful to avoid
contact with the monster.

"You've been very quiet, Observer. What do you observe?"

Carmot turned a drawn face to the Commander. "I

observe that an appalling display of force resulting in destruction and fatalities is insufficient to install suspicion in the nye. We all underestimate this unspeakable mass of alien obscenity."

He returned his gaze to the thing in question. "The display of electronic destruction put on by our engineers was quite impressive. It is possible that we may have exhausted the thing's resources, that its moment of terror was a last desperate attempt to avoid imprisonment and perhaps dissection." He looked at Parquit evenly. "But I would not bet a *southing* on it."

Carmot's pessimism did not overly bother Parquit. Rather, it was the Observer's unflattering intimations of ignorance on the part of the AAnn. Not fitting for one in the service of the Emperor.

"You would have us attempt to destroy it now, after the nye it has cost?" Parquit said sharply.

"Yes!" the Observer replied, with more violence than the Commander had ever seen him express. "Now, immediately! Before it regains the strength it showed. And for the very reason you yourself just said!"

Parquit was taken aback. "*I* said?"

"Truly! 'Attempt to destroy it,' you said. You cannot even conceal your own uncertainties, Commander."

"That may be," replied Parquit quietly. "But it is also for that very reason that we must continue to study it. Its ability to survive extraordinary assaults demands that we try to learn how this is accomplished. It promises us secrets to be learned nowhere else. I will not surrender these prospects to insubstantialities and personal fears."

Carmot sighed. "Let us hope they remain only that." The diminutive Observer turned back to his inspection of the dull hulk. Instinct betrays one, he thought perversely as he wildly wondered what the thing's flesh would taste like. The oddest thoughts occurred to one at the oddest times.

His nursery was light-years and real years away. He wished he were in it.

The Vom rested quietly. It was aware of the small army of intelligences poking and prodding at it. It was aware of instruments sending questing energies throughout its structure and it did not resist, although certain information was allowed to be picked up subtly changed, carefully mottled. It did not even resist when one cluster of figures set about removing a small section of physical self, an unforgivable insult. In time past the very thought would have meant slow death for the thinker. Now, the Vom did not react. It could do penance.

The mistake it had just made required a good deal of it.

Very well, it would continue to present an aspect of docility that bordered on death. Also, it had much thinking to do.

So, and so. It had underjudged its captors. It reminded itself that under certain conditions a large number of small intelligences could act as efficiently as a single great one. Demonstrably, they could sometimes surpass it. It had relied too much on its unmatched body to carry the attack through. In forgetting to reason it had forgotten everything. It had been fortunate, yes, fortunate to have survived. After retaining life for millennia of near-starvation, it had nearly invited extinction by a single rash act.

It perceived that a group of the small intelligences had been gathering large groups of lower beings to one side, outside its first retainer. The Vom could not read minds now, but it was an astute interpreter of emotions and actions. It detected the long tubes leading into the vault from outside and the devices whose function would be to remove much of the tame water. So its captors were going to supply it with organics. It contented itself and calculated the time needed to regain its former plateau—the various sections reported: surprisingly little. In addition to many other things, the Vom had forgotten its own recuperative powers.

The next time it took action it would be much stronger. A properly planned course would be pursued. The thought of having to endure captivity by another kind of intelligences was strange and repugnant. In fact, it was harder to bear the thoughts in the minds of its captors, which pictured the Vom as a prisoner, than it was the reality. The Vom firmed its resolution and counted this another form of penance for its errors. Soon it would be strong. Not as strong as it had once been (it had energy to spare now for remembering) but, yes, strong enough. Time brought power.

The little girl couldn't have been more than nine or ten. She crouched fearfully behind a moss-covered rock in the dense rain-forest. Warm water dripped off the trees all around. It was the only movement in the dead, humid air; the sound the only sound. Drops fell heavily from branch to branch in the riot of silent greenery. Filicales and bryopsids dominated the scene.

Clasped tightly in her right hand was a small blaster. Cautiously, she raised herself enough to peer over the rock. The forestscape showed nothing unusual. Nothing to see but the delicate trees, mistiphytes, and an occasional patch of chromatic fungi.

A dull maroon something moved between two mushroom things on her left. The gun twisted around and fired and the maroon thing exploded in steam and green blood. Bits and pieces continued to hump around in a horrible travesty of retained life.

The girl stepped around the boulder, keeping the blaster focused on the area of destruction. When the remnants of the still unidentifiable thing had ceased their life-burlesque, she lowered the weapon and moved forward.

She wasn't looking up, so she didn't see the fire-constrictor as it dropped silently from its branch. Just as she didn't see the double rows of tiny scimitar teeth which sank inches into the muscle at the back of her neck with the force of a hammer.

Kitten blinked as she exited the booth, rubbing a spot above her left ear where the head contacts had chafed slightly.

"Well," asked a foppishly clad Porsupah. He was sitting on a bench gayly lit from within, chewing a stick of arromesh. "How was it?"

She replied in a broadly accented, aristocratic tone. This, like Porsupah's suit, was for the benefit of the many who strolled the noisy, glittering pathways of the amusement arcade.

"Rather dull, I'm afraid. Oh, of *itself,* it doesn't fail. And the killer-illusion choice was somewhat different—slinkering is something I haven't done more than once or twost before. But compared to the simies of Terra or even Myra IV, it's not much. The cortex of a fire-constrictor doesn't permit much of the real pleasure of the kill to seep through, if you know what I mean."

"I told you we should have gone fishing!" Porsupah put on a petulant look. "How anyone can compare the thrill of hooking a parapike with the sterility of the imitation stimuli of a simie booth—it's all just so, so *gauche!*"

He handled the role of a spoiled merchant's nephew with a skill and verve Kitten couldn't hope to match.

"Fishing, fishing! Honestly, Niki, sometimes I swear you'd be happier a fish yourself. And I never compared the two." She flicked ashes idly from the long stick of Terran tobacco. "Even if some of the fish are bigger than your hoveraft, I can't see much of a challenge to someone using a powerhook and reel."

"The thrill's in the play and the landing, not the size of the fish. At least I don't use an explosive hook, like some. And it's a more honest form of fun than plugging yourself into one of those infantile joyboxes!" He waved contemptuously at the row of simies. A few had lights on over the doors, indicating they were in use. Each one they passed had a more garish sign than the next, promoting this or that forbidden thrill in safety and perfect simulation.

"Meretricious mental masturbation!" the Tolian concluded grandiosely. He rose and started to walk down another arcade way. Kitten followed, strolling on his left.

"And furthermore," he continued as they passed a stall

where a tall alien was vending home-cooked pastries, just like Emethra used to make, "there's nothing stopping *you* from trolling for giant groupert or malrake with plain old hook and line, you know."

She drew herself up haughtily. "I may enjoy taking risks now and then, it's true, but I'm not *crazy*, Niki."

"Does my lady seek something a bit more intense yet sure and private, then?" came a voice from one side.

They turned together. A portly human was seated in a wicker chair at one side of the still walkaway. In an age of multiple diet chemical controls and adequate cosmetic surgery, the man was a living fossil. He was fat.

It was moderately aesthetic fat, however. Perhaps the effect wasn't entirely unintentional. Rather than sagging, it ballooned tautly against his cheekbones and forearms. There is a great deal of difference appearance-wise between a fat man who looks like Santa Claus and one who seems composed of wet rags. This one was a Santa.

The blue eyes, set like lapis-lazuli on either side of the marquise-cut probosis, did not twinkle, however. They stared unwaveringly back into one's own.

The portatables surrounded the man like metallic pygmies attending an idol of gluttony. They were piled with tridee cubes of planetary scenery, hand-carvings of Replerian ivory and fine woods, and an occasional bit of good jewelry. The stock was a little better than the average of the type but displayed nothing extraordinary.

"Well now," Kitten began, "we're not averse to suggestions from even the most unlikely quarters, my pudgy purveyor."

"A lady who follows her soul, I see. Better than calling me plain 'fat,' which is what I be."

Kitten gestured with the tobacco stick at a rack of cubes depicting fishermen in time-honored poses with victims of the sport a Terran counterpart would scoff at as trick photography.

"Your miserable attempts at flattery do me no honor. Unless you've more for sale than pretty pictures favoring the local cretinisms, I fear you waste our time."

The man sneezed. "The administration really ought to do something about covering over these seaside amusement ways. At least the walkaways could be subheated." He wiped his nose with a big multicolored hanky and heaved himself forward in the chair, wheezing.

"If you've the inclination," he continued much more softly, "and the money—yes the money—for something most definitely different, I think we might do business."

Kitten moved closer and leaned over part of the tables. She pretended to examine a carved walrus-like creature with thin silver whiskers and rose-crystal tusks.

"The desire is always there, merchant. And I have enough credits for anything in the way of entertainment this damp sod-ball could possibly offer. Endeavor to provide specifics, please."

"Bloodhype," the man whispered evenly. "A narcotic, if you haven't heard of it. The finest, rarest, and most pleasureful drug this end of the opposite Arm. If you've the mind and guts to try it, that is."

Kitten drew back, sighing. "Oh my. And I really hoped you might have something worthwhile, too." She took in the whole City in a contemptuous jerk of her head. "Your market for such a product is *everywhere* evident. No doubt the sophisticated populace makes heavy demands on your thin stock. The woods must be aswarm with beboggled loggers and trappers!"

She handed the man the figurine and her credit slip. He went through the motions of recording the purchase. He pursed his lips in surprise as her credit rating flashed on his doublecheck screen.

"You do have the money, lovely lady-lady. Yes you do. As for your sarcasm, I am not offended. People migrate, m'lady, and so do many products. A number of such pause here on their way to other, more lucrative markets. But some is always available at points of transfer. That smokestick of yours, for example, is Terran tobacco, is it not?" Kitten nodded. "There, you see? For someone with the proper attitude and resources, anything is available anyplace." He was very jolly about it all.

"Then you're serious? It's really available in this back-water?" She put just enough disbelief and suppressed excitement into her voice.

He continued to wrap the little carving in decorative foil. "As serious and real as your beauty, lass."

"And you've samples with you?"

He chuckled lightly. "My ancient human history is not the best, but from the tapes I can recall, I believe the court fools were traditionally on the slim side. No, lady. The equal of Hivehom the local constabulary may not be, but their machinery is as good as that on many of the more metropolitan worlds. I trust that you would not be averse to a short sea journey?"

"Well . . . how long?"

"Less than a day."

"And we could leave . . . when?" she asked breathlessly.

"Immediately, if you wish."

She turned to Porsupah. "Niki?"

"These whims of yours, Pilar. Oh well, if you think you know what you're getting us into. Jaster is supposed to be 100 percent addictive, I recall."

"Oh, poo! Scare rumors the Church manufactures to frighten children!" The fat man was watching her closely. "Besides, if it's the real stuff, think what a coup I will have on the Marchioness . . . the bitchy little snippet!"

"This absurd vendetta you carry with your cousin . . . all right. But only if it all takes less than a day. I still have that flyer reserved to take us north day after tomorrow following—"

"Bother your fishing!" She turned back to the merchant. "We accept."

"Excellent! Then if you will permit me a few moments to pack up my simple shop, we can be off."

"I hope your mysterious rendezvous isn't terribly inaccessible. This outfit wasn't made for roughing it." She indicated the skintight black-spotted orange fur jumpsuit she was wearing, with open circlets on each leg revealing patches of skin up to her arms.

The man was folding the portatables—or rather, directing them to fold themselves. The stock automatically twisted and turned until it was contained in several odd-sized crates and rectangles. These quickly maneuvered themselves into a single featureless black block, like an automated jigsaw puzzle. He locked it, put a single CLOSED sign on the front, and started off in the direction of the sea breeze, Porsupah and Kitten following.

"Kind of chilly," said Pors.

"As can be seen—and smelled—this amusement area is quite close to the docks," their guide informed. Already they had left behind the hard lights and perpetual people-hum of the walkaways. Moving under their own power, they strolled along dimly lit seaside byways, kept clear of fog by City weather machinery.

Commercial craft mingled here with private vessels, each sidled close by its protective pier or slideway. They ranged from popcorn clusters of tiny one-seat water-skippers to huge bulk-fishers and transports hundreds of meters long. The farraginous flotilla threw alien city-shadows against the night sky. Phosphorescent foam the color of old newsprint lapped onto plastic hoveraft beaches.

When Repler's two moons were in the sky, as they were now, they threw a fair amount of light. Massed together, they would have made a body a little larger than Terra's Luna. September was nearly overhead, while August had just cleared the horizon. It would get lighter before it got darker, and the shadow of the old tom mewing on a broken piling would split.

The man led them down a long, telescoping dock. Hard by the dark water at its end rested a narrow, racy-looking hoveraft. Light showed in the open doorway and above the forecabin windows, illuminating the pebbled artificial beach. Despite its fine lines, the vessel was clearly more metal than plastine. That argued for a craft intended to transport cargo more than people. Quickly, too.

"We're expected?" said Porsupah on catching sight of

the lights. Kitten knew that he'd probably spotted them as soon as they'd turned down the quay. No point in letting their friendly pusher onto any Tolian abilities he might not be aware of.

"Hardly. No, I suspect the two pilots are up. The ship is normally engaged in transporting supplies to our host's place of business. Sedda and Franz are perfectly trustworthy. You needn't worry on that account."

"Let's hurry it up then," said Kitten. "We *do* have other engagements, you know."

The fat man slowed his pace slightly. "Someone is expecting you then?"

"No no! I just get impatient at times, merchant. I am ... high-strung, you might say. Besides," she added hastily, "hoveraft night-rides aren't exactly the most luxurious form of transportation, you know."

"The best at my disposal, I fear. Again may I say we will not be overlong. Our destination is but ... but why should that concern you, eh?" He herded them on board.

Two men looked up from a game of femin-de-fer as the three entered the cabin. Both were simply attired in plaid work-pants and light water-repellent jackets. They looked very competent.

The one called Franz gave Kitten at least as thorough a look-over as he gave his cargo. He spoke to the fat man, who was peeling off his own jacket. The thick arms thus revealed showed a surprising amount of muscle.

"Well! York, your taste in merchandise is improving!"

"Watch your tongue, Franz. The lady and her friend are to be our guests. Class A-1, you understand?"

The burly pilot looked startled, then pleased. "Your pardon, m'lady. No offense meant."

"None taken," said Kitten, smiling archly and lighting up another smokestick.

The other pilot, Sedda, was already warming up the raft's engines. A shudder went through the vessel as the big rotors began to turn over.

"Have a seat back among the cargo, then," said Franz.

He turned to the fat man. "I take it his Lordship's approval will be forthcoming for this unscheduled journey, York?"

"No doubt on it," the big man replied, making himself comfortable for the trip.

"That's enough for me, then." The pilot turned back to his position forward.

"If you'd give me a hand here first, Franz?" said York.

"My pleasure, enormous one."

York had rummaged through a side compartment and come up with two blindfolds. "I say now," began Porsupah uncertainly. "Are those things entirely necessary?"

"I fear that they are," York apologized. "You understand, where merchandise of so, ah, controversial a nature is involved, extreme precautions are the norm." He reached out and gently removed the stub of the smokestick from Kitten's lips, deposited it carefully to one side.

Kitten squirmed slightly as dark cloth took away her sight. "Surely you can't believe that, even if I were so inclined, which I am not, I could possibly retrace the route to your patron's hideaway from what I might see while racing through the night over the waters of an utterly strange planet?"

"No, I do not. But I do not share similar feelings with respect to your furry friend here. Where unknown qualities are concerned, it is best to be careful. And while potential customers you may be, you two do constitute rather an unknown."

"Really?" said Kitten. "I'd think we were pretty transparent. Certainly our purpose is clear. Why the 'potential' customer? Are you entertaining second thoughts about my credit rating?" She began to get a sinking feeling in her stomach that somewhere someone had made a ghastly blunder. This occurred whenever things refused to run in synch with her ideas of the cosmos.

"Not your credit rating, no," York replied conversationally. He finished knotting the blindfold. Hard. "But thoughts, yes. I'm especially curious about one thing. A triviality, really, but it bothers me. While you were conversing with me at my pitiable stand, several blatantly plainclothes lawfolk passed by and did not see fit to interrupt us."

"And why should they have?" she replied, tensing.

"Because," interrupted the voice of Franz, "as friend York's pickup relayed to us, your smokesticks are Terran tobacco. Ever since an early colonist discovered that the fumes were fatal to the young shoots of an especially rare and valuable wood, Terran tobacco has been a forbidden import on Repler."

Kitten made a half-hearted shrug. "Am I expected to know that?" She gathered her feet under her and began edging a hand up towards the blindfold.

"Possibly not," said York. "But those two officers should have, even if you slipped it by the oh-so-careful customs inspectors at the Port—"

She ripped off the blindfold and in one motion slammed a heel into Franz' knee, feeling the patella snap. The big pilot doubled over in pained surprise. She saw Sedda set the raft on auto and turn back towards her just as something very heavy descended on her head from behind. Darkness and silence descended with it.

When she regained consciousness she found that her position in the world had been altered. She was now horizontal. She tried to move her arms, then her legs. Results were not encouraging. Her limbs had been effectively immobilized. The bench she was securely tied to was hard, flat, and (she wiggled awkwardly) damn cold. The coldness was magnified by the fact that she had no clothes on. The bonds at her wrists, waist, and ankles disturbed her far more than her nakedness. Her clothing she missed mostly for the several miniature weapons sewn into the waistband.

Turning as far as possible to the left and leaning with all her weight, she tugged hard at the smooth bond on her right wrist. This accomplished nothing beyond bringing on a sudden onslaught of dizziness. Her body was weak from inactivity. The more-than-leather strap wasn't leather. And there was a lump at the back of her head that wasn't caused by her hairdo.

A familiar voice called softly from somewhere to her right.

"Sssst! Pilar!"

That was her cover name. Despite another restraining strap across her neck, she was able to turn enough to see Porsupah encased in a rough mold of polypane foam. He was packaged as neatly as the polished figurine York had sold her. Her head had cleared and she strained to see as much as possible. Because of the neck strap she could raise her head only a little, but could turn it all the way to left or right. Despite its strength, the strap still felt like fine leather and didn't chafe. Even so, she had doubts that they were so constructed because their owner wished to seem solicitous of her health.

When she looked up she saw an old man. He was seated in a raised chair at the foot of the bench. His clothes were garish, loud, and clashed badly. Gray-white hair was parted down the middle and combed off to both sides, tied at the back in a pigtail. She found the air of polite concern he affected while staring down at her positively revolting. She would have preferred some honest drooling.

He was an ugly old man. Not that his features were particularly repulsive; they weren't. But the aura of evil he carried about him was as perceptible as rotting wet vegetation. Some folk felt nice, some felt ugly. This one felt ugly.

"Hello, my dear," he said. The voice was high, almost girlish, but there was little hint of age in it—no quaver, and certainly no weakness. It wasn't even a tiny bit grandfatherly, although that was apparently the impression the man was trying to give. "Glad to see you're awake. Permit me to introduce myself."

"Not until you release me and my friend from these ludicrous contraptions!" she said, putting as much ice into her words as possible. The oldster didn't appear chilled. "And until you explain yourself. Then perhaps I may forgive you enough to make your acquaintance. This is a strange way you have of doing business."

"I suspect, my dear, that your concern with my business is not from the point of view of a purchaser. Meanwhile you should know—whether you 'forgive' or not—that my name is Dominic Rose, my title Lord, and that you are presently ensconced, however indelicately, in my own residence some several hundreds of kilometers from Repler City. As for releasing you, I have two pilots currently undergoing treatment in my private dispensary. One has a broken kneecap, the other six parallel wounds in his belly that your not-so-stuffy companion put there."

"I do apologize for that," broke in Porsupah. "I was aiming for his eyes, but he slipped. I will have the peasant's head and my Uncle his ears when word of this outrage is revealed!"

"You will have nothing but a short existence if you persist in upsetting my liver, Tolian. Your 'Uncle's' reality is suspect. Now then," he continued, turning back to Kitten, "if you will simply tell me who you and your friend are, we might avoid any messy unpleasantness. I should also like to know which of several governments or competitors of mine you are working for."

"I don't see that my identity should be in question," she replied venomously. "Surely you've gone through our private effects by now!" Inside she was beginning to shake a little. This fellow was too direct. Such men survived by a habit of discarding semantic chaff and going straight to the point. Cold men disdained word-play.

"Oh yes," Rose said. "They declare you, quite thoroughly, to be one Pilar van Heublen. A young lady of respectable means and impeccable pedigree here on a pleasure trip from Myla IV. Should I request confirming detail, I am sure you could embroider these facile evasions elegantly."

"Why should you doubt them?"

"There are several reasons, my dear," he sighed. "At least one of which, I am informed, you are already aware of. I wish you wouldn't try to bandy words with me. You openly brandish a forbidden import, Terran tobacco, in full view of several police. Not only do they not take you into custody, they studiously ignore you! This brands you as something other than what you claim to be. You might still be the same *person* your Ident claims, but I doubt it. In any case, I doubt your avowed purpose in coming here completely, wholly, instinctively.

"A false identity, influence of a high order with the police, coupled with interest in a truly rare drug only recently available again on the market, add up to more than a wealthy flit out for a new thrill. Your Ident and credit slip appear to be perfectly legitimate, and I assure you they have been gone over by experts. This makes you doubly suspect; such things are obscenely difficult to forge. Work of such a high order few organizations can afford. Governments are among these. A very few of my competitors, too. But they are not usually so subtle in their method. When they seek information they are more apt to send a dozen inquirers with persuasions of explosive mien. This leaves us where? Back with governments again. Now, I dislike bureaucrats on principle. If so, I dislike you. Anyone who interferes in the business affairs of a simple old man I dislike!

"I especially dislike pretty tourists who can throw a side-kick capable of breaking a man's leg, from a sitting position, no less. I think if you weren't tied down you might even try to break mine. Being an old man, I'd crack very easily. My bones are brittle, I'm afraid. Everywhere but my head. Perhaps you represent even more than our local police, umm? The Commonwealth, mayhap? Or even the Church?"

Kitten feigned a long sigh. "Old man, you have a maniac imagination. Or possibly it's simple senility."

Rose's expression did not change. "You're as feisty as you are lovely. I'd rather not ruin one to modify the other. And you may be right about my imagination. I'm using it right now. I'll keep on using it until you tell me what I have to know. The same will apply to your short friend." He gestured in Porsupah's direction.

"Perhaps you, Tolian, are more inclined to answer a few questions?"

"I vow vengeance!" Porsupah shouted. "Vengeance, when my family learns of this! You will *wish* we were merely government puppets! My great Uncle is the second most powerful metals manufacturer on—!"

Rose was shaking his head slowly. "Such fine acting! Still, there is always the long, *long* chance that you are who you claim to be. That your ease with tobacco was due merely to ignorance all around, or some fantastic bribes in the proper places. In that case, I will later apologize profusely for what I am about to have done. For now, I would rather proceed."

He pressed a button or switch below Kitten's line of sight. There was the sound of a door opening. Kitten looked up and to the left to see an opening appear in the side of the room. A tall male figure entered. It was well-muscled and nude to the waist. A black hood pierced with three slots for eyes and mouth covered the man's head down to the shoulders.

Kitten laughed—not easy, under the circumstances. "Oh . . . oh now, *really!* How terribly, terribly melodramatic!"

"Isn't it?" said Rose rather fondly. "Please forgive me, my dear. I'm something of a traditionalist."

The figure walked to a small wheeled cart and pushed it over next to Kitten's bench. He stopped it close by her head. A large metal case sat on the cart. The man uncoupled four metallic latches and swung the two halves of the case open. The contents gleamed in the soft fluorescent light like faceted gems. They comprised a complete portable surgery.

"Physical torture!" she said contemptuously. "How unutterably crude! If you would persist in this idiocy, I would at least expect a modicum of sophistication!"

Rose smiled for the first time. There was no humor in it.

"The allegation has been made before, my dear. As I've indicated, I'm pretty nostalgic about some things. Despite the great advances in human technology, certain basics remain essentially unchanged. Only the methodology is improved. Also, I confess cheerfully that my motives are not wholly practical. The procedure involved provides me with a certain amount of pleasure. I *like* hearing pretty girls scream. We all have our little affectations. Mine is neither new nor unique. It's a time-honored human pastime. At least you must give me credit for my choice of tools. You're looking at a complete portable laboratory for organic repair—a very expensive toy, I assure you. Not the slightest danger of infection."

"How considerate you are!" Kitten rasped. She tried the bonds at one ankle this time, pulling upwards as well as back.

"You won't break those strappings, my dear. Now, this particular surgery was made by the best thranx technicians on Humus. For different purposes, of course. Cost me a pretty credit, not to mention faking hospital credentials for the purchaser and a host of other details! But I have few hobbies and can indulge. If you look closely, you can make out the imprint of the noted Elvor laboratories on each instrument. See how they catch the light!"

Kitten was trying to look anywhere but at the objects of Rose's adoration. One glance had been more than sufficient. Where Rose saw beauty, she saw only a nightmare of piercing points and fine-honed edges. Things for gripping, things for slicing, things for scraping.

She shuddered for the first time. Even the most experienced operatives had only so much control.

"I understand," she continued drily, "that the sublimation of normal desires through the use of such devices is positive proof of the wielder's impotence."

"Such well-honed insults! Such delicately practiced invective!" Rose clapped his hands boyishly. "I've read formal psychology, my dear. That is true in a few cases. Only a few. Anyway, as you can see, I've turned the actual operation—pardon the pun—over to this fine young friend of mine. It is him you should be trying to dissuade. He requested most firmly that he be permitted to perform as my surrogate. I agreed, because of my persistent problem in such things. I have a regrettable lack of patience and tend to get carried away early. That spoils things much too soon. Very unprofessional, too. My youthful compatriot, however, brings not only the necessary patience to the task, but also a certain young enthusiasm. And he's received expert instruction, even if he remains less skillful than I."

The mention of the semi-naked young man reminded Kitten of his unspeaking presence. She turned, with difficulty, to stare curiously at him. On impulse, she gave him her best helpless-young-maiden look. It must have had some effect, because the young man finally spoke.

"I've always had a suppressed desire to play at lower abdominal surgery without bothersome encumbrances like anesthetics," he said smoothly. He was toying with a long thin pair of finely-crafted forceps with razor-sharp tips. They made a squeaky sound whenever the two blades snicked together. A hand came up and lifted back the black hood.

It was Russell Kingsley.

"Relax, Maijib," Hammurabi said to his First Mate. The hoveraft sped over the slick waters. "Rose won't try anything silly or unprofitable. He's old, but he's not stupid. Our best insurance is thousands of kilometers skyward. There's no way he can get to the dust aboard the *Umbra.*"

"Even so," said the diminutive Takaharu, "I'd feel a lot better about the whole business if you'd talk with him via comm and forget this needless appearance in person."

"No good, Maj. He wouldn't believe a word I said from the comfort of the *Umbra's* forecabin. He might consent to come aboard, but he's a tricky old devil. I'd rather not let him on ship. He needs something in the way of concrete proof of my seriousness. I'm it."

The hoveraft slowed as Takaharu slid the rented craft slowly around the rocky circumference of the island, searching for the landing. Hammurabi noted idly that the large quasi-evergreens grew down almost to the water's edge, where the green stalks of water plants took over from the land-dwellers. It had been the same on all the islands they'd passed thus far. It was the same on Will's Landing, the island on which Repler City was located. It was more intense at the equator and less so nearer the poles.

The docking area sat at the head of a natural inlet. Several other vessels, one a transport of fair size, were tied up or beached at the landing. As they rounded the last point the comm buzzed and Takaharu leaned to flip the channel open. The small vidscreen lit but no picture appeared.

"You in the blue raft—identify yourself and state your business."

Mal leaned forward into the pickup eye of the raft's vidcast unit and spoke towards the omni-directional mike.

"Malcolm Hammurabi, Captain-Owner of the free freighter *Umbra*. To see Lord Dominic Rose. Business. As was earlier agreed, my pilot and I are unarmed."

They sat quietly while someone on shore dutifully relayed this information to someone equipped to deal with it. The raft's fans droned like an idle beehive beneath the floor.

The screen flickered briefly, then cleared. An unremarkable middle-aged man appeared on the screen glass. He was trying hard not to look bored.

"You're early, Captain. His Lordship has just entered conference. I am instructed to direct you to land. His Lordship cannot meet you there, but there will be someone suitable to greet you dockside and conduct you to the residence. Take the third slip, please."

The light faded, taking the face with it.

"Efficient S.O.B.," Takaharu said mildly. "A lot like his boss, I suspect."

"You're familiar with Rose's reputation?" Mal said, slightly surprised. "You didn't mention it before."

"Before what? I didn't expect you'd have personal dealing with him. No, friend of mine once bought an ampule of thryacin from one of 'his Lordship's' dealers. For a pet doggish that had the gout. Turned out to be colored ink." The mate revved the engine, coasted around a small moored boat. "The doggish died," he added.

"Um." Mal flipped off their own tridee. "Haven't seen him myself in some time. Doubt if he's changed much. He's a funny character. As they get older, most crooks become more fearful of death. Not Rose. He just becomes a little less moral, if that's possible."

Takaharu turned a sardonic face to his captain. "I wouldn't think so, judging from all I've heard of him."

"All things are possible. But if he's still degenerating he must be down to fractions by now. Your question would amuse him."

"And you think you can deal with a thing like that?"

Mal shrugged. "For what I want to do, I'll have to. According to the Holy Books, to quote, 'the percentage of matter in the universe that is composed of intelligent organic matter is comparable to a typical human's casual expectoration in any two of Terra's oceans.' It's not too difficult to put such people in proper perspective, depersonalize them. Try to think of a rock with rabies. Here's the slip."

Throwing more power to the rear-right fan, Takaharu eased the raft around and edged up onto the dull plastic mat tacked down over the sand. A tall young man waited by the side of a telescoping ramp. Although far slimmer, almost gaunt, he was taller than Mal. Nearly two meters, he would have towered over the Mate. Dark complexion, red hair, and boyishly good-looking, Mal noticed. The youth extended a long arm to help Mal up from the cabin port, realized his error and flushed.

"Apologies, sir. I'm afraid I'm not used to this."

"Skip it, kid."

"I am to conduct you to his Lordship's residence."

"Fine. As agreed, my pilot will remain on board until my return." He waved back to a watching Takaharu, who promptly cut the engines on the raft. The craft settled gently to the landing mat as air was expelled from its cushion.

Mal turned back to his guide and with a start noticed that the ornament curled about the lad's right shoulder was more than simply well-crafted. It was alive.

Pleated wings unfolded to reveal a long neck topped by a flat triangular head. Wide yellow eyes stared down at him quizzically. The Captain took a step backwards and groped for the blaster that wasn't there. The youth noticed the flinching movement and hastened to explain.

"It's all right, sir. He won't harm you. He's harmless. Well, tame, anyway." He reached up and began scratching the reptile on the back of the slightly ridged neck. The snake closed its eyes and relaxed, the wings refolding. "He's just wary of strangers, that's all." The youngster gestured up a slight incline. "The residence is just ahead. If you'll come . . ."

Mal matched strides with his guide—carefully staying on his left. He continued to keep a wary eye on the somnolent minidrag.

"That *is* a flying snake, isn't it? From Alaspin?"

"Yes sir. I'm surprised you recognized him. They're not often found off their native world, I understand."

"First time *I've* ever seen one off it. Gave me quite a turn. I believe the poison they throw is almost always fatal."

"Yes," replied the youth without breaking stride. "If the poison hits an open wound or the eyes, death usually occurs within a minute or so. If it hits bare skin or organic clothing it takes longer. It's highly corrosive, too.

There is an antidote, but the chances of a victim receiving it before death occurs is slight. The speed it kills with doesn't permit much time for turning some up."

"Not hardly," Mal replied. "I've never heard tell of a tame one."

"A fact which has been pointed out to me often, sir. It's a childhood pet. I can't remember a time when it wasn't close by me."

They were walking among a scattered complex of structures. Done in neo-landscape style, they provided excellent dispersal and natural air-cover, making good use of island vegetation. The irregular shapes were all brown and green, blending easily into the forest. Few windows could be seen. The only well-exposed structure was a single, needle-thin observation tower which poked its disc-shaped crown above the top of the tallest tree. The upper surface of the disc exploded in all directions in a wild electronic hairdo. No question but that their approaching hoveraft had been visually spotted long before commtact had been made.

"For a quiet, peaceable trader his Lordship takes rather extreme precautions," Mal ventured, hoping to draw some useful information from the lad.

"I cannot judge such things, sir. I have been in his Lordship's employ for yet a very brief time. By the way, my name is Philip. I am aware that his Lordship has many acquaintances who would not be displeased to see him expire in violence. So he takes care. An interesting personage."

Mal peered more closely at the youth's bland expression. "You're a perceptive young man. Yet you don't strike me as the type Rose would hire. What is your job? I might add that your off-planet accent sticks out like a solar flare."

"As to that, sir, I know it well. I've been on Repler the same short time . . ."

"Damned if I can place your accent. Yet . . ."

". . . but one seeks employment where one can. I did

not know for whom I was to work when I took the job. One of his Lordship's subalterns hired me. I am good at my work."

"Which is?" Mal prompted.

"Well . . . watch out for that branch, sir . . . currently my title is 'apprentice sanitation engineer.' I work with the less popular by-products of existence. Keep finer sensibilities from contact with them. At least, that's what it says in the manual." He grinned, added by way of apology, "I'm afraid his Lordship's selecting me to greet you was a calculated offense."

Mal grinned back. "Don't let it bother you. Seeing that damned thing play arm-jewel on your shoulder makes up for it, plus some." He gestured at the deadly reptile.

They arrived by a building so well camouflaged it seemed a part of the hillside. Not the largest of the complex, it was clearly designed even from the outside as a place for living rather than for business.

The guide pressed a palm to one side of the green-brown wall. A wide double panel separated with a slight hiss, offering entrance. A long alcove was revealed within. It was completely walled with bronze-inlay mirrors and carpeted in synthetic furs. They entered.

The corridor made several sharp, twisting turns, and they descended at least one, possibly two, levels. Several doorways and electronic portals were met and passed. Some appeared without warning in the mirrored sides. If the setup had been designed to confuse, it succeeded.

After several minutes of casual if complicated strolling, they came to a moderate-sized room. It was furnished magnificently in antique Terran. The furnishings looked like the real thing, not reproductions or fakes. But then, old Rose was probably doing well these days and wanted to show it. Mal's eye was quickly drawn to an elegant old television set. It had to be non-functional. Just the chassis was worth a small fortune. Ancient precursor of the tridee, it sat alone on its own pedestal.

At the same time that he was estimating the thing's worth in antique shops on half a dozen planets, he wondered crazily if maybe it *could* still be functional. A familiar young voice interrupted his musings.

"You're to wait here, sir. His Lordship will join you shortly."

Mal shook hands with the likable youngster as the other turned to depart.

"Pleasure meeting you, friend. If you've ever a mind to learn spacing, my ship, the *Umbra,* is listed in all the registries."

"It's always been a wish of mine, sir." For a moment the youngster's face acquired the shadow of someone—oddly—much older. It passed and he looked down at the Captain. "But now that I might make use of such an offer, I'm too busy with other things. Still, one never knows. Perhaps some day, when I've settled one or two personal things . . ." He smiled easily and left Mal alone in the room.

After contemplating the portal by which the youth had departed, Mal turned and walked over to the incredibly archaic video set. He began examining it in some detail, wishing at the same time that he was more familiar with such profitable trade items as luxury antiques and similar oddities. He was in the process of trying to open the hinged back to see how much of the innards were original when Rose entered via another of the ubiquitous paneled doorways.

"Good day, good day to you, Captain Hammurabi! I've heard tell of you in shipping circles. They speak well of you there." The old man extended a hand.

Mal took it and immediately felt dirtier than when he'd entered the room. Without waiting for an invitation he sat himself down on a comfortable-looking old easy chair. It was covered in hand-stitched upholstery and was worth a few thousand credits at the least.

"Can I order something for you, Captain? Liquid refreshment, mayhap? The congenial companionship of a nubile young lady? Well-trained, I assure you."

"A fast shot of bloodhype, perhaps?" said Mal evenly. He'd taken the offensive since sitting himself down and intended to maintain it until he left the island kilometers behind. "Don't try and look startled. You knew I had it and you knew I knew what it was, or I wouldn't be here now. No, skip the oh-so-coy verbal byplay, too. I don't appreciate it and I've no time for it."

Rose sighed with great care. "So few of the accepted verities remain these days. You youngsters ignore the pleasures of a game you don't even understand. Such hurry, such rush, such haste to make money! But as you will. How much?"

"It's not for sale."

"Oh come now, Captain!" chuckled the old merchant. *"Everything* is for sale! I know. I've bought it. Your very livelihood depends on how astutely you hire your body and the bodies of your crew out to the highest bidder. And you profess to know what is and what is not available for sale!" The last words dripped contempt.

"I won't shoot words with you, Rose. You've more experience at it than I, for one thing. For another, long dialogues full of double-entendres and metaphors bore the crap out of me. Also, you might just trick me into saying the wrong thing at the wrong time and I'd feel bound by it. Now, this is what I want:

"I want you to halt all traffic in bloodhype. I want you to destroy any not yet shipped. I want you to supply a list of known addicts—addicts, Rose; not pushers, not dealers, addicts—to Church authorities so that those few cases which haven't passed the point of no return can be treated. I want you to make a respectable effort—if you have enough control, which I suspect you do—to shut off all production of the drug and to destroy whatever growths or synthetics that furnish the raw stuff for the re- fined product."

"That's interesting," Rose said, helping himself to a transparent chocolate from a silver dish nearby. "One thing for you, Captain. Your threats are specific. I like that."

"Shipwaste!" Hammurabi said in disgust. "I said I wouldn't bandy words." He slammed a fist the size of a small ham onto an ancient coffee table. The old wood groaned alarmingly.

Rose swallowed the last of the chocolate, licked two fingers daintily.

"Pardon, Captain, but somehow you did not impress me as the altruistic type."

"Any man's nature contains a certain number of variables, Rose. On rare occasions it behooves some of us to do a decent thing."

"Never suffered the urge," replied the drugger.

"Some variables are all at the same end of the psychological spectrum. In return for cutting off future profits, which are always speculative anyway," Mal continued, "I'll return all the other drugs to you. You can have back your aelo, mak, heroin-B, and all the rest. I'll mention nothing of any of this to the authorities and post a personal bondship to an independent broker to guarantee it. Only one other being on the *Umbra* knows what your little case of spice contains, and she won't talk without my say-so. Records of the initial chemical analysis of the contents of the spice jars will be wiped by my own hand from the ship's memory core."

"How good you are! And if I do not care for your terms?"

"Then I go straight to the padre in Repler City with the drugs and every scrap of knowledge I can gather concerning their origin, destination, and method of shipping. Not to mention a certain old man whose business it is to speed such filth on its merry way."

Rose sat quietly, smiling, thinking. The thoughts and quiet Mal could understand. The smile could be forced, or it could be genuine. A genuine smile would mean unforeseen and unplanned-for factors—to wit, an ace-equivalent in the deck. Wait and see.

Rose appeared to be fascinated by the fingers of his left hand. He turned his attention to the right, as though to assure himself that it did, indeed, match its mate.

"Now I'll introduce a little something extra into the universe, Captain. Since you insist on playing the role of the gallant, honest, good-samaritan type—ergo, civilized . . ."

"Words again?" Hammurabi said irritably.

". . . I believe I shall try you on damsels-in-distress. It should prove instructive. When I entered you were absorbed in an inspection of that lovely 20th-century video set—a genuine Victor, I might add. Like myself, the insides had long since reached an advanced state of decomposition. They have been replaced with especially adapted modern equivalents. Watch it. You'll see something."

Rose removed a pencil that wasn't from a breast pocket. He fiddled with it for a moment. A picture in full tridee appeared instantly. It displayed an exquisitely attractive young girl strapped naked to a low wooden table. Off to one side an alien being struggled futilely in a cocoon of surfoam. Mal's trader encyclopedia identified it as a native of the planetary system Tolus. A fairly handsome young man, nude to the waist, held some unidentifiable metallic instrument over the girl's body.

"Sorry to have to leave you, Russell," Rose said into one end of the pencil. "Have you begun yet?"

The young man looked up into the screen and grinned.

"I was just about to, Uncle Rose. We've been having a chat."

"Commendable," replied Rose. "But while I don't wish to spoil your esthetic conception—I'm sure you've the whole afternoon's work well choreographed—I fear I must ask you to modify things somewhat. We've a slight change in plans. A guest, you see."

Kingsley leaned forward. "Oh, I see. A fellow aficionado? Big chap, isn't he?"

"Not a fellow connoisseur, no. Now then, if you would be good enough to do something interesting to the young lady? Elicit a dramatic response, if you will. That's a good lad!"

The young man bent over and did something with the silvery instrument. His upper torso obscured most of the motion. A long, high-pitched scream came through the receiver. It held for several seconds, then broke into a series of uneven choking coughs. Surprisingly, this was followed by a heated series of strong, unfeminine curses worthy of any dock-loader. The instrument moved again. Another scream, a little weaker this time.

"Stop that," said Mal.

Rose spoke into the pencil. "All right, Russell, that's enough. Don't damage her." The screaming stopped. There were no curses this time. Just silence.

"Use that thing in your hand, old man. Turn it off."

Rose smiled, did something to the pencil and slipped it back into his pocket. After a second's thought, he removed it again but did not activate the picture.

"I'm afraid I'll have to ask you to postpone your fun for now, Russell. But I promise you an equally interesting toy later tonight. Sorry to disappoint you, lad. I know how you were looking forward to this."

"Aw, Uncle Rose . . ."

Rose tut-tutted into the mike. "Business, my young friend, business." Once again the device was returned to the oldster's coat.

"We are about to make an exchange, then? Don't you even want to know who she is?"

"No. I may trouble to find out later; I don't now." The shipmaster obviously did not wish to talk.

"I'd think you might." His Lordship's leer invited a helping of knuckles. Mal had practiced controlling himself too long to let it lapse now.

"As to the protocol of exchange," began Rose briskly, "I'm a reasonable man. Things will be kept simple. Oh, you might promise me the young lady's silence in this matter. She is a government operative and will be difficult to convince. Likewise her furry friend. But I have confidence something workable can be arranged. It's a little thing now, anyway."

"Yeah," said Mal. He was staring at the converted video.

"So." Rose moved to a complex-looking desk and produced a small book with a pressure seal. He activated it with a twist, began riffling pages. "I don't expect you to have someone deliver the stuff to my front door, as one would receive dinner at his home in the city. I'll supply you the address of an operative of mine near the main Port, in Repler City. As soon as the case is delivered intact into his possession and he considers himself safe— you may keep the spices if you prefer, they're quite good —you, the young lady, and her friend will be permitted to board your craft. You will call your pilot and explain the delay. My men will do nothing to make him believe things are other than normal. You may consider escape, if you wish. Quite impossible.

"You will be released, as stated, when my operative cannot be touched by the weaponry of the City. At that point he will be here before you can reach safety and/or notify patrol craft to try and intercept him. My word on this. I've never broken it where business is concerned. You may think me a nasty fellow, but I'm an honest nasty fellow. I won't shoot you in the back—for at least a day. Then I will do my level best to see you exterminated."

"How kind you are," Mal muttered. He stood. "You're really going to let the girl and her friend go? I can't guarantee her silence."

"About that, now. Just keep her from contacting her superiors for, oh, three days local time. Then I'll consider that part of the agreement fulfilled. At that point she can babble her pretty head off. The Church will understand. No court would prosecute you. You see, I will have relocated myself by that time. The mere fact that an operative of her age was able to penetrate this far indicates that my business position here has become untenable. Apparently the local intelligence—damn that bug!—knew quite a lot, but weren't sure what lot was what."

"If you'll supply me with a caster, Rose, I'll notify my Mate and inform him of procedure. He'll listen."

"How will he know you're not saying anything under the muzzle of a blaster?" Rose asked, curious.

Mal stared down at the aged drugger. "Because he knows I wouldn't be in that situation, mister. Either the blaster-pointer or I would be dead, so it couldn't arise. I don't trust people with guns. They're apt to act rashly. I'm glad you didn't opt to employ one. I want to see that girl as soon as possible."

"Oh, she's all right. Kingsley's young, but talented. He'd barely begun. I'll see that you and she are put in the same room. In fact, I insist on it. You may find this arrangement more to your profit in the end. I would. Although I don't believe the pretty-pretty will be in the mood for idle conversation for a while. Or anything else." He gestured at the video. "As I said, my young friend is talented. Still, he hasn't yet acquired the delicacy of touch long practice brings."

Mal held up a massive fist, held it out where Rose could get a good look at it. "Let's skip the morbid dialogue, shall we? In the interests of logic. Otherwise you may push me to the point of breaking your scrawny neck. That might throw a crimp on the whole elaborate deal, mightn't it?" He took a step towards the drugger.

Instinctively, Rose stepped back. "Um, yes, it could complicate things if I were to prematurely pass on. This way, if you will."

Mal sat in a chair in the single room to which they'd all been confined. Dressed now, the tall girl lay sleeping on the couch across from him. She'd been treated and given a mild sedative. He didn't look at her. Porsupah, the Tolian, was busy at a single cabinet. He was mixing something liquid that had a faint aroma of sage. He walked over to the girl and gently shook her. Instead of talking he handed her the glass. Taking it without a question, she sipped, glanced up at the smiling Tolian, and downed the rest in a series of long swallows.

"Whew! What was in that, you offspring of a comet-cat?"

"Sorry, culinary secrets are reserved. Clan oaths, you know."

"Clan oaths, my sweet Aunt's grape juice!" She blinked several times. "Whoo!"

"What a quaint remarking!" said Porsupah. "That is a bit of terranglish slang that's completely new to me."

"It's not really accepted slang, Pors. My Aunt . . . Jo, on my father's side . . . was really sweet. She also drew produce from grapes. Only it wasn't exactly . . . well, the vines wouldn't have recognized the results of their efforts by the time she was finished with them. My father used to swear by it."

She swung her long legs off the couch, wincing slightly. She breathed long and evenly. At this point she seemed to notice Hammurabi for the first time.

"Thanks . . . whoever you are." Her gaze was direct, the feeling of thankfulness clear as quartz. It made him acutely uncomfortable. He squirmed. He'd hoped that when she sat up her evening outfit would show a little less flesh. No such luck. Gravity and the manufacturer conspired against it. Not that he'd mind, ordinarily. But whatever their situation was, it was not ordinary. He didn't need anything taking his mind off the business at hand. Speaking of business and hands . . . there, see?

Despite the ordeal she'd just undergone, the girl was reacting calmly. This also was not ordinary. He couldn't rationalize it. This also made him nervous.

She was staring at him. "Well, telepathize my thighs if you must, but say *something!* I'm not asking for a biography, you know."

"Qua? Oh, name's Hammurabi. Malco . . . Mal Hammurabi. I'm captain and owner of the free-freighter *Umbra.* Puts you one up on me."

"Kitten Kai-sung. And scrunching your eyebrows down like that doesn't hide your line of sight at all."

"Sun-father!" Mal sighed in frustration. He continued, a mite belligerently. "Does my staring at your legs make you so full-fission nervous?"

"No. Does it make *you* nervous?"

"*Yes,* goddammit, and we're not in a position where I can spare time to do proper appreciation to them, and that makes me a deal more upset!"

Kitten rubbed the edge of her right index finger slowly over her lower lip.

"What sort of alternate position did you have in mind?"

"Give it up, Captain," advised Porsupah, drink comfortably in hand. "She'll drive you to null-hike."

"Meaning I'm not free-floating already?" Mal responded. The pseudo-pserious atmosphere broke like a light fog, dissolving into laughter. No one minded that it tended a little too much to the hysterical.

"Okay," Kitten said finally, gasping. "Truce declared. Lieutenant Porsupah here and I are both in the Intelligence Arm of the United Church. If that old bugger has this place wired he's welcome to the information, since your presence has apparently persuaded him to let us live." She glanced at her partner, then back at Mal. "Might as well tell you that our purpose was to try and tie this creature Rose to renewed traffic in bloodhype, an especially vile drug."

"We were discovered through one of those careless little slips that always happen to other operatives," Porsupah continued philosophically. "It's always the little slips. Of the myriad *jukill* ways to ruin an assignment! And we as much as had sealed proof that he was running the stuff through Repler! I don't mind telling you, friend, you pulled us out of a whisker-thin spot." The appendages in question gave a humorous twitch.

"Now, don't get me started again," said Mal, grinning. "If it's any consolation, you were lined out the right way. I've seen a shipment. Several grams worth."

"You *have?*" Kitten shouted excitedly. She shot to her feet, then hunched over suddenly. She sat down slowly, muttering. After an uncomfortable silence she looked up and continued as though nothing had happened.

"There are several things I must do when we get out of here, Captain. One of the first is to shut off—as slowly as possible—a narcissistic amalgam of fermented proteins named Russell Kingsley."

Mal perked up more, interested. "So that *was* old man Kingsley's boy? I'd heard about him. Appears they weren't all rumors. Only the good things. You work for a man and you really only know him professionally."

Now it was Porsupah's turn to express interest. "You are friends of the family, then?"

"Only as far as the bank. I'm on Repler now because the *Umbra's* making delivery on a major shipment for Chatham Kingsley Fisheries and Goods, Ltd. The old man's a bit of a decadent type himself, but only healthy stuff. I really don't think he's aware that his itty-bitty baby boy's a romping sadist. Mother died when the boy was a kid. I'd assume Russell's been left to develop his own life-style since then."

"I'm touched," said Kitten in a voice that would chill molten copper.

"He does dote on the kid," Mal added.

"I am sorry for that," she continued in the same tones. "I had hoped his imminent extinction wouldn't inconvenience anyone else. I still can't really believe it would. Still," she continued a little easier, "to know that you've actually seen the stuff . . ."

"About that. Appears that Rose's latest shipment accidentally got mixed in with Kingsley's cargo. Mixup was discovered accidentally by Rose, intentionally by two of his operatives, and accidentally by me. I came here with the idea of striking a bargain: In return for him halting traffic in the jaster, I wouldn't go to the authorities with enough warrant for a mindwipe. Don't get me wrong. Most drugs I could care less about—let the idiots who need them have 'em. May they kill themselves off quickly and quietly. Bloodhype is something else. It sheds filth on everyone who's seen what it does. I've seen . . . but instead, I had to use it to bargain you two out. He fully intended to kill you, you know."

"You still shouldn't have agreed to it," Kitten said.

"You had no say in the matter," replied Mal.

"Suppose I kill myself now and Porsupah does likewise?"

"Fine. Then he threatens to kill *me* unless I have the drug turned over to him. If you take away his major bargaining point he'll forget niceties and try something like that. And I'd give him the drug to save myself, selfish fella that I am."

"I see." She sighed deeply. "I apologize for the difficulty we've caused you, Captain Hammurabi."

"Mal," he said.

"All right . . . Captain Mal." She grinned, frowned, got confused. "I can't let you do it. Do you really know what that stuff does to people?"

"A good deal better than you, I suspect, infant."

"Call me that again and I'll break your arm."

Mal smiled. "Might be you could at that. Point remains, however, that I've already made arrangements for the exchange to be carried out."

"There's no way to cancel it?" Porsupah interrupted.

"Oh, if I could get to a transceiver—say, the one on the raft that brought me—before Rose's contact receives the drugs, it could be done. I'd consider that a very unlikely possibility, however—even if I wanted to do it, which I don't. See, I intend not only to save my own life but yours too. Even if you don't appear to value it too highly."

"It remains a question of proportion, Captain," began the Tolian philosophically. "The number of lives at stake here far exceeds three. And despite what you may think, I happen to have become quite attached to mine."

"Right on both counts," Kitten added.

Mal was getting a bit exasperated. This damsel-in-distress was not reacting properly at the prospect of salvation.

"Listen, you altruistic femin . . . !" he began heatedly.

She glared back at him, and seemed quite willing to shift the argument to a physical level.

Auspiciously, the door chimed. Porsupah threw them both a look that was more wilting than any words could have been, and they relaxed—somewhat. The Tolian spoke towards the door pickup.

"We can't lock ourselves in, you know."

The panel slid back to reveal the tall figure of Mal's young guide. The youth carried a tray filled with a multitude of small dishes: white-brown shellfish, bread, several kinds of butter and other condiments, cinnamon bark, steamed tubers, smoked snails . . .

"They called me to the kitchen," he said as he set down the tray, "and ordered me to bring this to you."

Porsupah and Kitten saw the flying snake at the same time. They froze.

"Don't worry," said Mal easily. "It seems pretty tame."

"I know what one of those things can do," replied Kitten as she edged over towards Mal. "Victims don't die easily." He resisted an impulse to put an arm around her. She might decide to break it.

The youth straightened and turned to leave, then paused and looked back at Mal.

"You're being restrained against your will, aren't you?"

"I'd sort of think it was obvious," said Kitten.

"Not necessarily. His Lordship often has guests whose status is not what it seems." He rubbed the scales at the back of his pet's head. The snake looked up, then relaxed on the lanky shoulder.

"I might say that I know about the drug, sir." Three faces looked up in surprise. "Your arrival has made it easier for me to find out some things I'd been curious about for a long time. It's not very pretty." There was a long pause, then the youngster stared sharply at Mal. "If I help you escape, will you promise to see that something's done about it? The drug, I mean."

Kitten leaned forward eagerly. "You really think you can get us out of here?"

Philip smiled at her most unyouthfully. "If you don't fear a fair chance of getting shot, electrocuted, or drowned, yes."

"You know a way out of this maze, we'll try it," Mal replied.

"Not only will we see about the drug," added Kitten coaxingly, "but I'm sure the government will arrange something material in the way of gratitude."

"And protection from whatever is left of Rose's petty empire when the Church finishes with it," added Porsupah.

The youngster looked over at the much smaller alien. When he spoke again, his voice was a good octave higher and the words momentarily unrecognizable. Mal knew a little Tolian, as he did about half a hundred languages. Only enough to trade by, though. The musical syllables rolled off the youth's palate fluidly and without hesitation.

Philip broke off in what seemed an abrupt manner but probably wasn't. He left, the panel sliding shut quietly behind him.

"Well," said Kitten, "what was that all about?"

"His High Tolite is excellent, really remarkable. He even has the diphthongs down, the epiglottal stops, everything."

"I'm sure he can rattle off the local equivalents of c-a-t and d-o-g without a second breath," said Kitten, "but what did he say?"

Mal was looking at the closed portal. "Rather surprising talent to find in an apprentice sanitation engineer, wouldn't you say?"

"Is that what he is?" asked Porsupah. "Well, besides exchanging a regional prayer with me—nice to hear the amenities again—he just asked us to wait. Said he'd return soon and to be ready. He reiterated his feelings about the drug traffic and disclaimed any need for protection. Said he would take care of himself."

"Also pretty cocky for an apprentice sanitation engineer," Kitten said. "No matter, if he can slip us out."

"He added that he hoped both of you were strong swimmers." Porsupah sat down and began to remove his flexible mukluks. He wiggled each webbed hind foot as it appeared. "The question, of course, did not arise in respect to myself."

"Really think he can get us out?" Mal queried. He was interested in the little alien's opinion of their youthful benefactor.

"Why ask me?" Naked, the furry Tolian walked over to the table where the tray of delicacies had been set. He commenced a serious study of the smoked escargot.

"I can say with assurance, however, that I intend to do nothing for the next several minutes, barring earthquake or Redemption, but eat. I've had nothing in my belly since we arrived here save memories."

"Just don't overdo it," said Kitten, moving to join him. "It seems we're in for an extensive journey by water. And if you get a cramp out there, I'm sure as hell not towing you."

They were down to the last pair of hors d' oeuvres and Mal was dreaming of distant steaks when the youngster returned. His clothes were dirty, with patches of grime and oil staining the coveralls. The flying snake was perched on its same shoulder. It was coiled tight, the triangular head holding steady and unwinking a foot in the air. The pleated wings were only half furled, ready for instant flight. The snake gave them a soulless once-over, decided that no one in the room was a candidate for instant destruction, and relaxed somewhat.

Philip's voice was low and he was panting hard but evenly.

"After me now, quickly!" Without looking back he turned and left.

They followed. In the lead, Mal saw that the youth was already at the end of one hallway, waiting where it intersected another. As soon as he spotted Mal, the youngster disappeared around the corner. He reappeared a moment later and beckoned urgently. They ran to join him.

"Stay low and quiet, and along the far side," he whispered. "And watch out for the bodies."

He turned and led them up a corridor.

They passed several doors, all unopened. Once their

guide gestured for a halt and they all froze while voices got louder somewhere up ahead, then faded. They continued forward. The only sound was of controlled breathing. They came to a door set in a low recess, which was slightly ajar. Philip disappeared inside, returned almost immediately. Kitten and Mal both had to stoop to get through the sub-two-meter overhead. Mal noticed the metal engraving in the door.

BIOENGINEERING PERSONNEL ONLY
ADMITTANCE RESTRICTED

Besides bending, Mal and Kitten had to step high to avoid stumbling over the two corpses that lay crumpled just inside the entrance. Even in the dim light Mal could tell how one had died, from the unnatural angle at which his head rested. Dressed in mechanic's overalls, the other lay prone with an unfired sonic pistol in one hand. His other hand covered most of his face. Which was just as well, if the long grooves seared into the revealed cheek were any indication of what lay beneath. Milk-white bone gleamed at the bottom of one groove. The muscles in the man's face and arm were frozen at full contraction. What the hand covered would not be pretty, no. The flying snake had been at work here.

Kitten was busy examining the numerous long tunnels which led from the small room. Clearly they were in the maintenance arteries of the island. Water trickled along the floor of several dark corridors, disappeared into unseen drains. The natural stone walls were damp at the entrances to some, hot and dry at others. None rose higher than the cramping height of the room they were in. Philip turned without speaking and plunged down the one closest on their left. At least it was a little wider, if not really spacious.

There was barely enough light from the widely spaced red fluorescents to make out the form of the lanky youth moving ahead of them. The otherworldly figure moved with a slightly bloody tinge to it from the safety lights. It was leading them who knew where? Maybe it was all a stunt of their captor's. Kitten had experienced his sense of humor. Maybe he'd decided on some especially gruesome way of disposing of them, decided it would be safer to write off the fabulously profitable shipment—unlikely as it seemed. At any moment their guide could disappear around a turn, leaving them to wander in a maze of filthy underground passages among unseen terrors while Rose's whining laugh echoed from hidden speakers.

She found herself dripping inside the fancy evening dress. It had not been designed for running over slippery floors in a hunched over position.

"Too frigging humid!" she muttered.

"Nonsense!" replied the disgustingly cheery voice of the Tolian. Excepting its lack of large land masses, Repler was much like his home world. Like many races, however, the Tolians did not go in for colonization on any significant scale.

"If it bothers you, just think how nice and dry you were a short while ago—on his Lordship's playtable."

"You're not being funny," Kitten replied, panting heavily now. No doubt the damn tunnel ran out under the ocean and they'd run like this all the way to Repler City. "How'd you like me to tie knots in your whiskers?"

"Have to catch me first." The little alien was the only one whom the low ceiling didn't inconvenience. He had plenty of room. His webbed feet made loud slapping sounds, like sponges, wherever they hit the trickle of water which flowed along the center of the floor.

"Where does this highway lead, anyway?" asked Mal. Kitten stared at him enviously. Despite his huge bulk, he didn't even appear to be breathing hard. "And where does this water come from?"

The youngster's voice drifted back from close ahead. "Condensation. The tunnel—this one, anyway—is a service access to the sewage plant. Both the intake for fresh water and the outlets for treated sewage are monitored from there. Each has an electrified gate at the end which is controlled by the master island defense computer. But they can both be shut down from the plant for up to an hour. If I can cut the power to the gates from the plant console, I can probably also powerdown the alarms without alerting anyone. That way, if someone comes in and inspects the system after we've started out, nothing will seem amiss. Unless he thinks to check the gate power lights, in which case we'd be finished. But since the entire system is automatic, that's not likely. We shouldn't have any trouble."

"He says," added Mal sardonically. Even he was beginning to pant a little now. "Assuming all this works, how do we get from the plant to the hoveraft?"

"One outtake tunnel comes out at the mouth of the harbor inlet. The gates at the end of each are designed more to keep out undesirable marine fauna than intelligent beings. It's an efficient design but not very sophisticated. From the gate it's a short swim to the landings. While powerful, the real island defenses are located further out. And don't worry about the water. Compared to the seas of most worlds, the salt content here is very low. Of course, the treated sewage, while thoroughly sanitized and thinned, wouldn't taste particularly good."

"Oh thanks," said Kitten drily. "I'll keep that in mind."

The tunnel made another sharp bend. Abruptly they found themselves in a small, well-lit room full of banks of automated machinery. Mal and Kitten stretched luxuriously.

Down a short, broad rampway to their right were two wide channels of water, one slightly greener than the other. Clear plastic domed above both. One end disappeared into the floor, while the other flowed off into a black hole in the stone wall. Philip noticed Mal's stare.

"The one on the left carries out the treated sewage. The other draws in seawater for purification."

"Surely the two don't open to the ocean next to each other," asked Porsupah.

"No. The intake channel leads out almost at a right angle from here. It opens on an untouched section of coast. The sewage channel exits near the inlet. The current is strongest there and aids in carrying the mixture out to sea. We'll be hugging the shore there, so the current shouldn't bother us. And swimming out with a current will help considerably. I don't know if we could make it against the intake pumps . . . The roof of both tunnels is uneven, but air shouldn't be a problem."

"What do you mean, 'shouldn't be'?" Kitten asked.

"Well," Philip glanced at his wrist chronometer, "it ought to be getting dark out by now. I didn't get a chance to look at any tide tables, and to ask would have been awkward, let alone suspicious. Sometimes when both moons are in the sky and Aug. is at its highest, the water level rises all the way to the roof of the channel.

"Not a drawback," said Porsupah to Kitten. "It'll do you well to hold your breath for a while."

She looked at him appraisingly. "I don't know whether to start with the whiskers on the left or the right. What do you think, Captain?"

But Mal was watching Philip. The youth had already removed the metal panel that protected one heavily in-strumented locker. He'd magically produced several com-plex but tiny tools, including one intricate-looking screw-driver affair with a head that was geometrically insane.

Philip put the tools neatly aside, looked up. "Captain, I think you ought to station yourself by that door over there." He added apologetically, "It's the only entrance from the complex proper. Miss Kai-sung, Porsupah-al, if you could remove a section of that plastic doming large enough for us to slip through, it would save a little time. The left-hand channel—there are transparent pressure-sensitive bolts on each side. It takes four, two to a side, to release one section."

Mal was sure the minutes were not being split into 60 equal parts. He found himself glancing anxiously from the access tunnel they'd used to the single doorway, then back to Porsupah and Kitten, who were working feverishly on their second bolt. Not having been removed for some time, the bolts were proving stubborn.

After a while, he found himself watching their guide intently. The youngster was working quickly and steadily. The long fingers moved spiderlike over the web of wiring, impulsistors, solid and fluid state components.

"Think we've been missed?" he asked.

"There's no way of knowing whether anyone's been ordered to visit you after I delivered the food," said Philip without looking up from his work. "I do know that there wasn't any tridee pickup in your suite. It doesn't make any difference now. I don't advise going back to check on it."

Mal wasn't surprised to see that the youth was sweating heavily. Whether from the concentration he was applying to his work or from nervousness, he couldn't tell.

The young engineer worked carefully now. "I just negated the alarm system. It should only take a minute now to cut power to the sewage gate—damn obsolete solid switches . . ."

"Isn't there an override on the computer for emergencies—like an unauthorized interruption in the power flow?" Kitten asked.

"This is where it would be managed. I'm handling that, too. It's tricky . . . I'm more worried about someone coming in while we're trying to swim the gate and switching power back on. We'd still get out . . . well-done."

"Hey, what . . . ?"

Mal didn't think, didn't look. He whirled and chopped hard, using his weight. The man never finished the sentence. Mal had become so absorbed with Philip's manipulations of computer innards he'd completely forgotten he was supposed to be watching the door. The man had entered unseen and uttered the single exclamation of surprise. Now he was lying motionless against the half-open portal.

Mal carefully closed the door, repressing an almost overpowering desire to look out and see if anyone else was beyond. He turned and bent over the fallen figure in the green biotech uniform.

"I didn't mean to hit him so hard," he said quietly. "He startled me."

"Yes," said Philip. He craned his neck for a better look, turned back to the console. "I believe you've broken his neck. Remind me to announce myself in advance if we're ever to meet on a dark street." He carefully replaced the exopanel and stood up, brushing his hands. "No sense letting them know what sections have been toyed with." He looked over at Kitten and Porsupah. "How are you coming with that doming?"

"A second," said Kitten, struggling on the last bolt. It came loose with a soft pop as the vacuum was broken. Together they lifted the released section and slid it over the doming in front. The revealed space left plenty of room for even Hammurabi to slip through with centimeters to spare.

Mal took a step towards the channel, then paused and looked at Philip.

"Yes, I concur, Captain." Mal nodded and went back for the body of the dead technician.

"Even if they've discovered our absence, they'll have no reason to suspect you've come this way," the youngster continued. "There are dozens of branches leading from the maintenance pod we entered."

"Let's discuss it later, over a mug of hot ceebeetea at some suitable city saloon," Mal said, hefting the corpse over his shoulders. Porsupah and Kitten had already slipped into the greenish liquid. They waded easily into the deep channel, holding onto projections from the sides to prevent the light current from pulling them down the dark cave.

"What do I do with the body? Like you say, the current carries sewage away. But this island isn't big. I wouldn't want some detection device to discover it floating about Rose's defense perimeter while we're trying to reach the raft."

"When we leave the gate, I'll hold it up while you center it underneath," said Philip. "The grating will pin it on the bottom securely enough." He put a hand on either side of the opening, slipped into the gentle flow. "I'm going to replace the panel from underneath. Since the bolts are clear plasticine, too, it won't show tampering unless someone looks hard right at the seals."

"You're awfully proficient at escapes for . . ."

". . . an apprentice sanitation engineer?" The youngster grinned. He helped Mal lower the limp body into the water. "I read a lot of cheap adventure stories." He reached up. Despite his height, he had to jump to grab hold of the edge of the removed section of doming. Successive jerks and tugs, with Mal holding him around the hips, slid it neatly back in place over their heads.

"What about this 'gate' you keep talking about?" asked Kitten. "With the power turned off, will it open?"

"Oh, it can be raised manually, all right. The positive charge it normally carries is considered sufficient to discourage nosy visitors, intelligent or otherwise. Nothing so crude as a manual lock on it." He turned and let himself drift into the brackish flow, moving easily with an occasional long, sinuous stroke. The others followed.

The water in the channel was comfortably warm, a carry-over from the sewage sterilization procedure. Still, Kitten found herself shivering slightly. There were no lights in the long cave and darkness was total. She swam with slow strokes, letting the current do most of the work. Now and then her hand would give notice of a slight bend in the channel. The youth hadn't mentioned anything about side tunnels, so she wasn't afraid of fumbling off into some fish-trap or heat chamber—much. She could sense pressure waves from a large mass moving parallel on her right. The faintly neanderthalic ship-captain, no doubt. She recalled how easily, accidentally, the big man had snapped the technician's neck, and mentally resolved to put a moratorium on all threats of arm-breaking.

Porsupah was somewhere behind. Being capable of swimming circles around any of them, it was decided that he should follow at a distance. This would enable him to give them a little time if any pursuit should develop. That beggared the fact that there wasn't a thing they could do about such pursuit, but it seemed too reasonable an idea to ignore.

Somewhere up ahead their youthful guide felt for a gate that might or might not be charged with lethal current. She took another breath. He'd been right about the tides. In some places there wasn't enough room to get one's head above water. In such spots she had to turn on her back. Then she would drift with only the upper part of her face above water, sometimes scraping the cold stone of the roof as she drew in long draughts of moist, stale air. Then it was turn, dive, and swim, heading for the next air pocket, pushing off the wall for a little extra distance and hoping she wouldn't miss it.

That happened only once. She surfaced and the air pocket was a blob of water-weed. She had to swim frantically ahead until a small pocket appeared. Panic would have used too much air, so she stayed ever so calm.

It was indeed totally black—cave-black, coal-sack black—in that tunnel. Blacker than the inside of your eyelids when closed. The only light in that mile-long, dayslong swim was the glow from her own wrist chronometer. A numerical firefly, it followed obediently, seeming a separate existence and not a part of her arm.

A few eons later, her outstretched right hand encountered something hard and cold. There was enough clearance so that her shoulders could rise out of the water. She held onto the grating for several seconds. Then she remembered that if certain circuits were reconnected, thousands of volts could shoot through the damp steel. She let go hurriedly. A voice sounded on her right.

"Hinges are a little stiff, Miss Kai-sung." It was Philip. "Ah, there!"

A moment later something broke the surface on her left with a loud whoosh. It was Hammurabi. He was followed seconds later by a thin whistle: Porsupah. Even the Tolian was panting. Not because of fatigue, but because the air here was anything but fresh.

"Everyone okay? All right, I'm going down to lift the gate," said the youngster. "Miss Kai-sung, you and Porsupah-al wait ten seconds and come after me. This tunnel descends slightly and then opens into the sea. It's

not a long drop, just deep enough to ensure that the outlet opening is always hidden from surface view. The shore
here is pretty rocky. Find a spot shielded from land. Captain, after they've slipped out I'll resurface inside. Then
you follow me down. I'll be holding the grating open from
the sea side. When you feel the bottom of the grate, tap it
with your watch and trail the body just behind you. I'll
hear it and let the gate drop. It ought to hold the corpse
to the seafloor solidly."

Without waiting for comment the youth hyperven-
tilated, then ducked under. Porsupah and Kitten counted
off the seconds together and followed. Water splashed the
perpetually moist walls and Mal's face. Several millennia
later Mal heard the youngster break surface.

"Ready, Captain?"

Mal took an unbreakable grip on the corpse's neck with
his right hand. "One question. I'm no herpetologist, but
I don't recall noticing any gills on your scaly companion."

"Oh, Pip? I discovered—quite by accident—that he
can go without oxygen for a surprising amount of time.
Some day I'll run across a xenoherpetologist who can
explain it to me. I'm going now." Deep breathing, an
echoing splash in the confining air bubble. Mal followed
shortly, the tech's body a tugging, naggingly buoyant
parasite. Fortunately, as Philip had said, the gate didn't
go deep. He felt for and encountered the prongs at the
bottom of the grating. Carefully, he eased the body belly-
up against them, then tapped one-two-three times with his
wristband. The grating immediately dropped with surprising speed, pinning the unlucky, unnamed man to the
muddy channel bottom.

Immediately Mal turned and swam, away and downward. He could feel pressure waves from another body
swimming alongside. The shipmaster had a moment of
worry. When the power to the gate was switched back on,
the body jamming it open ought to trigger every alarm on
the island.

But by that time they'd be long gone.

They'd better be.

The two men broke the surface together. Only one moon was still in the sky, but there was enough light to make out two dim figures on shore, huddled close by an overhanging block of gneiss. Two shadowed faces, one human and the other not, stared back. Mal and Philip swam over and hugged the boulder, catching their breath.

"Nice to breathe fresh air again," said Mal.

"Yeah. I'd like to rest too, but in the city. I'll feel a lot better when we're on board that hoveraft of yours."

"Which direction is the inlet?" Kitten whispered. "My sense of direction is scrambled."

"Just around that point," the youngster replied, pointing ahead. "The island's not very big, but parts of the complex go quite deep. Miss Kai-sung, you and Porsupahal don't know where the Captain's raft is beached, so be sure and stay close. The harbor is crowded enough to be confusing."

"Don't lecture me, my skinny samaritan. I'm a big girl now."

"What about harbor patrols and interior alarms?" Mal asked, to change the subject.

"Aren't many this close in. There is a transceiving shield, quite illegal—and efficient. Our best bet, therefore, is to get out of the landing proper and skim like hell until we pass the defense perimeter. Then we can cast unblocked to the Rectory in the city. Once they pick us up, his Lordship should be too busy packing to worry about us."

"You hope," said Kitten.

"The best of all possible Illities," he replied. He began paddling towards the point of land he'd indicated.

"Any other vessels expected tonight?" Mal asked, swimming close behind.

"I don't know for sure, but I don't believe so. Why?"

"Going by your description of Rose's setup and what I know of similar ones, this defensive situation is designed primarily for detecting boats trying to get in. It just might ignore any going out. With luck it will be quite a while before anyone notices our disappearance."

As they moved up the inlet, hugging the shoreline, Kitten couldn't escape the feeling that Rose was watching from somewhere in the trees. At any moment a light would lance out from the shadows and spear them with its unblinking glare. But they reached the raft landing without anything other than a few disturbed mollusks detecting their passage.

There were few lights on at the artificial beach. Nothing moved. Philip led the way up the pebbled plastic-sand cover. No one stopped him to ask what a sanitation engineer was doing out for a late-night swim—in full workwear. A gesture brought the others out of the water. Slick and hard, the plastic gave excellent purchase to hover vehicles. The little group had no trouble making their way towards the beached rafts, although there were places where some frantic scrambling was necessary. They huddled next to the deflated sac of one raft.

"I can make out one guard at the head of the loading pier," Philip whispered. "We ought to be able to slip inside your craft without his noticing us."

"I'd rather make sure he doesn't," said Mal. He disappeared quietly under the metal piering. Several minutes passed while the others waited and the moonlight grew dimmer. The dot that represented the guard abruptly doubled in size, then disappeared completely. After a short pause, Mal's voice floated across from the rampway of his raft.

"All clear now. Philip, you boost Miss Kai-sung and Porsupah up, then I'll pull you in."

It was a short dash to the side of the raft. Kitten felt two massive hands envelop her wrists. Suddenly she was standing on the ramp alongside the Captain. A second later Porsupah, then Philip, appeared.

"What about the guard?" Philip asked.

Mal was opening the lock. "Under the pier, in a clump of bushes. He shouldn't be spotted. Still, he might be required to report in on who knows what schedule? We'd better move." He noticed the young man's gaze still on him. "No, I didn't kill him."

The door swung back to reveal bright light and the muzzle of a small gun. It was wielded, fortunately, by a familiar small man.

"You gave me a start, Captain," said First Mate Takaharu. "I wish you'd apprise me in advance of these middle-of-the-night parties."

Mal moved past him to the center control console. He flipped switches, began warming the drive fans as gradually and quietly as possible. "Wasn't practical this time, either, Maijib. Neighbors would have resented not being invited. Lieutenants Kitten Kai-sung and Porsupah, Philip—my First Mate, Maijib Takaharu. You should all exchange greetings later, but just now let's get the shining hell out of here. . . ." He gunned the engines all at once, throwing everyone for the nearest support.

The raft backed at high speed into the water, sending a shower of spray across the inlet. Gears whining in protest, the little craft spun 360°. Skimming the surface at 200 kph, it kicked up a wall of faintly phosphorescent spray as it shot out of the harbor. A few night-prowling mudducks saw it go.

"I don't recall sending for you, technician."

The man in the blue serge uniform was obviously badly frightened. Also out of breath. "Your pardon, Lord. The two suspected Church agents and the freighter Captain you ordered held with them have disappeared."

Two birds sang in a cage to one side of the room. Rose turned and stared at them. One was bright blue, slightly milky like chalcedony. The other was a mottled yellow. He watched them for a while before pivoting back to face the tech.

"They've left the island." It was not a question.

"It must be so, Lord. The hoveraft the freighter Captain arrived in is missing from its landing. The guard assigned to watch was found under the piering nearby. He was paralyzed, but the meditech believes he will recover."

"How awkward all around," Rose replied evenly. He

had given no evidence of upset, evinced no loss of control. He was too old for that now. "Is it known how this was done?"

"Two men stationed near the confining suite were found dead in a service alcove. A check of the central recorder indicates that a portion of the immediate island restricted perimeter, specifically the gates protecting the water intake and sewage outlet channels, were powered down for some thirty minutes earlier this morning. A subsequent check of personnel revealed that two men, an apprentice sanitation engineer and a senior biotech, were missing. The body of the latter was discovered jamming open the gate guarding the sewage outflow channel. Also, one of the first two fatalities displayed clear evidence of both acid attack and nerve poison. The engineer was known to keep a poisonous reptile with him at all times."

"Quite ingenious," Rose murmured. He turned and depressed one of many switches set inconspicuously in the arm of a luxuriously upholstered couch. The ceiling of the exquisitely wrought bird cage began to move gently downwards.

Rose spoke without turning. "Any indication of how long ago the craft left the harbor?"

"Computing from the time of the power lapse and that of the pier guard's last report, Lord, it is estimated they have been gone now for about an hour."

"Far too long for any of our exterior defenses to be in range. Hmmm." The space inside the cage had been reduced by about half. The faint hum of a small electric motor could be heard. The song of the blue bird had grown uneven.

"This has been checked, of course?"

"Immediately, your Lordship. They are nowhere within the perimeter."

There was barely enough room now in the cage for the birds to stand upright. The mottled yellow was bouncing frantically between the unmoving floor and the descending roof. The blue's song had risen to a series of hysterical chirps and squeaks.

"I will be forced to run off-planet."

"An attempt to slip you into the Port could be best made now, Lord. Or arrangements might be made for a daring shuttle pilot to try and pick you up from one of the larger uninhabited islands."

Rose shook his head sadly.

"As soon as Major Orvenalix receives the report of those two agents, the first thing he will do is relay a full order to the customs' frigate. If he hasn't done so already. They'll relay his request to the nearest Navy port for a cruiser and a flock of stingships. Shuttles that don't land at Repler Port or Masonville are rare to nonexistent under any conditions. With the word out on myself, anything large enough to produce detectable atmospheric friction, down to a smallish meteorite, will be tracked to point of landing from point of tangency with every scope available."

A singularly penetrating chirp emanated from somewhere between the two layers of cage. They came together. A few barely discernable popping sounds resulted. From between the two metal plates oozed a tiny trickle of red. Two drops of crimson fell to the shining carpet, staining it.

Rose sighed deeply, turned back once more to the technician. "I'll want a single-seat raft, the fastest available. There is only one way for me to get safely off-planet in one piece. If it works, the authorities can fume till they obscure vision. I'll be completely untouchable. Not safe, necessarily, but untouchable. If it doesn't work out, why, my problems will be solved and an old man will finally get some rest. For now, though, I'm not sleepy."

"Will you require a driver, Lord?"

"No. I have to do this myself. You can't tell where I'm going if you don't know. Same goes for a driver."

The man turned to leave, paused. "Luggage, your Lordship?"

"A small packing case," said Rose thoughtfully. "Change of clothing in a collapsible packet. My credit slip, no gun. That's all."

The man paused once more by the door. "Good-bye, your Lordship."

"Good-bye, Masters. I'll be in touch—maybe."

"Sir." The blue-clad Masters closed the door quietly.

Vibbbraations stronger getting getting. The Vom had departed from its resting place of centuries so precipitously that the Machine, even with its tremendous speed, had not been able to analyze the results and react properly with sufficient speed. However, it still retained suitable thread of Vom-consciousness to follow it through the plenum. By the Machine's standards, the length of the Vom's travels was not far.

The basic problem remained unsolved. The Vom had escaped its ancient prison. The ring of monitoring stations were unpowered and sealed in fixed orbits around the dead planet. They could not be moved. Therefore a different solution was called for. The Guardian would have to be awakened from his long sleep. Without that, the Machine could only analyze and observe. It could not take action.

Not only was the situation unprecedented, there also remained the additional problem of obtaining sufficient stimuli to activate the Guardian. This required the mental presence of another conscious mind of an ability that at least approached that of the Guardian himself. Surprisingly, there was such a mentality somewhere ahead. It existed on the very planet to which the Vom had traveled. The Machine could no more analyze the moods and substance of that mind, however, than it could that of the Guardian or the Vom. That was not one of its functions.

The Machine Considered. It was dealing with a quantity as vital as it was unfamiliar and unpredictable. It would be best to bring the Guardian into activation proximity in such a way as to make it appear natural to the activating mind. All evidence of manipulation must be avoided. The key mind was clearly still in a state of stabilization. If handled improperly, it could be permanently damaged. This would be fatal.

The utilization of a number of smaller minds was implied. Fortunately, there were a multitude of suitable ones present on and about the planet. Operating in this fashion would also prevent the Vom from becoming alarmed.

A point: It would be vital not to stimulate any belligerence on the part of the small intelligences. This could produce a crucial delay which could not be afforded.

All in all, it seemed a feasible plan.

"Hey Ed, come 'ere, will ya?"

M'wali tossed in his suspension cradle. There wasn't another freighter loading or unloading due for another three hundred years yet. Well, three hours, anyway. They'd just completed an unloading about an hour ago. Therefore his shuttle partner, Myke Reinke, should not have been calling out to him. He should most definitely not have awakened Edward from his sound and beautiful sleep. Edward M'wali was upset as well as up.

"Friend Reinke, do I maliciously pull you from the soothing balm of Morpheus? Is your sleep so uneasy you must take from mine? Be your watch so dullish that you fracture courtesy to serve your simple brain some interest?"

A short shudder traveled the length of the ship. M'wali sensed a shift in position and forward motion. His partner's sanity was abruptly suspect. Moving the ship required reaction mass, ergo credits. There was no reason to be moving the ship. The equation was simple but infuriating.

"Offspring of sand-hogs, what are you about!?"

"If you'll move your pseudo-poetic ass out of that bunk, Ed, and take a look through the NV scope, you might see something."

M'wali considered a last possibility, discarded it. Reinke did foolish things, but he did not, ever, drink while on duty. Still, there was a first time for . . . He floated out of the bunk and over to the control console. When he saw what the natural vision telescope was holding in automatic focus, all thoughts of sleep vanished.

"Oooeee! Munguenma na juaekundu! Great God and Red Sun, what is *that?*"

"Never seen anything like it, eh?" said Reinke evenly. His hands were playing lightly over the controls. "Me neither. Looks like the Yellow Giants' jackstraws as arranged by the March Hare."

"March Hare?" said M'wali, not taking his eyes off the fantastic object.

"Skip it," replied Reinke.

"Just what are you thinking of doing, anyway, partner? We might get the shuttle inside that thing. We'd never get half of it inside the shuttle."

"Look a little lower. Down where those three long spines just about intersect."

M'wali took another look at the scope. The object now took up most of the field of vision, even though the tracker was automatically reducing magnification as they slipped closer. Yes, there was definitely a smaller, slightly saner looking bit of machinery floating slightly detached from the main body, near its south pole. It would fit— maybe—into the shuttle's cargo bay.

They sat unspeaking for several minutes, staring at the approaching object—which was actually retreating from them.

Closer inspection did not breed familiarity. The impossible merely took on greater detail.

"We *do* have a loading job in three hours. Think it's all right to shift station to fool with this thing?"

Reinke's reply was muted. He was busy maneuvering the shuttle closer. "I can recognize a rhetorical question when I hear one. When the boss sees what we done gonna bring him, he'll supply us with another ship—apiece."

"I'm not picky, myself. I wish only a very small space yacht—KK drive equipped, of course—with a platinum head."

"Kind of cold, hmmm?"

"Just to look at, idiot."

"Mighty strange taste you've developed in art."

"A direct return to the seat of human thought, you

might say. Besides, all geniuses cannot expect proper appreciation from the lower depths of the herd."

"All right, genius," Reinke smiled. "Suppose you suit up and lay some cables on that carp. When we've first got the thing secured we can arrange surface transportation. Meanwhile, I'll register salvage in case any of the other hock jockeys come nosing around. Take out a buoy first. As soon as it's positioned I'll transceive its frequency to Port Control. Then we can play with this thing at our leisure."

Which occasioned a brief, horrible thought. Turning to the transceiver, he rapidly scanned normal salvage frequencies. The computer noted nothing not previously listed in the book.

They had moved hard by the gleaming central object. It floated just above them, relatively speaking. A gold, be-spiked, glassblower's nightmare. The smaller body held sharp and clear out the fore port. M'wali had left to suit up, so Reinke occupied time in studying the immediate object of their attentions.

Interestingly, it appeared to float at the focal point of the three large, spiky projections of the central bulk. The pylons, or whatever they were, were a milky white, with faint shades of rose and light blue flowing across their surfaces every now and then. Glass or ceramic, looked like.

The detached spheroid had a few knobs and projections of its own, but nothing like the crazy-quilt above. It was pyramid-shaped. The base of the pyramid faced the larger object.

A body composed of more familiar curves and angles entered Reinke's view from the right. M'wali trailed vacuum cables and powerful pulse-jets behind him. The readyspark strapped to his partner's back sparkled in the glare from Repler's sun.

No conversation passed between the two men. None was needed. Both had performed similar operations dozens of times. The subject was new, but the procedure wasn't. Besides, M'wali liked quiet while he worked. He busied about the smaller object, setting himself for the routine task of arranging cables and jets on the alien construct.

Several moments passed. Reinke noticed that a single rectangular block, four times the height of a man and equally deep, had separated from the base of the pyramid. A single vacuum cable trailed from it. He perked up a bit, flipped open the ship-to-suit comm.

"Hey Ed, what's up? Is that thing going to come apart like a jigsaw puzzle?"

"Damnifino." M'wali's voice was sharp and clear across the intervening vacuum. "I got close to the thing and this thick lid or whatever retracted. Nothing else happened, so I decided to go ahead and hook up the first cable. When I activated it, this big hunk detached itself and pulled right out, like a plug."

"What's it made of? Any indication of origin?"

The space-suited figure was down on the surface of the block. "Doesn't look any more familiar close up than it did from a hundred kilometers away, Myke. Damndest looking stuff you ever saw, though . . . **fssst . . . sput** . . . corrugated in places, like carved fluting . . . almost has a greasy look . . . seems to be a port or something a little higher up . . . whole thing isn't very big . . . yes, there is a transparent section . . . got a reddish tinge to it . . . I can see inside, I think . . . OH SWEET JESUS . . ."

"For summasake, man!" Reinke fairly pounded the console in frustration. "Open up!" Heavy breathing came back over the comm. "You sonuvabitch, if you don't say something fast-quick I'm coming out there and—"

"Easy, Myke, easy. I'm fine. Just a little shocked. Calm down. You'll need all your expletives later."

"Okay, I'm calm. See? Now, what is it?" Reinke had to resist an urge to stomp on the floor. Breaking boot connection would send him floating helplessly about the cabin.

"It's small enough to bring back on the one cable.

You'll see it soon enough." M'wali's voice was unnaturally subdued. "And brother, don't eat anything until you do."

"If we weren't in such an awful hurry, I could almost enjoy the ride," Mal said. "Despite the crowding."

The five of them cramped the small forecabin of the hoveraft badly. Mal, in the only other seat, was trying to relax. Takaharu was handling the driving.

There was a slightly larger space for luggage and such located behind the forecabin, but it was completely enclosed. No one felt like sitting in the dark just now.

"I'll be pleased to clear all this up and get back to work, Captain," said the First Mate. "Devious intrigue isn't my line. I'm not mentally constructed for subtlety and evasion."

"We concur," Mal replied. "Not only don't I care for it, I'm not very good at it, either. But this young man, here . . ." he indicated the lanky form of Philip, draped angularly over an empty packing crate.

"What will you do now, Philip-al?" asked Porsupah.

"Well, I hadn't given it much thought. I could look for another job, but I think maybe I'll just kick around for a while. I can always get work. Something more interesting might turn up."

"Well, you shouldn't have to worry about credit for a time," broke in Kitten cheerfully. "We promised you a reward in the name of the Church. They've a special fund for such situations. Even if they disagree with our recommendations, which they won't, they can't violate a promise made by one of their field operatives. Let alone two." She looked over at Porsupah and he nodded affirmatively.

"You're authorized to make that kind of decision?" asked Mal, a little skeptically.

"Ordinarily, no. But this isn't the sort of assignment we'd ordinarily draw."

"I'd guessed that."

"Now look," she said heatedly. "I admit Porsupah

and I might not always have been right on top of the situation . . . what are you laughing at?"

Mal had doubled over. Long, basso peals of amusement filled the cabin.

"Listen to me, he-who-struts-like-an-ape!" she yelled.

"About that reward. I'm not much in need of credit yet," Philip interrupted hurriedly. "There wasn't much to spend on, here. I've enough put away to keep me floating for a while."

"It needn't be in the form of credit, if you wish," said Kitten, calming slightly but still keeping a jaundiced eye on the snorting ship-Captain. He was trying unsuccessfully to muffle his laughter. "Something equitable can always be worked out."

"Okay, then. I want you."

Mal stopped chuckling. Porsupah only twitched his first pair of whiskers.

"I beg your pardon?" said Kitten.

The voice of the young engineer had changed slightly. It was no longer distant, half-subservient. Not that it had deepened or changed physically. But the inflections were different, assured, more confident.

"I said I want *you*. The government owes me a reward, promised, in your name."

"Well, sure, but . . . hey, you're serious, aren't you?"

"Look, lad," began Mal.

"My name is Philip, Captain." He looked evenly at Mal. "In certain situations I respond to lad, kid, youngster, young fella, and many analogous appellations. This isn't one of them. The *young* lady can be no more than a year or two older than I—if that. It's rare enough that one chances across someone so attractive, intelligent, and, yes, of a compatible size. I want to take advantage of it."

"Now just a minute, Philip—"

"Just a minute yourself, Captain," interrupted Kitten, a trifle upset. "I don't need you or anyone else to bargain or moralize for me." She turned and looked over at Philip. He stared back unflinchingly. "It's up to me to decide whether I want to reject the proposal or not. Under the circumstances, I think it carries the flavor of an almost forgotten gallantry. Not to mention compliment. I accept your offer, Philip."

"Thank you, Miss Kai-sung," he replied gravely, executing an awkward half-bow.

"Under the circumstances, don't you think you ought to," she glanced archly at Mal, "call me by my first name?"

"Agreed . . . Kitten." He smiled broadly.

"You're quite right," Mal said evenly. "It's none of my business. Go and fantasize, if you will."

Kitten stood up and stretched . . . lazily, languorously. Mal gazed unswervingly at the ocean, which gazed back.

"There's room in the storage area, wouldn't you say, Philip?"

"I believe so, Kitten." He unfolded himself, extended a hand. She took it.

"See you shortly, gentlemen. This won't take long." She pulled the sliding panel closed behind them.

Takaharu hadn't budged throughout the entire exchange. Mal continued an unprecedented fascination with the sea. Porsupah stifled a laugh.

"You'd best get used to this if you expect to be around sweet Kitten awhile, Captain," the Tolian offered. His whiskers twitched. "I don't doubt that she agreed partially to enjoy your anticipated reaction. You came through in marvelous style."

"Thanks," Hammurabi said drily.

"Which brings me to another point, Captain." The alien took another glance at the ocean, then the console panel. "It occurs to me that we are not headed northward any longer."

"Right. However, that's the way we shall go."

"Yet that is not the way to Will's Landing."

"Two straight, Lieutenant. Very good."

Porsupah pondered a moment longer before replying.

"Forgive me, Captain. I had believed my terranglo beyond reproach. Yet there seems to be a nuance here that I fail to grasp."

"Apologies are mine, Pors." Mal sat back, rubbed a hand across his eyes. "I'm irritable. When I get irritable, I grow unnecessarily obtuse." He smiled easily.

"You see, one other question needs immediate answering. I intend getting it where we will arrive."

"Keep going," said Porsupah interestedly.

"I've performed a good deal of work in the past, as well as quite recently, for a merchant-trader name of Chatham Kingsley. Always played square with me; paid me well if not generously."

"Kingsley? Then that—"

Mal nodded. "The old man's favorite—and only—son. Why he bothers about him is beyond me. Even adopted blood is thicker than water, I suppose."

"Depends on the race. Here now! If the father is anything like the son—"

"No, no. I don't think the old man is even aware of his offspring's hobbies. I suspect the kid's managed on his own ever since he was big enough to order the help around. Chatham's a bastard, true, but he's a sane bastard. He only enjoys cutting people up economically.

"See, the shipment that the bloodhype and other drugs turned up in were all consigned to Kingsley's agents. I met Rose's by accident. It's a possible tie-up there that I'm concerned about. Before I run any more of Kingsley's goods around the Arm, I've got to know if they're going to be full of silly spice."

"I appreciate your problem, Captain. Yet we are expected, especially after transceiving that report on Rose, to file reports in person to our superior."

"Look, Pors. Everything we could do about Rose has been done over the transceiver already. If this Major Orvenalix is but half up to his reputation . . ."

". . . He is . . ."

". . . then there's no need for you to show up immediate-like, right nowish."

"Regulations . . ."

"Will be adjusted for a few hours," Mal replied gruffly. "The drug shipment is safe, you are safe, I am safe, and

our good and kind acquaintance his Lordship might as
well be pinned under the grating with his technician back
at the island, for all the chance he has. When a few of the
good Fathers finish with him, he'll wish he was . . . And
while I'd normally not bother to even mention it, you and
your effervescent associate owe me nothing if not a little
time. Seeing as how I'm in large part responsible for returning to you the balance of yours."

Porsupah didn't reply.

An hour or so later, the panel separating the forecabin
and the storage compartment slid back. A clearly tired
Kitten Kai-sung, Lieutenant in the service of the United
Church, temporarily attached to Intelligence Branch,
stepped into the cabin. Her dress, which had never been
designed by its manufacturer with the contortions of the
past twenty-four hours in mind, looked as worn as its
wearer. The long black hair fell haphazardly in directions
not always directed by gravity. The face was drawn.

There was also an unevenness to her gait, which was
not caused by the slight sway of the hoveraft.

"Nice to see you again," said Mal. He found himself
smiling in spite of himself. "Glad you could make it back
shortly."

Kitten flopped down in a corner. She brushed an errant
strand of hair from her face and glared at him. The
youthful apprentice sanitation engineer redraped himself
over his packing crate without a word. His expression,
revealing absolutely nothing, was significant for that. He
folded his arms across his chest and fell promptly asleep.

"Get a little more than you bargained for, rewardwise?"
Mal prodded.

"Let's just say, Captain, he's been amply repaid for
his help. Also for any help he may render in the next, oh,
ten years or so. But to satisfy your morbid interest, there
was one thing that did get to me a mite."

"Oh?" said Porsupah, giving every evidence of surprise. "I must know of this wonder!"

She pointed. "Well, bristle-fur, it was that damned thing. It stared at me the whole time."

She was pointing to the recumbent form of the flying-snake, which lay, blue-black and shiny, curled about its master's left shoulder.

It was either a glance at the instruments or else maybe the angle of the sun, rising over the horizon slightly behind them, that told her.

"Hey, whither the hell goest we?"

"It seems," said Porsupah, "that the good Captain feels strongly the need of an immediate confrontation with his employer. To determine if same is in any way implicated in the drug traffic. I informed him that it was necessary for us to return to central control, but he was adamant."

"Yeah," said Mal, looking straight at her. "That's me. Adamant."

"Investigation of all suspects in this matter is the government's business," she said.

"Later, maybe. Your Major can have proper seconds. I do my own dirty work."

"I will not stand for it!"

"Then sit down!" he shouted angrily. "Patrick O' Morion, I've never come 'cross such an obstinate woman!" He made a heretical gesture heavenward. "First I rescue you from a proverbial fate worse than death. Then I rescue you from death! Then I save your assignment. I even, Kelvin knows why, try to protect your virtue. How old *are* you, anyway?"

"Twenty-four T-years. Why?"

Porsupah interrupted sarcastically. "See, Captain, you're about twenty-three point nine years too late for that." The Tolian then found much of interest in the workings of his seat.

"Black holes have both of you!" she yelled. "I'll treat with you later, water-rat." She turned back to Mal. "And you, baboon-that-walks-with-fundament-forward, just because your grotesque carcass isn't up to the performance of our resident sewage-dabbler . . . !"

"Watch it, little girl, I . . . !"

First mate Takaharu swiveled half-way round in his chair. He actually raised his voice slightly, a thing reserved for extraordinary occasions.

"I am known as a patient man," he murmured in a steadily rising voice, "but if there is not some silence about this cabin immediately. I shall direct this craft onto the nearest reef and allow your souls to drift in violent converse for eternity! Please all to shut up?"

Glaring across the tiny cabin at each other, the Lieutenant and the freighter-Captain sat.

Philip chose that moment to fill the air with a stentorian snore.

The Vom was aware of the Machine, orbiting directly above it. It had been aware thus for some time now. Yet it recognized that the intelligence needed to transform the Machine into a potential threat was not present. As long as this remained so the Vom had nothing to fear. The Machine could not act without the direction of the Guardian, and there was nothing to wake the Guardian.

Yet clearly the Machine was aware of this too. Then why would it trouble to track the Vom across parsecs? Obviously it hoped somehow to activate the Guardian. The Vom sensed lack of key knowledge and this troubled it.

However, its strength was multiplying rapidly. It was a geometrical process. Each new, reactivated facet aided in unlocking or strengthening others. Since the Vom was maturing only internally, it aroused no suspicion in its former captors. Former, because for some time now the Vom had remained in place merely as a matter of convenience.

Regrettably, the Vom could not read thoughts. It never did have this ability. But it was regaining another talent, the ability to pick up and interpret the emotional discharges of other minds. It could sense no threats around it. A real threat would have had unshakable confidence behind it. The confidence here was purely superficial. The only ones the Vom was at all concerned with were those few who projected utter fear. Under unfavorable circumstances, these might conceivably panic the others. That would be inconvenient now.

Soon, however, it wouldn't matter. The Vom would act as it pleased. It had already passed the point where its peculiar composition could be threatened by sudden discharges of energy. Even the arrival of the Machine did not upset it. Not with the Guardian inert, inoperative. In fact, only one thing bothered it at all.

Was there something it had not discovered on this small planet that might conceivably activate the Guardian?

"A thousand moltings, your Excellency."

"What is it, sergeant?," said Parquit RAM irritably. They had finally managed to detach a section of the creature. Arris had just brought him initial analyses, spectrographic readings, and such—and now interruptions. He'd prepared his mind for revelations, for some practical return on an already enormous investment in time, credit, and nye-power, and this under-officer had shattered the mood.

"Ten thousand days of precipitation on my ancestor's graves if I have disturbed you, Excellence, but—"

"Oh, get on with it, nye!" That was the trouble with military protocol. Took up too much military time.

"Excellence, a small hoveraft was just detected within the concession perimeter. It appears to be piloted by a single human."

"Is that worthy of an interruption? Human and thranx fishermen and fortune hunters occasionally stray within our boundaries. Hold the man for half a day—just long enough for him to flow from the apoplectic to the apologetic—inform him we do not regard his person as sacrosanct, issue the standard missive of protest to the governor, and then let the fellow go."

"Well," he said when the sergeant did not absent himself. "Do you then find my physiognomy so fascinating? Why do you still inflict your presence on us?"

"Commander, Excellence, your indulgence. I do not make a standard intrusion. I would never bother you with such trivia. It is that the human . . . sir, he desires diplomatic sanctuary . . . with *us!*"

Parquit pushed the folder of spectrographs aside. "That *is* truly different, sergeant. I applaud your evaluation of the situation. My curiosity is piqued. Does the creature appear sane?"

"He does, sir."

"What sort of man is he? No, bring him here. I want to see this for myself."

The sergeant bowed, clasped his throat in salute, and left.

"Shall I go too, Commander?" said Arris, moving to gather up his papers.

"No. Stay, xenobiologist. This should amuse and possibly interest you."

The sergeant returned, along with two other soldiers. A single human walked between them. He clearly came under his own will, walking as briskly as his evident age permitted. Parquit raised a clawed hand and the sergeant returned the salute. He left, taking the escort with him. The human was left standing alone before the Commander's desk.

He wasn't a particularly impressive specimen, as humans went. Clearly of advanced age, if Parquit's eye was any judge. Yet the body appeared fairly healthy. The man was dressed well if not luxuriously. He carried a single small metal case, half a meter square and thin. He was unarmed, of course.

After a cursory examination of the room, the mammal stared back at the Commander. If he was nervous, he concealed it with the poise of one used to such elementary psychological ploys. A bold type, certainly. He'd have to be, to come *here* seeking asylum. Parquit could conceive of only one reason for a human or thranx to do such. He must be desired by his authorities—strongly enough to throw himself on the mercy of those controlling the only autonomous bit of surface on the planet. As mercy was not a trait the AAnn were famed for, the human would have to be desperate indeed.

"I believe I have you evaluated sufficient for my needs," Parquit began. "In any case, I most surely will not waste you by returning you to the authorities who doubtless are seeking you. That need not concern you. I will at least have the pleasure of denying them that. In this way you will perform some small service for me. If you can somehow convince me that you may be useful in ways other than by denying your person to the government, I may consider not turning you over to the officer's chef for this evening's sun-down meal. Scrawny as you are. As you no doubt well know, we regard human flesh as something of a delicacy, the more so because of its unavailability. Admittedly a sore point between our races. Your justification for continued existence on a plane other than as dinner better be substantial."

The human made a recognizable gesture of affirmation: He nodded his head. "That's about the kind of greeting I expected. Now I will tell you who I am. I am Lord Dominic Estes Rose."

"A natural or acquired title?"

"I bought it, if that's what you mean."

Parquit did not congratulate himself for this bit of insight. The creature had neither the bearing nor appearance of the nobleborn. Not that this bothered him. Even today among the AAnn there were those who had purchased their nest in the aristocracy. It was necessary to adapt to change, needed to preserve the monarchy and the succession. Parquit himself had a near-nest relative who . . .

"Your business, man?"

"I am a simple merchant."

"No merchant is simple who remains one. For that you find reason to flee to us?" Parquit added sarcastically.

"I also run illegal drugs."

"Ah! That explains a good deal. Do you specialize?"

"I'm what you might call a high-class general retailer." The human chuckled. "I'm not particularly particular. If it'll bring a profit, I'll broker anything. What I want, Commander . . . um . . ."

"Commander is proper."

The man shrugged. "If you want it that way. What I want is help in getting off-planet. I'll handle the reopening of my lines of supply myself. In return for this I can be of some help to you. I have contacts all over the Commonwealth."

"You'd sell yourself away from your own race?" Arris spoke for the first time.

Rose responded. He laughed.

"Do you believe in souls, friend?"

"Naturally," said Arris.

"Well, as far as forty Terran years ago, mine had been mortgaged several times over. Many races own a piece of me. A number have been trying to collect for years. I always stay one jump ahead of my un-friends. And my credit is excellent, which helps. I'm for bartering with anything that holds a convertible credit slip. That's the only race I owe allegiance to, the race of figures in my account with the Bank of . . . but that needn't concern you."

"I believe it all, man. Suppose, though, that I still decide you are more valuable to me as this evening's entrée than a man of business?"

"For a lizard, your symbospeech ain't bad. I might choose to blackmail you into a formal promise. How sounds that?"

"Illogical. To blackmail one must be able to threaten. Prospective dinners rarely possess anything to threaten the diner with."

"Well, I have what's in this case." Rose shifted the container in front of him.

Parquit sighed. This man was going to turn out to be a disappointment after all.

"Man, that case contains nothing of metal other than

what is embodied in its basic construction. Nor anything of plastic, glass, wood, ceramic, nor any object of artificial construct greater than a few millimeters of your measurement. If it had, you'd never have been permitted past the landing point. Let alone into my personal presence. All you might do is throw it in my direction. You would be incinerated along with it before you could half complete the motion."

"Don't doubt it. See Commander, what this case contains is a number of *kuysters*—your measurement—of the pure drug bloodhype, in powder form and under pressure. If I let go of this handle, this case will fairly explode from internal pressure. I think I'm too close to you for any destructive beam to be certain of destroying all the powder without killing you too. If the least of it, however tiny an amount, reaches you, you'll be as hooked as the worst addict in the filthiest dive on Terra or Dust-Dune. Since I currently control the only supply in the known galaxy, you'll die later than I will, but a good deal more uncomfortably. As will your companion," Arris stiffened, "and anyone else who breathes it. . . I presume your air circulating system is efficient. You might consider your men. I might also remind you that if my intentions had been basically antagonistic, I could have safely released the dust at any time, if my object in coming here was to do you harm."

"You are bluffing. You are not the type to welcome suicide."

"Commander, I invited it by coming here! If you want other proof, you can find out real quick."

Parquit did not make Commander by hesitating in awkward situations. "All right. I grant your sanctuary."

"Swear by your Shell and The-Sand-That-Shelters-Life."

Parquit made the AAnn equivalent of a smile. Naturally he did not bare his teeth. "You are a knowledgeable rogue, soulless Lord." The Commander lowered his voice, rumbled through the archaic hisses and croaks of the ancient oath.

"There. Are you satisfied?"

"You forgot the sealing of the membrane and the last three wind atonings."

"A simple test, man. Compliments." This time Parquit did it properly. It was impressive.

Rose nodded when the AAnn had finished. He turned, set the case down on the floor. Arris winced involuntarily when the man took his hand from the handle. Rose turned back to face them.

"You were bluffing, of course," said Parquit.

"Don't let the either-or keep you awake nights, Commander." Rose looked around, helped himself to an awkwardly shaped chair.

"I might say that any being who deals in bloodhype is a living scab to all AAnn as well as to your own race."

"Insults are a sad way to begin a long relationship, Commander. Besides, I've heard them all already."

Chatham Kingsley's island-home, Wetplace, reflected wealth—new wealth, as opposed to traditional inherited types. Kingsley could have built an old-Terra type baronial mansion (they were currently in style). But he eschewed the false reproduction and opted instead for the maximum in modern convenience. This left a good portion of the island's interior for a wilderness garden. Most of the necessary business edifices, such as warehousing, were built offshore on a complex of struts, pylons, and floating platforms.

The central residence consisted of a single tower, which rose some 50 meters into the air while plunging an equal distance into sea and bedrock, on the side where the island fell off steeply into the shallow sea.

The island thus remained almost entirely in a virgin state. The natural profusion of greenery was encouraged by judicious additions of organic fertilizers, powerful plant foods, and professional verdurement. Thick cycads, ferns, sporophytes and horsetails grew to the waterline, dipping graceful fronds into the slightly salty tideflow. In some places they even mingled with the sea-plants which grew sunwards from the seabottom, forming an unbroken wall of green against which water lapped viscously.

The Tower itself was constructed of parallel vertical bands of a coppery bronze alloy and panes of opaque black glass.

Takaharu guided the raft among the few small commercial craft which plied the artificial harbor. They headed towards a single long, floating dock. An anchored walkway led towards the Tower.

Mal glanced at the console. "All right, Maijib. You can acknowledge their calls now." Since Kingsley was overtly legitimate, they could expect to approach his property closely without fearing the gift of a missile or mine. But now at least a cursory greeting was in order.

The first mate flipped on the comm. Immediately a harried voice filled the cabin. It was also officious and slightly bellicose.

". . . a private residence! Identify yourselves, please! This area is defined as . . ."

Hammurabi leaned over the mike for the second time in two days. "Malcolm Hammurabi, Captain-owner of the free freighter *Umbra,* and First Mate, along with Lieutenants United Church Kitten Kai-sung and Porsupah, and engineer Philip . . . Philip . . ." Mal glanced back at the lanky youngster. In all this time he hadn't thought to ask the fellow's last name.

"Lynx," the engineer replied.

". . . Philip Lynx, to see merchant-trader Chatham Kingsley, and is the old S.O.B. at home or not?"

"I beg your modification, Captain! I might inform you that . . ."

"Never mind, Hulen," a cultured, even voice broke in.

"Yes sir," the unlucky Hulen replied. He sounded subdued. The voice returned.

"Is that you, Hammurabi? This is the old S.O.B. himself. What brings you down from orbit? I thought you hated anything over half a gee. Your credit, in full, has already been transceived to your ship's account on Terra. I'd have thought you'd have checked on that long ago."

"I did. That's not why I'm here."

"Well, then?"

"I'm peeved, Kingsley, peeved."

"And presumably I'm the one who's peeved you, eh? All right, come on up. Or down, rather. And bring your friends with you. We'll see if we can't unpeeve you."

Firm as its footing in the sloping *Pecces* was, the wide delivery-way shifted slightly under their feet with the action of the tide. A human butler met them at the entrance to the black and gold structure.

"The master awaits you in the viewing room, sirs and lady. The sixteenth level." The elegantly appointed servant directed them to a room-sized elevator. It was more than large enough to hold them all comfortably. Kitten depressed the stud marked 16 and the lift started to move.

"Feels like we're moving downwards," said Porsupah.

"I sense so too," Philip added.

"The building is half below sea level," Mal informed them. "I've never been here myself, but I'm acquainted with the schematics for storage reasons." He indicated the lights over the front door. Number 18 had just winked out and 17 on.

"We entered at midpoint—about the 20th floor." The door slid back silently. He stepped out into an enormous, unfamiliar room. It had a concave ceiling and was crescent shaped. The elevator shaft formed its apex.

The far wall was entirely glass. It revealed a breathtaking panorama of the sea floor that disappeared in a turquoise haze. Fish and sea mammals swam lazily back and forth in front of the glass, catching the sunlight which filtered down through the clear water. Some clustered around feeding platforms. A number differed sufficiently from the familiar vertebrates to be classed as eye-catching, if not exotic.

No, it was the room's decor that deserved the latter

label. There was no individual furniture. Seats, tables and chairs were formed by rises and depressions in the floor of the room. The entire compartment was covered in a rich, reddish-brown fur. Artificial, but still exorbitantly expensive. The hairs ran as long as five centimeters. The lining—it couldn't be called a carpet—covered every space: floor, ceiling, walls, everything but that single panoramic window. Like the skin of some misshapen behemoth turned inside out. They were in the belly of a dream.

"Fascinating concept," Kitten whispered. "Kind of like being inside a marsupial's pouch."

"A fine analogy, Miss Kai-sung," boomed a voice from near the window.

Chatham Kingsley reclined on a low, fur-covered platform. He was shorter than any of them, with the exception, of course, of Porsupah. A good three centimeters shorter than Mal or Kitten. He affected a blond crewcut, a short, thick brush mustache, and a gold and topaz ring in one ear. Angular cheekbones, a pointed chin, Roman nose, and falsely innocent china-blue eyes completed the face. A curious mixture of putty and flint. The mind behind the baby-eyes was at least that hard—a fact which Kingsley's ever-polite chatter strove to obscure.

"Well Malcolm, you arrived in time for lunch, anyway. Sit yourselves down, all of you. I've instructed the cook appropriately."

"I'm afraid, Chatham, that there are a few things that are more important than—"

"Hold on," said Kitten. "Porsupah and I haven't had anything but a few scraggly canapes and fish sandwiches in the past 36 hours. At the moment, *nothing* is more important than lunch."

"I myself have no intention," added Porsupah, his eyes glued to the subterranean scene, "of staring at all those delightful and no doubt edible swimmers without taking a bite of something. Your obviously well-nourished bulk not excepted, Captain."

"So we accept your invitation," finished Kitten firmly. She stared challengingly at Mal, who sighed deeply and chose not to fight back.

"Marvelous! Bless you, my dear. Miss Kai-sung, wasn't it?"

"Call me Kitten."

"And you must call me Chatham, yes. Are you and your friend—Porsupah is a Tolian calling, I believe—are you really ranked officers in the Church forces? I've not seen you around city before."

"Really and truly we are, Chatham. We're only temporarily attached to the Rectory in Repler City."

"A shame. But old Orvenalix's taste is improving." The merchant stared at her approvingly.

Kitten turned to Mal. "That settles your question. He's innocent!" The freighter-captain groaned.

"Innocent?" said Kingsley uncertainly. "Then I am presumed guilty of some wrongdoing?" He shifted to a sitting position on the lounge, looked questioningly at Mal.

"Okay, okay. Let's eat first, as voted. I confess I've been overruled by my innards, also. I'm famished."

The others were playing with dessert. Mal was cleaning off his fourth leg of Garvual, a large, carnivorous wading bird, when their host cocked an inquiring eye at him. Mal had long since decided that subtlety would be as useful with Kingsley as it had been with Rose. For different reasons. He wiped his hands and mouth with a hot towel, stifled most of a gargantuan belch, and began.

"Chatham, I found a consignment of drugs mixed in with the *Umbra's* last cargo. That shipment was 92% yours. We completely deshipped at Largess, so I know it came aboard there. It included a significant milling of refined bloodhype. Yes, bloodhype. Nearly pure, I'm told. Also a number of other nasty types, but nothing in jaster's class. Don't try and play coy with me. I know you'd be aware of the stuff's reintroduction onto the market."

Kingsley tapped delicately about the corners of his

mouth with a towel. "It is true I am not entirely uninformed where information concerning trade in this section of the Arm is concerned." He sat back and folded his hands contentedly over an emerging pot-belly. "Cordials will be forthcoming. Your implication, then, is that I am somehow involved in this traffic?"

"Are you?"

"No."

"Why wouldn't you be? You live conveniently close to Dominic Rose, who we know is responsible for distributing the stuff."

"We live on the same planet, that's true."

"This is too serious for sarcasm, Chatham."

"Pomposity invites sarcasm."

"Okay. Look, modern transport reduces a planet to nothing, distancewise. Your contacts are broader than his, better established, legitimate across the lanes, and have strong financial support. With his illegal connections, the two of you are logical partners in an enterprise capable of pulling astronomical profits."

"I'd heard rumors that it was that old reprobate who'd been transshipping the stuff, but there was no way to confirm any of them. He covers himself too well. Or did, apparently. You're wrong on several counts.

"For openers, much as I respect Rose's business sense and his ability to handle complex transactions across parsecs with a maximum of secrecy, I personally hate his guts. That would put a crimp in any relationship of needs founded on complete trust. Second, I'm doing quite well, thank you, trading in legitimate goods. Too well to risk jeopardizing everything for a single line. However profitable. And don't think I don't envy him the margin of that trade. I do. Not that I'm averse to handling something a little off-grain, understand. I'm no saint. A respectable stimulant like Kepong, now. The authorities frown on it, but it is not, strictly speaking, under edict."

"According to whose lawyers," said Kitten.

"Yes, a point of contention. But while the powers that be debate, I see no harm in making hay while the sun shines, as the saying goes. Wonder what 'hay' is? But bloodhype? That's a little too filthy. A decent gun will kill a man honestly. That stuff eats as it kills. The thing that finally dies isn't a man anymore. Or whatever race. No, no. Absolutely not."

"What about your son?" broke in Philip. He'd finally turned away from a close inspection of the window view.

Kingsley swiveled in surprise. "Russell? My son, I fear, is not interested in anything remotely indicative of work. He is averse to business in all its manifestations, excepting his allowance." The merchant sighed. "A deficiency which I fear I encourage overmuch."

"Among other things," Kitten said flatly.

"You've met him then, Kitten?"

"Briefly. Twice."

"I'm not surprised." The trader helped himself to a flagon of imported honey-pollen brandy from Calm Nursery. A second human servant had arrived with a rolling cart of drinkables. Clearly, people were still regarded as a status symbol on Repler. Porsupah opted for a tall bottle of Bitterind, a common mixer, and poured himself a straight glass.

"Yes, Russell would hardly miss a new arrival arranged like yourself, Kitten." The trader chuckled. "The lad's a terror with the ladies, I'm told."

"Chatham," began Kitten, "you don't know the half of it. Matter of fact—"

Mal interrupted hastily. "It's not that I don't believe you, Chatham . . ."

Porsupah put a restraining paw on Kitten's arm, felt the tensed muscles relax. "Softly treading now, smooth-skin. The other is clearly not present. It is bad manners to think of killing the son of one's host. Especially while drinking with him."

"Relax, Pors. Obviously if he was around the old boy would have presented him. As for manners, I'm not going to consult a book of etiquette the next time I meet that chap. I'll be very polite at his funeral."

"Sssss! Listen, for a change."

"I've as much as given my word on this drug thing," said Kingsley amiably. "However, if you like, I'll provide the strongest proof. I will post a bond with an intermediary to the effect that, should I ever be implicated of trafficking bloodhype or any of the commonly fatal drugs, you will receive thrice your payment for this last shipment—from my estate, if need be."

"A grand gesture, Chatham. You almost convince me. I'll take that offer. You'd better hope no one tries to frame you."

Kingsley chuckled. "On the day someone manages that, I will hire in with an AAnn consortium as kitchen inspector. The bond will be drawn up tonight. By tomorrow morning it will be posted with the central exchange computer here and at annexes on Terra and Hivehom."

"Fine." Mal downed a straight glass of orange Couperanian brandy. He could trace its tactile path down his throat and into his stomach. It formed a pool of glowing warmth there, a small non-nuclear furnace.

"There now," said Kingsley expansively, polishing off the remainder of his own drink. "If everyone is suitably fueled, I'll give evidence of my openness in another manner. To all of you." A conspiratorial tone had entered the trader's voice. "I confess the action will not be entirely unselfish. I need some fresh, outside opinions. Surely you can't do any worse than my own technicians."

"Is it interesting or just profitable, your proof?" Kitten inquired.

"A deal of both, my dear. Come and decide for yourself."

Leaving their silverware and glasses and such behind, awkward alien shapes in the smooth furry sea, they followed the merchant to the central elevator. Kitten noticed he limped slightly. The conveyance dropped them another ten levels but did not stop there. Instead, a series of lights running horizontally across the control panel blinked on. Apparently they were traveling parallel to the surface, deep into island bedrock.

Kitten estimated that they had traveled roughly two-thirds of the way into the island and slightly downward, when the doors finally slid back. The trader led them out.

Two men stood ready to greet them. They both relaxed at the sight of the merchant.

"Good evening, sir," offered the one on their left.

"Evening Willus, Rave. Taking some guests to see the salvage." Both guards hefted heavy, no-nonsense weapons: Paxton Five's. The thick-bodied guns launched tiny self-propelled missiles with explosive warheads. They were clumsy and awkward at close range, but reflective laser armor would be useless against them.

There were guards at two more checkpoints, located at sharp turns in the tunnel.

"Never been through here before," Mal said, staring at the smooth, machined walls. "Quite a hidey-hole. What do you keep down here, your trousseau?"

"Abandoned any need for that when my credit account first passed six figures. There are several storage chambers of varying size cut into the rock. We're headed for the biggest."

Mal nodded. "I noticed several other passageways branching off when we left the elevator."

"This one is particularly well fortified. I use it to store the more expensive imports and exports. Also goods which require controlled atmosphere, peace and quiet. Delicate scientific apparatus, for example. Just now it happens to house a very intriguing hunk of cosmic jetsam a pair of shuttle-pilots—semi-regular employees of mine —found drifting in indifferent orbit. They had the good sense to plant a salvage beacon on it and contact me right away . . . The thing they hauled down is interesting more than as a mere representative of alien manufacture. You'll see why."

They turned another corner abruptly and stood in the described room. There was a thick door, retracted into the ceiling. Several other men and thranx were already there.

"Engineers and technical consultants from my staff in

Repler City," said Kingsley at an inquiring glance from Kitten. "Brought away from their regular jobs to work on this thing. Expensive." He pointed. "That's it."

He indicated a huge rectangular block of metal standing slightly apart near the back of the chamber. At first glance it was not particularly impressive. It stood near a host of other carefully stacked crates. One of these stood unpackaged. Mal recognized the device as a commercial class Seatoler. This was a thranx-developed instrument which could accurately predict changes in ocean currents, water temperature at various depths, and even track and predict fluctuations in the height of the thermocline. In other words, a very valuable and exclusive hunk of fishing equipment. No doubt consigned to one of the larger fishing concerns on Repler.

One of the engineers noticed their arrival, walked slowly over to greet them. Skinny afterthought arms dangled from a short-sleeved workshirt. The man had a hooked nose and artificial corneas that gave his gaze an unnatural sparkle. Kitten could make out the silvery threads that ran around the edge of the implants.

"Sir, we still cannot locate any kind of button, switch, lever, or even a sign that this thing is meant to be opened. It took us four hours just to find a seam, you know."

"I know, Martinez. I'm paying for it. Keep at it. I'm not ready to resort to slicing it open. Not yet. Haven't you been able to learn anything about its insides?"

"Well, the metal—we're pretty sure now that it is metal, by the way—resists normal xerographic and skeletonay probing. But one of the guys got the idea of trying a moliflow scan at very low power. We got some interior pickup that way, enough to take rough measurements of the body inside . . ." The man wiped sweat from his brow.

"There's a creature in that thing?" asked Kitten.

"A genuine, certified new-to-science, bonafide alien. Yes, my dear."

"About three meters tall," the engineer continued. "Pickup was faint, and it's hard to hold focus at such low power. We couldn't get much more than that. It seems to be in an excellent state of preservation. I didn't want to take a chance on harming the tissues by using the scanner at a stronger level. As far as direct visual observation goes, we've only found the one transparent section that the pilot marked. The red tinting of the glass, or whatever, is heavy enough to render it opaque in spots. Even so, you can make out more than is pleasant. It's not pretty, Kingsley."

"I've seen the frozepix, Martinez, I know. As I said, keep 'em at it. This amounts to a paid holiday for some, and I won't tolerate loafing."

"Yes sir."

The group moved to the base of the metal ziggurat. It was mostly gray, shading to a bleached-bone white in places. Tiny pits were visible over most of the surface, scars from micrometeorites and null-flies.

"Another point, Hammurabi." The trader was examining a particularly large pitting. "Analysis of a scraping from this thing—and you've no idea what we had to go through to get it—places it between five and six hundred thousand years of age. Now me, I'm fond of antiques, but this gives me the shivers."

"And it's been floating around in your backyard for that long?"

"No one knows for certain. According to what the smart boys tell me, that's not likely. It would have been noticed before now. Still, Repler hasn't been inhabited that long and large-scale commerce is pretty recent. More likely, though, it was floating free and happened to be captured by the planet's gravity. There's certainly nothing to indicate it was built around here. It doesn't correspond to anything built by other known space-going races."

"It might have been built on Repler," Mal persisted. "Lots of things could disappear in that span of time."

Kingsley shook his head. "Doesn't add. If the builders of this and the battleship-size sphere that accompanied it could make things last this long, we'd find similar constructs on the ground. In an advanced state of decay, sure, but at least a foundation here and there. While it's true much of Repler is still unexplored, enough survey has been carried out to indicate that not even a primitive sapient race once lived here. This is what the brain-boys tell me, anyway. You ought to see that mother object, by the way. Haven't even scratched that, yet. Looks like one of Mother Nature's more grandiose invertebrates, blown up to gigasize."

"Mister Kingsley!" The shout came from behind the massive relic. The merchant looked up.

An engineer peered around the edge and down from his precarious perch atop the makeshift scaffolding.

"There's some paneling back here, sir." The man expressed confusion and puzzlement. "I could swear I've been over this spot a hundred times already. Anyhow, it just slid back under my hand."

"How big an opening?" yelled Martinez. Then, lowering his voice, "Anything visible?"

"Damn right there is! There's a light underneath that's flickering like it can't make up its mind whether to stay on or off. It doesn't appear to be blinking in any kind of recognizable series. Now it's staying lit. I can't make out a bulb or filament of any kind."

"You can come down now, engineer," said Kingsley quietly. He started to back away. "In fact, I suggest everyone move back."

"A commendable suggestion," Kitten added.

"Martinez," the trader whispered. The room had grown suddenly silent. The engineer tore his eyes away from the relic.

"Go back through the main access and send all six guards in. Then contact stores and get Cady. Tell him I want a small cannon and crew down here. As of two minutes ago."

"Yes sir." Martinez departed on the run, glancing back often over his shoulder.

Oblivious to human concern, the front of the ancient relic continued to open.

No one breathed. The slowly opening panel was similarly noiseless. People avoided bumping into things.

The cover of the capsule, or whatever it was, finally stopped. It had swung out and back about 120 degrees, revealing a padded interior. A rainbow of wires, pads, and things with unknown and unimaginable functions enclosed and criss-crossed the inert body of the alien. When nothing else happened, a small cluster of engineers and technicians, men who had been halfway out the tunnel at the first movement, began to edge back for a closer look.

The first two guards arrived, panting heavily. They took one look at what was taking place and immediately ran around the perimeter to the right. That way they would have a clearer line of fire into the capsule.

First sight suggested a mating between a crab and a Kodiak bear. The being was clearly constructed along lines with power commensurate to size. The trunk was broad and deep. Lines of muscle showed clearly under the skin at the bare spots. Most of it was covered by a bristly silver-white fur centimeters in length, fading here and there to a light brown. Plastrons of some shell-like substance, mottled white, covered the chest area. The fur there was sparse and stunted around the edges.

Four thick, jointed legs, bare of fur and armored like a battleraft, trailed from the limp torso. A thick tentacle at each shoulder point divided almost immediately, splitting four-fifths of the way down into four smaller, finger-like branchings. There were sixteen manipulative members, then. The branching limbs descended to a point just above where the legs began.

There were four eyes, two on either side of the curved white beak. Two large ones close to the center, with a smaller to the far left and right. Furred lids shut tight over all four. The beak was closed, but four short, pointed canines projected outside the mouth, two up and two down. There was no external evidence of ears or nostrils.

Six guards now focused their weapons on the thing. Mal, Kitten, Philip, Kingsley, and a batch of fascinated technicians and engineers stared open-mouthed in its direction.

"Ugly thing, isn't it?" said Porsupah into the silence. The engineers immediately started to buzz among themselves, a dozen conversations suddenly going at once.

"I'm not in love with its features either, Pors," Kitten replied. "Anyone recognize the species?"

"I don't want to interrupt any fascinating dialogue on alien cosmetology," said Philip quietly, "but I believe I just saw an eyelid flicker. Yes, there it is again."

Kitten backed away, moaning. "Oh god, I think I may suffer a lapse of training. I'm going to scream."

She didn't, although funny sounds came from her throat. One of the technicians wasn't so bashful and did scream. Another fainted. All four eyes did open, slowly, all at once. The pupils, Mal noted as he took four large steps backwards, were slitted like a cat's in the two big ones but were round in the small peripheral ones. He drew his own pistol. If the thing decided to charge he had more confidence in running than in the gun's stopping power. The alien looked frighteningly efficient, was clearly carnivorous (that hooked beak, never mind the teeth) and powerful enough to shred armor-plate.

"Hey, I can't scream. I'm too scared."

"Scared, Lieutenant?" said Mal, immediately regretting the unkind dig.

"Fang you, ape. This isn't in the manual."

They all heard the voice at the same time.

It was similar to the voices one hears in dreams. Precise, sharp, but very far away.

"Do not be scared, female-image-of-small-furred-animal-with-long-claws. After such Time, it is sad to be awakened to thoughts dissonant and unfriendly."

"Interesting," she said, recovering rapidly. Whatever else could be said about the voice, it was completely devoid of any hint of malice. She was instantly, perhaps unreasonably, reassured. "Telepathy."

"A serviceable label, given lack of proper referents," the creature murmured. The eyes shifted slowly, slightly.

"Also for want of a better term, you may address me as 'Peot.' I am quite immobile. I can, however, detect a number of your species pointing what I ascertain to be lethal devices in my direction. While I do not believe they could do me harm, I would prefer to avoid the possibility that one may stumble accidentally, thus forcing me to find out. I assure you I mean you no evil."

One of the guards, an older man with some gray in his sideburns, turned his head to face Kingsley. His weapon did not move.

"Sir?"

Kingsley had not become wealthy by hesitating. "Take the rest of the boys and resume your normal stations. Stay there unless you're sent for."

"As you wish, sir. I protest, though." He gestured to the other five and, without taking their weapons off the alien, they began to edge out of the chamber.

"Oh, and Haddad?"

"Sir?"

"Call Martinez at stores and tell him it seems we won't be needing that cannon after all. Tell him just to get back here himself."

"Aye, sir."

The engineers had edged back and were slowly resuming their multiple conversations—quietly, this time.

"I've a million questions and no place marked 'begin the game here,' " began Chatham, "so . . ."

"A moment," said Peot solemnly. The eyes closed and the alien went incommunicado for several minutes while the humans shifted about restlessly. They reopened.

"There were a number of things I had to determine. It is difficult also for me to adjust to the span of time that has passed."

"No more so than it is for us to adjust to your presence," said Kitten.

"Perhaps not, small female. My Machine tells that I am the last of my race. This fact is not entirely unexpected, yet it is heavy on me."

"Characteristic number one," Porsupah whispered to Kitten. "Facility for understatement."

"You might say that, and there's no point in you whispering, Pors."

The Tolian did a blush-equivalent.

"I am here now because the Machine felt it needful for the continuance of my work."

"Your work. What is your work?" Kingsley asked.

"I am a Guardian . . . *the* Guardian."

"And what must you still guard . . . after half a million years?" The small attempt at levity fell flat. The alien's visage did not encourage humor.

"The Vom."

"I see. The Vom. Pray tell, what is the Vom? Or Voms, as the case may be."

"Long ago, my race encountered a being . . . if 'being' is indeed the proper term . . . so alien that we suspected it must have traveled here from another galaxy. Although the concept of crossing the intergalactic abyss was one before which even our finest minds shrank it always seemed the only rational explanation of the creature's origins. It was discovered that the creature was powerful beyond imagining, sometimes in ways difficult to understand. Also, it did not invite close study. . .

"Attempts at contact proved fruitless. The thing destroyed whatever life it encountered. It began with the higher forms on a planet and moved to the lower, until it had eliminated even the miscroscopic existences. A planet stripped by the Vom was as thoroughly sterilized as if it had passed through a sun. Conventional weaponry proved useless against it. New machines were tried and offered some hope, but the thing was too clever to be trapped. Several times we appeared to have destroyed it. Always it escaped by avoiding rather than inviting a fight until it had discovered a method of combating each new development we threw at it. Its caution convinced us of its mortality, so we at least knew it *could* be destroyed . . .

"Always it grew stronger. At the cost of a great many planes-of-existence, time, and effort, a way was found to contain it on a single planet. The life on that planet was forfeited so that we might protect ourselves."

Peot did not comment on the thoughts that passed through the chamber following that remark.

"This new device prevented it from leaving the planet by its familiar method. We believe it could at one time travel through space on its own, but had clearly forgotten or lost this ability eons ago. After consuming all life on the planet, it shrank rapidly in size and power."

Kitten discovered that her palms were damp. She glanced over at Mal and was mildly surprised to see the freighter-captain rubbing his own against the legs of his coveralls.

"I don't think I like the way your thoughts are leading," said Kingsley.

"It is greatly weakened. So much so that it may now be possible to destroy it forever. To have survived to realize that end would make even the sleep of millennia worthwhile."

"The thing is here, now, on Repler," said Philip. It wasn't a question.

The eyes swiveled to rest on the young engineer. "Yes, that is so." (Something/there/veiling/physical youth/ hiding??/determine/what?/not now/standoff?/more than/ less than/query-query?/silence/*silence*/ *?*/.)

Those present got only the confirmation.

"Well for Solsake, where? Let's be about rooting out this archaic bugaboo or whatever! The military base at the capitol can—!"

"I have evaluated your thoughts on the matter and those of the two military attachés present," came the thoughts firmly. Both Kitten and Porsupah started. So much for classified information. "The Vom is weakened, true. Enormously so, yet it is still powerful enough so that simple energy devices will not harm it."

"Simple, hell!" snorted Kingsley. "The rectory there mounts energy rifles on an anchor core that—"

"All is relative, my young friend. I know wherewith I say." Kingsley subsided. Maybe, Kitten figured, the certainty in that voice got to the trader. Or maybe it was the "young friend."

"I should, however, be glad of some help," Peot continued, perhaps with an eye towards assuaging any feelings of racial impotence. "Yet I fear that such an attempt would but provoke a devastating response on the part of the thing, which I am currently powerless to prevent. Something simple, on the nature of gleaning the central city of all intelligent life. No, it is best to try none such . . . yet."

"You did say it might be killed," reminded Mal.

Kitten reflected while observing this by-play that the adaptability of the human wasn't bad by half. Here they were standing and chatting amiably via telepathy with a completely improbable alien, only recently resurrected, about some other unknown and equally outrageous creature from another universe as though everything had been politely arranged by faxpax and when will tea be served, thank you?

"Although immensely powerful by your standards . . ."

"Look, how do you so all of a sudden know so much about our standards and such?" said Kingsley, a trifle belligerently. He was doubtless a bit put out that his prize possession had taken over its own introduction.

Peot, however, had no time for idle converse. He began again, patiently.

"Although immensely powerful by your standards, it has degenerated considerably from what it once was. The major portion of the Machine is in synchronous orbit directly above the Vom's current location. It will stay that way regardless of how the creature moves. The Machine is directed and operated from this capsule. Certain repairs to critical functions must be made before any attempt to attack the Vom can be made. As a matter of self-protection and your own safety . . . the Vom grows stronger each day it is unopposed . . . these things must be done as soon as possible. Some of the required elements are rare. Others have deteriorated, I fear, because their life has been reduced to a point where they will no longer activate the instrumentation they affect. These must be replaced."

"All well and good," said Kingsley, argumentative to the last. "But what guarantee have I that you'll use these no doubt expensive supplies as you say, for the purpose you claim? In fact, what guarantee have I that you're even telling the truth about this fantastic, impregnable boojum of yours? Maybe you're really preparing for some large-scale nastiness of your own, hmmm?"

"So. In the first place," Peot reached out suddenly with a long tentacle and swept up the nearest technician, "I am also not convinced of your intentions towards me. These are immaterial. As stated, I have no wish to harm you. No, do not send for your weapons, Chatham Kingsley. I wish simply to demonstrate that I could have killed everyone here quite easily. War and its arts were the reason for life among my folk. I knew the location, abilities, and probable fighting capability of everyone in this chamber before I opened my eyes. So, a demonstration of good faith on my part."

"Well, that's certainly reassuring," said Kingsley, not at all reassured. His voice wavered uneasily as the giant stepped easily from its padded capsule, stretched. "My apologies. As many as you want. I accept your story, whole, complete, in toto. Now if you'd be good enough to put my technician down? I think he's fainted."

"I did not mean to harm!" came the alarmed voice.

"No, no, he's fine; it's nowhere near a lethal condition. Just put him down, please. Gently. Yes, that's fine." The towering alien backed away a couple of steps as two of the man's companions bent over him, dividing their attentions between the unconscious tech and the all-too-close Peot.

Sensing their discomfort, the alien moved to examine the interior of his capsule.

"Planning any more surprises like that?" asked Kingsley uncomfortably.

"I am not such a poor bargainer myself, that I would tell you everything at once," the alien thought. An unmistakable undercurrent of humor came with it, then faded. The voice turned somber again. "I shall endeavor to work as rapidly as possible. So much to be done!" A mental sigh accompanied the last. "I have a professional concern only in this. But I also cannot stand by and loose the thing again on an unprepared galaxy. Not while I have such a fine chance to destroy it once and for all."

Kitten, seeing that no one else was about to, moved close to the alien. She reached out and touched the thick pelt that encircled the alien's waist.

"You speak of war as your race's favorite and foremost activity. Yet your actions indicate noble and altruistic motives. I don't understand."

"Noble? Yes, we were noble. Altruistic? On the contrary. If this were my race's time and not yours, you would unquestionably be an enslaved folk. War was not merely an activity with us. It was, as said, everything. Your enslavement would seem as natural to us as the freedom of others might to you. And there would be neither malice nor hate involved in the action."

"That's ghastly!"

Mental shrug. "All things in the universe are relative."

"But you're still helping us. And I don't believe that 'sacred duty' wave of yours, either. Not after millennia. And you put that engineer down carefully, as carefully as I'd handle a kitten. Why?"

"I happen to be a gentle person," came the soft reply. "I prefer life to death, peace to war, tranquility, order, plants that blossom, small beings that produce pleasant sounds, the feeling wind gives, all such things."

"More contradictions and none of the originals resolved," said Kitten.

The alien turned from its inspection and stared down at her with all four eyes. Involuntarily she took a step back, then angrily moved forward.

"Small female, what sort of being would your kind place in such a position as mine, to float in confined aloneness, aloneness, for eternity? What sort of specimen, whose mind only is needed—the neural network, the electro-organic nexi? With only occasional voices of your own kind, in passing, for companionship. To be brother to a machine. To drift only, in ignorance of time and motion. Yet an important task now and then to be trusted to such . . . A voluntary position, also, for such we were. One that had to be taken of choice and not order. Love, comfort, ease, rest, kindliness, smoothness, stroking, friendship, so pleasant . . . Oh yes, I was quite insane . . .

"And you, rabbit-with-fangs." Kingsley started. "If you still need further proof of my words, I fear you will have it sooner than you wish." The alien turned back to face the interior of its capsule.

"Umm. Well, for now, I'll see to it that you're supplied with what you need," the trader said evenly. "Inform me, and I'll—"

"No."

"No?"

"No. A negative. I shall relay my needs and requests through another . . . that one, I think."

An image formed alongside the wordpicture. Or maybe it supplanted them. It was difficult to tell. But it was not ambiguous. The others turned to stare at the subject of the thought.

Philip shook himself as though returning from a sleep. He looked very young again, suddenly. "Well, gee," he said.

"Now listen," began Kingsley. Mal put an arm on the merchant's shoulder.

"When a being confesses to insanity, even if he's sane by our standards, it might be in everyone's best interests to humor him, Chatham."

"All right. All right. I just don't like the feeling that things are slipping out of my hands right in front of my face. I just don't like it."

"Rabbit-with-fangs," came the voice, "things were

getting out of your hands before your ancestors were
conceived."

Peot connected a circuit unused for millennia. And
thought.

A thousand kilometers away, the Vom jerked. Mentally.
Outwardly it had not changed. Inside, it seethed. Somehow the Guardian had successfully been activated. Despite constant monitoring, the actual stimuli had completely escaped the Vom's scrutiny. Even now the ancient
nemesis was preparing itself.

The Vom was not ready to act. Not yet. It was torn
between two possibilities: to attempt an immediate, all-
out attack in hopes of destroying or crippling the Guardian, or waiting until it had reached the next level. The
decision properly involved a million considerations, a
hundred thousand details, a millimultiplex of calculation.
Yet the great mind did not deliberate long.

It would wait.

Midmeal time. Sun directly overhead. On the Replerian
AAnn chronometer, half past ℳ. Relaxation and off-duty.
Freetime.

Well, not for all. But the three on-duty AAnn technicians took a vote. It went unanimously for participating
with most of the base. One, Cropih LHNMPGT, was
thirteen point eight credits ahead. His two companions
were not about to halt the *Jinx* game at that point.

So no one observed a certain gauge (measuring mental
output of the thing below via bioelectrochemical scan-
ners) jump from a fraction of ONE to over a HUN-
DRED. Jump once again, only this time off the gauge
before settling back, the thin metal of the arrow-indicator
bent at an angle from being slammed over so hard.

Nor did they notice the several sections of burnt-out
wiring and melted insulation. They might have noticed
the trickle of green liquid from a shattered fluid valve,
but it evaporated while Cropih called six-twelve on an

angle roll and it came up. No one turned until the liquid was but an insignificant stain on the sandy floor.

"It's a beautiful idea, isn't it, Malcolm?" Kitten murmured.

"Just Mal, if you please." The freighter-captain sounded pained.

Along with Porsupah, they were seated in the undersea view room. The magnificent sub-surface panorama shifted continually in front of them. They'd been given the run of the place "for the duration," as Kingsley had put it. He'd installed them in guest quarters on the eighteenth floor. Mal and Porsupah shared only one fear: that Kingsley's son Russell might put in an appearance when Kitten was around. That happenstance would assure a variety of mayhem, none of which could be beneficial to anyone. So far, however, the young bastard hadn't put in an appearance, nor even a transceiver call for all they knew.

Philip was off performing some errand for the alien. Peot never seemed to rest—not that he hadn't had his fill of it, Kitten reflected.

They remained, enjoying the view, relaxing a bit. Kitten had said nothing for some time, her mind obviously elsewhere. She abruptly informed them where it had been.

"So I say again, I feel like a fool just sitting here! We can do something. Besides relaying information to Orvy . . . the Major. If Peot is right—well, I think it ought to be checked out."

"I might have guessed," said Porsupah. "You want a look at this entity for yourself."

"Well, Peot could be mistaken. If he's not, visual observation still ought to be useful. Maybe he won't attack the thing now because he can't get near it yet, for some reason. Perhaps it can sense his presence the way he senses it. Maybe he's holding off for other reasons. But *we* ought to be able to get near it."

"Oh great," groaned Porsupah. "Here we have a creature that's survived half a million t-years plus. It supposedly has crossed intergalactic space, destroyed civilizations, and you want to hop on a raft and go sightsee it. Do I make arrangements to pack a lunch?"

"Don't be snide. Peot as much as said that it wouldn't do any harm yet. All the more reason for gathering what first-hand information we can, while it remains inactive. Are you saying that you're not curious and don't want to go?"

Porsupah sighed through his whiskers. "You always tie things together. I'm curious as hell. Of course I'm going."

"Me, I want to get back to my ship and forget this entire abomination," said Hammurabi. "But if you think you can manage it, I'm damned if I'll pass a chance to get a look at this thing. Might be some money in it, if Kingsley hasn't got this end sewn up too tight. Just one thing, though."

"What?" said Kitten.

"How do you propose to find it? I doubt Peot would tell you. He seems to feel strongly that humans should stay far away from it."

"But I don't think he'll stop us. You know how his 'voice' fades as you leave the chamber. His telepathic range, on our level, anyway, can't be that great. Even if he can detect the Vom at a distance . . .

"As for locating the creature," she continued brightly, "that's simple. Peot said that the main body of his 'Machine' is always positioned directly above it. I can get the beacon's location from salvage authority without Kingsley or anyone else knowing about it. Drop a line downwards, plot map, find creature."

"You make it sound so easy," sighed Porsupah again.

The borrowed raft sped rapidly over the calm sea. They reached Repler City ten minutes earlier than Mal had estimated. This was due at least in part to Kitten's habit of making turns around intervening islands and reefs that threatened to overturn the craft. Fortunately the hoverafts were practically incapable of capsizing.

She almost managed it. Twice.

Instead of docking at the City harbor, they headed
straight for the auxiliary landing nearest the shuttleport
itself.

The Port was located on a long peninsula. The surface
had been planed off, smoothed over, and pitted with
sheds, warehouses, coking areas, launch pits, hangers,
fuel balloons, and a small but growing atmosphere dock.
It could handle shuttlecraft of all but the largest classes.
The fine-grained paving ran a running battle with the
profuse island vegetation. The flora took advantage of
every crack and bare spot to press a vigorous, verdurous
counterattack.

The Port harbor area, for ships and hovercraft, wasn't
designed to handle much in the way of cargo. Those
activities were carried on mostly at the central city landings. But there was plenty of room for small commercial
and pleasure craft. Some of the island's wealthier in-
habitants had yachts and personal submarine vehicles
moored there. The landing was located in a small man-
made cove at the U where the peninsula met the main-
land. Commercial buildings rose to the right, with private
homes and botels behind and to the left, hidden behind
carefully controlled vegetation.

There was a muted thrumming. Mal glanced briefly upwards. To their right a shuttle of medium class was
descending on a tail of fire. He'd watched thousands
of similar landings and equally conventional liftoffs.
There'd been a time when such displays filled him with
wonder. Now only a few figures passed through his mind.
He could estimate the amount of thrust the shuttle was
putting out, its probable mass, even the position of its
mother ship. All in an unfamiliar atmosphere. Given a
visual check of the mother vessel, he could probably
gauge its home port and basal cargo.

There was a single check at the cove entrance. Kitten
and Porsupah's military credentials eased them past that.
Kitten docked the raft with a flair that displayed either
tremendous skill or fantastic luck, sliding in and spinning

between two larger craft. They were so close their cushions brushed.

A fast walkaway brought them to the Port Control buildings. They were a humorous parody of the giant complexes maintained on major trading worlds. As was typical of such smaller ports, certain offices were often combined. This proved true of salvage and registry. The office itself was no different from dozens of others they'd passed. Once inside, they were greeted by a thirty-ish gentleman of nondescript physiognomy and few words. He was casually attired in mesh and tropical lederhosen.

"Sit yourselves down. Be with you in a sec."

The slightly pallid official escorted them into an even tinier inner office cluttered with charts and microfiles. A plethora of pins, tacks and variegated markers swarmed over the maps and diagrams cluttering the walls.

"What'll I have for you, then?" he sighed, propping his feet up on the desk. On a major planet the official would have crossed his hands, not his ankles.

"Well . . ." began Mal.

"We'd like to confirm," interrupted Kitten, "the validity of a recently reported salvage claim."

"You got the beacon number?"

Kitten prepared to consult her vocorder. She didn't even get a chance to activate it.

"Never mind," the man said. "It's sixty-two."

"Yes. How the hell did you know?" asked Mal.

The official smiled slightly. "Wasn't hard. You're all clearly extra-Replerian visitors. This is the first registry we've had reported in several years. It seemed logical enough you wouldn't be interested in any several years old . . . I can tell you everything's in order. It's quite legal. Fees were paid almost immediately after the beacon was registered. Registration and claim are already recorded on Terra."

"Still, we want to make absolutely sure it's valid," persisted Kitten. "Not that we've any thoughts of claim-jumping, or anything along those lines."

"Perish forbid," the man grinned. "Wouldn't be my business if you did."

"In order to be valid," she continued doggedly, "all details on the registration regarding location must coincide with the beacon's actual positioning in space, right?"

"Naturally."

"Well, I'd like to have a check made on it. It's pretty important to us." She purred, a semi-vocalization she was astonishingly good at, having perfected it after considerable use: "We'd be ever so grateful."

"I'm sure you would, but I'm afraid I'm not permitted to pass around that sort of information, m'lady."

Kitten breathed deeply and dropped her voice an octave. "Not even for special requests from special friends?"

The official leaned close and breathed deeply. He lowered his voice an octave.

"No."

Mal couldn't help grinning. If Kitten was fazed, she didn't show it. Instead, she removed the vulcanite band from inside her left sleeve. On it was the embossed symbol of the United Church: an hourglass enclosed by a circle, with her name, number, and rank imprinted beneath it.

"Of course, if you put it that way, your command is my wish." He pulled a bit of paper from a pad, swiveled, and began punching buttons on a computer console.

"Isn't that saying the other way 'round?" queried Mal.

"I'm inherently masochistic." The official pulled a card from the printout slot, viewed it on a small gray screen, then handed it to Mal. The freighter-captain gave it a brief glance, nodded to the man.

"Thanks, old boy. You've been a help," said Kitten. They rose and turned to leave.

"Curiously speaking," said the official hurriedly, "why didn't you just tell me you were Church authority in the first place?"

"April Fool," said Kitten.

"But it's August."

"See?" She shut the door gently.

It was raining out, a warm, humid drizzle. They took a private transit car to the Port Library. Mal had informed them that it would do as well and be quicker than returning to the *Umbra*. He checked charts and figures while Porsupah and Kitten amused themselves by thumbing through samples of the local literature—bad shorts, mediocre novels, some good poetry and fair dreamschemes.

Mal shifted his notes to a time-renting station and did some fast figuring with the aid of the computer. After a bit he sat back, staring at the readout screen. He was still staring some time after the green light on top, indicating time-stop, had gone out.

"Well," said Kitten finally.

"Well, hell."

"I'm already aware of the proverbial location for the traditional one. We're supposed to be looking for one a bit more localized."

He looked over at her, past the anxious Porsupah. "Guess where our intergalactic boojum has chosen to hole up?"

"The governor's mansion," offered Porsupah, almost hopefully.

"Funny. Here." He pointed to a chart covered with rough lines and scribbling, half in and half out of the printout slot. "Somewhere right offshore the AAnn Concession."

"So?" she said.

"So? *So?*" He rose suddenly and stood glaring eye to eye with her. Hands tightly clenched on hips, he controlled his anger with an effort. "Do you have any idea what can happen to you if our peace-loving neighbor lizards acquire even temporary possession of you?"

"Captain," she said boredly, turning her head away slightly, "kindly keep in mind that I am an officer in the armed forces of the United Church. I am fully aware of the consequences of being discovered without permission within a diplomatic sanctuary. I am also more conversant than most with the oh-so-delightful hobbies and habits of our reptilian friends. Including their less savory ones. We shall avoid all potential unpleasantness through a simple expediency."

"Oh? And what might that be?"

"We shall endeavor not to get caught."

"Oh lovely! Universal beauty and logic! Kurita smite me if I've ever heard such lucidity in the midst of storm. We will avoid being shot by dodging the nerve-beams. I rhapsodize!" He was so upset he spoke in pidgin Centaurian, a tongue especially suited to flights of sarcasm.

"A poor analogy," said Kitten.

"A poorer idea," Mal replied.

"Well, we're going anyway. Aren't we, Pors?"

The Tolian sighed. "I suppose so, soft-and-warm. I know that tone too well to try mere reason on you."

"Marvelous, fine, delightful. I hope you have a charming tour, and that when the AAnn prepare you, they use plenty of hot pepper!" He turned away from them and began refiling the charts and maps.

Kitten turned as if to leave, stopped short, and turned again, smiling. She performed one of the many small things she was adept at, that of relaxing her body in certain specific places.

"Mal? Mister Hammurabi? I . . . I'd really feel better if you'd come along. Even if only as a gesture. To sort of, well, stay on top of things, you know."

"That won't work with me," he mumbled. "And stop blowing in my ear. It only gives me a headache."

"Oh, I don't really believe that. Besides, if you don't come . . ." she did something educated with her tongue, ". . . I'll inform the Major that you're withholding information and material evidence concerning the transfer of bloodhype. Specifically, the drug itself."

"That's my word against yours. And the stuff can, and will, be obliterated if anyone, anyone at all, tries to grab it."

"Of course you can do that," she whispered, "but the

charges and resultant official actions during investigation would tie you up in orbit for the *longest* time. Wouldn't that be awkward? You wouldn't be able to perform your primary function, that of moving things from here to there in a reasonable amount of time, like your customers like you to."

The freighter-captain wheeled slowly, like a tank, to face her.

"All right. Have done, then." To her surprise, he smiled back. "You've acquired a companion candidate for suicide, I promise. And I'll add another promise. If we get out of this with neural networks intact, I shall, despite whatever obstacles, writs, legislation, weaponry and so forth you try to put in my path, despite arguments, questionings, philosophy and couth, whale the tar out of you."

"I knew you'd agree with me," she said briskly. "Most people do, sooner or later. And I might add that my body contains no petroleum extracts or by-products of any kind. Nor am I affected by archaic threats which invoke the cetacea as a verb." She stared hard.

"That's good," he said, deactivating the computer terminal. "You keep telling yourself that."

It had been a difficult day, but the AAnn officer was too tired to be more than moderately upset. First, an unchecked circuit had accidentally tripped, setting off the alarm at one of the new, hastily installed subsurface warning points scattered about the island. This automatically activated two remote underwater defense stations and a whole subsection of personnel directly attached to his command. The result being that a large school of *corvat,* a medium-sized skate-like fish, had been incinerated before he could bring things under control.

But Tivven hadn't been punished. He hadn't even received a dressing down. His superior, with unusual restraint, recognized that the result was entirely due to the haste with which the alarm unit had been installed. And he'd shared Tivven's disgust at the hysteria which attended the absurdly complex system's installation, secret project or no.

Besides, his superior had problems of his own, equally upsetting to the liver.

And now this.

He stared again at the assemblage before him, debating again whether or not to trouble the base commander with it. According to Colonel Korpt's dictates, it shouldn't be necessary. Tivven saw no real reason to argue with an easy way out.

True, two violations of the Concession boundary in as many days was unusual. Still, there was nothing to distinguish the antics of this particular group from any other, nor to ascribe hidden purposes to their arrival. They were nothing as extraordinary as the single crazy human who'd sauntered in deliberately the other day, as though he owned the place. What Tivven and the others couldn't understand was why the Commander hadn't ordered the arrogant primate dressed and potted immediately.

So here he was, stuck with an obnoxious Terran female, an impatient, gaudily dressed Tolian, and a stolid Terran male of dull aspect and rather formidable size and strength.

The Terran female had been rambling non-stop for a good twenty time-parts now.

". . . and rest assured that once the governor hears my complaint, this is going to be brought to the attention of the highest authorities . . . !"

"Madame, silence!" Tivven tried to substitute belligerence for boredom, partially succeeded. "I shall explain one more time. You are guilty of territorial incursion into a restricted area. As such, by law you are now in Imperial Territory. This places you under my jurisdiction: not that of this planet, not that of the Commonwealth. Whatsoever I decide should be done with you, will be done."

The female threw him a sharp expression. Tivven was good at primate expressions. He could recognize a sneer.

It suggested several things, among them that his threats had been somewhat less than intimidating.

"Confine them to their vessel and secure them for the usual day-period." Those were the suggestions of Colonel Korpt. "And issue the standard protest to the governor via our representative in the capitol. Yolk, it's damp in here! Now get out."

A check with Commander Parquit had produced similar action. "Do whatever Korpt says. I'll sign the orders later—whenever. I'm busy now. Oh, and make certain, Lieutenant, that they stay on board their craft . . . I assume they came by hoveraft?"

"Yes, Excellency."

"I don't want them wandering around. They sound like a typical tourist bunch, and so I don't expect otherwise from them. But if one is found strolling about loose, front canines will be lost. Understand?"

Tivven understood.

He looked up at the group, tired.

"You are hereby confined to your ship until further notice. . ."

"Just who do you think you are, ordering us around, mister luggage-covers?" piped the Tolian. His whiskers bristled angrily. "Such an insulting attitude is here perpetrated! By a scaly underling, no less, who . . . !"

" . . . where you will be placed under guard. You are not to leave the vessel under any circumstances under penalty of a swift death," Tivven concluded doggedly. He gestured to the guard at the door.

"Escort them back to their vessel, sergeant, and post guard on it. They are not to depart until ordered. *If* ordered."

The sergeant, who had played this game before, saluted snappily—he was a fifteen-year veteran of this egg-forsaken post. He gestured towards the door with his stungun.

Tivven could hear the shrill voice of the Terran female echoing back up the corridor long after the three

had departed. Swiveling in his chair, he activated the
autolog and commenced dictating the ponderous official
report. He wondered if anyone ever read the things. He
doubted it. This particular time he would be right. But
not for the reasons he suspected.

The guard, like all guards since the beginning of time
assigned to boring, monotonous, unrelieved, insipid
night duty when most sensible beings were asleep, was
wishing he was. Perhaps the wishes were effective. More
likely it was just coincidence. Certainly, if he'd been
questioned about it later, it wasn't likely he'd recall the
small sting at the back of his neck immediately prior to
his lapsing into a period of extended sleep.

He probably would have wished to observe the being
responsible for inviting Morpheus. Likely, though, he
would have argued the method.

Kitten approached quietly after spotting the all-well signal from Porsupah. The Tolian stood by the body, searching the surrounding darkness. She ran lightly over to
him. Her goggles picked up and intensified the starlight
to the point where it seemed bright as day. Porsupah
didn't wear them. He didn't need any.

She joined him in scanning the grounds, paying special
attention to the three big crates stacked on the pier. That
was one of their prearranged ambush points. She bent
over the inert reptile, felt for its pulse. The tiny puncture
made by the drug-carrying dart had already closed. There
was practically no blood. After a moment's consideration she put a second dart next to the first, just to the
left of the armored spine.

A larger, blocky figure joined the two.

"Other one's taken care of," Mal murmured. "No
sign of activity from the building we were herded out of.
I'm a bit surprised its been so easy."

"They weren't exactly expecting it," she replied.

"Witherest fly we now, and how, princess?"

"If that's poetry, it's execrable."

"No, as a matter of fact, it's Whalen."

"Buffon. I thought you were the one afraid of being soup."

"I still am," he whispered tightly. "So I make jokes. So get your ass moving and I'll follow quietly."

"I could use a little more information first."

"Why don't you ask our somnolent companion here." Mal nudged the sleeping guard, who didn't stir.

"You're the one who did the map plotting on the creature. Didn't you pinpoint it?"

"At that range? With a library 'puter?"

The first moon was climbing rapidly. In a while the second would be in the sky, brightening the island considerably. Kitten turned and scanned the area again. A few lights glimmered in buildings half-glimpsed through thick vegetation. Nothing moved but branches.

"I wouldn't bet it was close inshore. It can't be all that enormous—the island certainly isn't. I'd think the AAnn would have noticed it if it were close in."

"Maybe we're not on top of it, but it *is* close to shore. Could be the AAnn are myopic from so much moisture. My calculations weren't that far off."

"Still, if we can spot it," added Porsupah, "you'd think the AAnn would have."

"Yes, you would," said Kitten thoughtfully. "Still, they've no reason to suspect its presence, as we have."

"Could be it has a way of evading alarms similar to the one we tripped coming in," said Mal. "Why it would want to hang around a populated, armed area like this one beats me, though."

"Maybe to study," replied Kitten, shuddering slightly.

"Too many imponderables," chipped in Porsupah. "Let's circle the island. We might not spot the thing itself, but we'll be looking for signs of its presence, whereas the AAnn wouldn't be. If you two just want to argue about it, go back to the raft."

The two humans said nothing. They followed the small alien at a comfortable trot up the pebbled beach. Neither of the two humans could still believe that the AAnn hadn't spotted the creature. But then it was hard to believe the creature, too.

They'd been jogging along the curving shoreline for perhaps five minutes when Porsupah halted them. He was staring out to sea.

"Well, what have you spotted? At this point I'm not too choosy," Mal said. They'd already had to put out two more AAnn and avoid or inconvenience several elaborate alarm systems. At this rate they'd never cover a tenth of the island's perimeter. Assuming they weren't shot or blown ship-high first. But Kitten and Porsupah seemed to recognize the concealed triggers as though they'd set them themselves. Mal hadn't noticed a one.

The question of what such an extensive network of alarms was doing in a supposedly innocuous area was another problem that defied logic.

What they needed, dammit, was a few answers!

Porsupah had knelt and was examining the sand. He took up a small pawful, rubbed the grains between his fingers, sniffed at it. Abruptly he turned and walked back about ten meters along their route. He performed a similar ritual there, then returned. To their questioning stares he replied, "This section of beach and forest wasn't arranged by nature. Not only is the sand different—taken up from a respectable depth, I think—but the rocks and overall landscape have an unnatural feel to them that I can't explain in terranglo or symbo-speech. Everything is just a little bit cockeyed."

Mal took a long look at the sloping beach, the thick semi-jungle. "I can't detect anything out of the ordinary."

"Nor I," said Kitten, the landscape glowing eerily in her goggles. "But I believe you, Pors."

"There is only one structure visible, too." The Tolian pointed.

A long, low building, set back in the trees. It ran perpendicular to the beach and was a little over a story high. As they walked towards the windowless structure, Mal noticed that an occasional tree—not all, by any means—

was tilted at an angle that deviated sufficiently from the norm to be noticeable. If you happened to be looking for such things. There was no question about it now. This section of Replerian real estate had been rebuilt, delicately rebuilt, to suit some specific purpose. Moreover, it had been done recently, according to Pors. This suggested hurry, which in turn suggested a need for secrecy. And it had been rearranged to look like it hadn't been rearranged, which hinted at a deal more.

The building proved to be unguarded. It was painted, almost enameled, a dark gray-green. A dull roaring sound emanated from somewhere inside. Kitten put a hand against the wall. It vibrated slightly.

"Look for a door," Porsupah suggested. "I'm going to check something else."

The Tolian disappeared into the jungled darkness. The door turned up almost immediately, recessed in the side they were on.

"Interesting," murmured Mal. He was staring at the AAnn lettering on the airlock-type portal. "It says—"

"I can read AAnnish," said Kitten.

Porsupah returned a moment later, puffing out short, whistling breaths.

"Where've you been?" asked Kitten.

"Up a tree. Whoof! I wanted a quick look at the top of this thing, and we didn't truck along a ladder."

"See anything?" asked Mal.

"The building runs I couldn't say how far back into these trees. Top of it is all ventilators. Big ones. You can see the fans from high enough. They're well screened and you'd never notice them from the air, but this close—no mistaking them."

"Well now, this is interesting," said Kitten, staring at the door. "This inscription here declares solemnly that anyone who enters without six kinds of ultra-top-high-security passes is assured all sorts of lengthy and painful deaths."

"Ultra-secret ventilator complex pulling lots of air

someplace, combined with a thoroughly dug up and re-
planted section of beach and forest. Need one say more?"
the Tolian announced.

Kitten was already examining the lock.

"It doesn't take an expert to tell this whole setup was
put together recently," said Mal. He ran a hand over the
gleaming guard rail. "Practically factory fresh."

They'd been descending helical steps for what seemed
a small part of a year. They'd found an elevator inside but
after some discussion had passed it up for fear of not
pushing the proper button and setting off hidden alarms.
Not to mention the possibility of meeting someone unpleasant at the end of the shaft. The stairwell seemed a
better bet. The only place it registered a power drain was
in the back of Kitten's legs.

"The construction is solid, but still far from well in-
tegrated," Mal continued. "Place was built in a hurry, for
sure."

With Porsupah in the lead, they reached the end of the
stairway. It terminated in a small room filled with tools
and boxes of unknown content. The Tolian started off
down a long, dimly lit tunnel. Their goggles made it as
bright as the main terminus in Terraport. The direction
led out under the sea.

The tunnel opened abruptly onto a brightly lit corridor
lined with doors and hastily thrown-together decorative
tiles. A surprised shout in a guttural voice sounded just
ahead.

Kitten pulled her tiny pistol, dropped to her right knee
and fired, all in one motion. The AAnn technic crumpled
after taking two steps away from them.

They dragged the still body a few meters into the dark
of the tunnel, reemerged cautiously into the light of the
corridor.

"We can't keep this up indefinitely, you know," said
Mal, trying to look fourteen ways at once. "They're going
to start finding these bodies eventually."

"Eventually is not immediately," whispered Kitten,

panting slightly. The technic had been heavy for an
AAnn. "It will be assumed for some time yet that those
we put under are asleep or elsewhere. Hopefully, even if
one or two are discovered by accident, no one will think to
connect them up until we've departed. Anyway, the AAnn
hate to be out at night and do so only when ordered. They
certainly need their beauty sleep."

"It won't be assumed they fell asleep if some casual
passerby spots a couple·of those darts sticking out of his
friend's neck."

Kitten answered between breaths as they jogged around
another corner. "The darts themselves are made from a
specially constituted gelatin. It dissolves untraceably into
the bloodstream. It also contains a coagulating agent to
halt bleeding around the wound. Thirty seconds after impact, it would take careful chemical analysis of the blood
to tell that a target's been drugged, much less shot."

Mal examined his own pistol with renewed interest as
they swung to their left. A trade item with excellent possibilities. True, it might not be for sale by the Church, but
still . . .

"Here's one that says 'Life-Systems Monitoring,' " said
Kitten. "It's the first one I've seen with that blue danger
seal on it. Let's try it."

The latch lifted easily to Porsupah's soft touch and he
slipped inside, Kitten following close behind and Mal
covering.

There were three AAnn in the room. All wore similar
expressions of surprise and bewilderment at the nocturnal
alien invasion. One soldier and two scientist-types, judging by the toga-chainmail of the intellectual elite the
others wore.

The soldier's hand got about halfway to the ugly pistol
strapped to his haunch before he collapsed on his snout,
unconscious. The younger of the two scientists continued
to stare in disbelief until he was sent sleepward. The
oldster, however, made a dive for something at the far end
of the big central console. He didn't reach it. Singeing
Porsupah's left shoulder, Kitten caught the scientist in the

midsection. He doubled up in midair and she shot him again, to make sure.

Mal took a fast glance up and down the corridor, then closed the door. Kitten was replacing the gas cartridge and dart cluster in her pistol. At the same time she was examining the section of console the scientist had been trying to reach. Mal looked at her questioningly and she indicated a clearly marked azure button.

"General alarm. Close."

Porsupah was rubbing his shoulder where the hot gas from her pistol had singed him. "Good! If it were anything less, soft-and-round, I'd mark you."

"They're all quite alive, if not kicking," she said, turning over the last of the three. Mal and Porsupah had moved to a wide glassite panel and were staring unmoving into it. She put hands on hips. "Well, aren't you even interested?"

"Come and take a look at this," whispered Porsupah without turning from the glass.

"What could fascinate you cretins so . . ." She caught sight of what lay beyond the panel and stopped talking.

A Brobdingnagian chamber showed on the other side. It was brightly, almost painfully, illuminated. Small silver-suited figures of what were clearly AAnn technics clustered in groups about the wall to their left. Most of the chamber was filled with a gigantic spheroid of nightmare black. It quivered slightly here and there, like jelly. The fur at the back of Porsupah's neck stood on end.

There was a sharp crackling sound, audible through a speaker set above one cabinet of instruments. A small bolt of electricity jumped from a far device to the ebony mountain. Ponderously, the massive bulk shifted away from the generator. It flowed/crawled towards them. Another crackling followed and the second bolt drove the thing back to the center of the chamber. It halted just short of three silver-suited figures.

"Well, that explains a lot," Kitten murmured. "The AAnn have some peculiar tastes, all right. Can't say I care for their style in pets."

"That winds down the 'invincible alien' theory of our resurrected friend," said Mal grimly. "Our bescaled neighbors seem to have managed to keep it in hand."

"Directing it, too," put in Porsupah thoughtfully. "Moving it from place to place via electrical stimulation. Conditioning."

"Could be Peot overestimated its powers. Just sizewise, though, it's plenty big enough to do a lot of damage, improperly directed," said Kitten.

"Direction depends on your point of view," said Mal.

"You're always looking for an angle, aren't you, throwback? That's the sort of evaluation I'd expect from one of them." She pointed at a cluster of techs.

"Listen, I've had just about—"

"Surely," Porsupah put in hastily, "it is of sufficient mass to destroy a good-sized village. And it may be an especially tough organism. Such a creature could indeed prove a formidable threat on a world as undeveloped as Repler."

"We've no assurance they plan anything along those lines," said Kitten. Mal snorted. "Still, I think it's time we concluded our temporary circumvention of the official policy on non-intrusion into Concession territory. Let's get back to the raft." She headed for the door, Mal and Porsupah following.

"Do I detect the advocation of violence in your words?" asked Porsupah. "It would amount to an act of war."

"You think the AAnn would risk a full-scale confrontation over violation of territory on this tiny base?"

"Of course not," the Tolian continued. "But if they feel this project of theirs could develop into something significant . . ."

"I see. Well, I wasn't considering it seriously, anyway. Fortunately, it's not our decision to make. I have a hunch that if the Major calls the AAnn Commander for a friendly chat and just casually mentions that he's fully aware of what's going on here, the AAnn won't be as inclined to try anything drastic. Not if they know they'll be held accountable."

"By the time the Commander here figures out how to proceed," she continued, "something appropriate will have been worked out in the way of restraints at the ambassadorial level. Which is all that needs to be done, I think. Obviously Peot has grossly overestimated this thing's abilities. Or else it's been dormant so long it's lost whatever it once might have had in the way of strange powers."

"One thing," said Mal. "If they follow what I understand is their usual procedure in cases like ours, we ought to be let go some time tomorrow. Next day at the latest. With a verbal reprimand. But there *is* always the chance something might hold up our leave-taking."

"Oh, I didn't intend to wait until they let us go," said Kitten, jogging easily on the sandy flooring. "We'll broadcast from the raft first thing in the morning. Their own transceivers ought to be busy then."

"They're certain to be monitoring us as a matter of course," he replied. "You know they'll pick up any broadcasting you do."

"I expect them to. But all they'll hear is a typical screeching performance via my alias to Church authorities. That alone ought to be enough to make any listeners switch off. The real message won't be transmitted in words."

"Phycode," said Mal, pursing his lips. "You can do that?" He sounded surprised.

"Of course, silly!" Unexpectedly, she giggled, green glass chimes. For a battle-rated officer, it was indecently infectious. A corner of her mouth went up; then a cheek, the left one, twitched twice. An ear wiggled.

"I just made a long, involved comment about your probable ancestry. An AAnn wouldn't have detected a thing. To a perceptive human I'd appear to be afflicted with a slight case of the fidgits. But to someone versed in the code . . ."

". . . I'd have seemed properly insulted, I know," Mal said. "I've heard about it, but never seen it—or have I?"

"That's what I mean," she grinned. "I'm very good at it." They'd reached the bottom of the stairwell. Porsupah started up.

"You're sure that when all these lizards come around, they won't remember what happened to them? Those three in the monitoring section, for example."

Her voice drifted back from just ahead. "They'll be out for at least another hour yet. No, they won't. In addition to being a strong soporific, the drug conveniently wipes out memory just prior to being administered. An intentional side effect. But if we'd taken a minute or two longer with those three, they'd remember enough to make things awkward."

The sun and the first guard were just coming up as they reentered the sleek sportsraft. Kitten was the first to her own cabin. She changed from the skin-tight, light-bending black crawfit to something suitably grotesque and flamboyant for a young lady of her assumed station. It wouldn't do for an AAnn vidcast scanner to pick her up transceiving in a one-piece suit designed to create an effect of semi-invisibility.

Mal and Porsupah changed a bit faster, not having to be concerned with such details as, for example, coiffure. Kitten essayed a few eloquent twitches, paraphrastically speaking, and felt up to the task. She'd have to trust to memory and improvisation to handle the verbal part of the act.

Porsupah waved as she entered the plush control lounge. He was adjusting the transceiver. The AAnn would almost surely pick up the cast, but it didn't hurt to try for as tight a beam as possible, anyway.

"The arrival of your friend with the shipment you requested is due shortly, I am told," said Commander Parquit. Rose walked comfortably at his side.

"A few necessities and items of nostalgic value."

"I'm sure," Parquit replied drily. "If the shipment is as small as you claim, then both you and your materials will be removed to orbit, there to await an appropriate transport as rapidly as can be managed, as per our agreement. An event which I look forward to with more than a modicum of pleasure." The Commander was making no effort to hide his dislike.

"You don't seem to care for me especially," offered Rose.

"I am not fond of your race, as few of my kind are. You strike me additionally as a particularly loathsome example. We can bargain without friendship. It is not required I kiss you."

"Not sure I'd care for that myself."

"I advise you not to have worries on that account. Must you carry that thing everywhere?" He indicated the metal case with its explosive, deadly contents. One breath of the powder could kill any of his command slowly and painfully.

"Oh, it's not activated just now for my, ah, bargaining purposes. Sorry if it makes you nervous. It's just that I've gotten in the habit of not letting it out of my sight. Not that I'd expect you ever goin' back on your word, you understand."

Parquit made an AAnn expression indicative of nausea, coupled with unconcern.

"Just that I feel more secure with it near me, see?"

"I neither pretend nor care to," the Commander replied.

"Incidentally, where are we headed?"

"Harbor Control." They halted outside a door. Sensing their body heat, the semi-transparent portal slid back.

They entered a wide room that was completely transparent from walls to ceiling. Only the floor was opaque. They were not terribly high. Still, there was no sense in subjecting some timorous controller to vertigo. It wasn't necessary to see beneath one's feet. They were in the approximate center of the island, just above the tallest trees of the forest.

"As your companion is due with your possessions soon, I would prefer you to be here. There should be no confusion if the agreed-upon coding is properly utilized. A proper visual identification, however, is far preferable. I have reasons for such precautions. Someone else could have intercepted the coding. This way we will be certain."

"Afraid of something, old skin?"

"No more so than normal. Besides, anything that will aid in expediting your removal gives me enjoyment. Other matters press heavily on my time. Rest assured, however, that getting rid of you is foremost in my mind."

"Flattery'll get you nowhere."

The Commander was already talking to a detec operator. "Communication from the anticipated arrival yet?"

"No, your Excellency. The channel is held open, though."

"Good. Notify if—"

"Excellency?" Parquit turned.

"What is it, Harbormaster Third?"

"Pardon, your Excellency, for disturbing. The Terran female is broadcasting. Directionally, it appears, to somewhere within the central city."

"A logical place." Parquit was only mildly interested. "I did not know that a raft of that class could beam so far directionally."

"Some have the capability, Excellence. Boostering and expensive modifications."

Parquit grunted. "Nothing of interest, presumably?"

"No, Excellency. Nothing unique. It appears to be a series of complaints distinguished only by their vituperativeness. Should I try to damp her out?"

"No, let her rave. Hopefully she will annoy the humanx authorities as she has us. I would not personally inflict such a female on the most desperate mate-seeker. Such selfrighteousness! I understand this grouping has been an abnormally difficult one."

"Abnormally vocal, anyway, Excellence," smirked the Harbormaster.

"You're holding a group of people?" Rose inquired. He'd understood enough of the preceding conversation.

"No, not people. Humans, and one other. Tourists. Along with an occasional commercial fisher, who hopes to find an unfished area close to the center of population, they sometimes stray within Concession boundaries. Most such are the result of honest errors of navigation. Others do so, I suspect, in the hopes of achieving a small thrill. Unfortunately, I cannot react as I would prefer. This would entail frying the lot of them. We are 'at peace,' you see. So such actions are proscribed by treaty. I believe some would actually enjoy the threat. Most merely express outrage that we constrain their sacrosanct person. You are the first, I regret, to arrive here with purpose."

"What *do* you do with them?"

"Hold them over for a day, make brief suggestions of bodily dismemberment, lodge a protest with the authorities, who, I understand, sometimes even actually levy a fine on the offenders."

"You said humans and 'one other.' "

"A Tolian. Petty aristocrat. These small mammals . . ." Parquit paused. Rose had turned away and was trying hard to control himself. "Does it shame you so much?"

"It's laughter I'm trying to hold back, not shame, your scaliness! Two humans and a Tolian. One large male and one exceptionally attractive female?"

"By your standards, as I vaguely comprehend them, yes. How do you know?"

"And you don't want visitors. Oh, Luna! . . . Listen, brighteyes. The female and the furry posturer are Church undercover agents, both officers. The male is an independent freighter-captain with more connections than an all-purpose 'puter linkup. In the words of ancient hue, me boyoh, you've been took!" The drugger burst into laughter, causing heads to turn in the control room.

Parquit did not betray any emotion beyond a slight tightening of horny lips.

"Harbormaster Third, damp that broadcast!"

"Excellency!" The reptile jumped at the sting in the command.

"Controller! Kindly inform the sergeant in charge of that landing section to conduct our visitors to my rooms. Under guard. Put their raft under cross-coverage from harbor turrets. If they make the slightest move to depart, destroy them."

"It is done, Excellence."

"Hey, no reason to jump on them like that! They're probably lookin' for me," said Rose.

Parquit turned and gave the drug-runner such an intense stare that the normally stolid Rose looked away.

"You flatter yourself, human. As you said, it gets one nowhere. I have reason to believe they are here for reasons and purposes other. I am admittedly curious as to how *you* know them."

"They're the ones—the two agents, anyway—who've forced my reluctant and hasty departure from these parts."

"I see. Reason enough to condemn them, for inflicting you on me. I sometimes wish for more primitive days, when decisions were a simple question of sharper teeth and stronger claw. Yet I endeavor to cope with civilization. Come along. You may be of some use, Sand knows."

Parquit headed for the door, paused at a word from the Harbormaster.

"What is it, Third?"

"Excellence, the human's expected shipment has contacted us."

"Monitor it closely." He turned back to Rose. "You will remain to make visual identification. Following that, direct yourself to my rooms."

The series of rapid, ultra-high-frequency numbers was picked up, recorded and transcribed by the Rectory 'puters. Coupled with the phycoded information just received, they were sufficient to send the padre in charge scurrying for the Major's office.

"You realize your confession of your profession is a mere formality now," said Parquit. "I am as certain of it as of my own ancestral tree. It is your purpose that concerns me more. You no more landed here by accident than I did by desire. Why not observe courtesy, be polite, and tell me freely? I shall be courteous in turn. I will not have you shot out of hand . . . No, please, young female. Subside. No more imagined insults. Surely the maintenance of this act is as wearisome to you as it is to me. I could search your vessel. Interesting things would no doubt turn up. But should they, I would be impelled by precedent to have you exterminated. I would far rather have answers to some questions—before."

"Poo! Commander, this has now become exasperating. The sheer size of this illusion you have drawn for yourself makes me fear for you."

"Your sudden solicitation for my good health is out of character, female."

"You are perfectly welcome to search our ship, if it will cure you."

"Those who have no options are generous . . ." began the commander.

"You won't find anything more espionage-oriented than a few typical, if expensive, cameras. The tapes in them contain only shots of water and island scenery—not this island, nor its surrounding water. Where your suspicions arise from escape me."

"They arose from me," came a voice from the doorway. "Dear me, a pun." The drugger strode past the startled group. "I'm surprised, yes, and disappointed, to see you still tied up with these two, Hammurabi. No profit in it, no profit at all." He shook his head slowly, mournfully.

"I think I see your point now," began Mal reasonably. "It sure looks like you've been right all along. Maybe we ought to reconsider . . ."

The drugger lit one of his few remaining dopesticks, ignoring Parquit's expression of disgust. "Uh-uh. Too much hate in your eyes. Angle of lips, position of head . . . no, you'd strangle me first chance you got, on general principles alone. Besides, judging just from your plain stupid relationship with these two," he gestured at Kitten and Pors, "you'd be a poor risk."

"You find some funny holes to crawl into, drugger," said Kitten.

He smiled. "I only go where I'm wanted. Commander, here, is a spiritual relative."

"Hold your insults, you push me too far!" said Parquit.

"Easy, Commander, easy." Rose hefted the ever-present metal case, shook it gently. "I've still my little surprise box."

"If you coerce me to the edge," the Commander said tightly, "a momentary insanity on my part could destroy us all. Your package of *supposed* drug concerns me less and less."

"Okay, okay. Forget it."

"No wonder the local police couldn't find you," broke in Porsupah.

"You contacted your supplier?" asked Parquit.

"Yep."

"You have now that which you require for departure?"

"Pretty much. Can't be as picky as I'd like at this stage. At least everything got here intact. I was worried about him having to dodge humanx patrols. Young for the job, but he managed. If they bothered to plot his course, it would provide another reason for not troubling him. Your reputation for hospitality isn't supposed to encourage visitors."

A young man appeared in the portal. He was tall and good-looking.

"Everything you wanted's been transferred off the raft, Dom, so—"

"*You!*" The scream of recognition was only half feminine. Kitten threw herself at the figure. A guard, energy rifle at the ready, interposed himself. She stared at the weapon for a long moment as though debating whether to try passing the guard anyway, hands at her sides, breathing heavily.

"You appear to be acquainted with this slug's associate," said Parquit in lucid understatement. He'd been surprised himself by the violence of her reaction.

"We've met," said Russell Kingsley. He eyed her warily across the room.

Peot was alone. In a universe of a trillion souls, he was, would always be, had been, alone. He'd lived non-life too long and now must live an unwanted real-life a while longer. Hurry. Hurry hurry hurry.

After several eternities, it was not easy to move with concern.

Orvenalix deliberated about two minutes before flipping a switch on his desk com.

"Get me the governor's residence, operator."

"Processing, sir."

After a few seconds the haze on the screen cleared to reveal a spectacularly pneumatic human female. She was seated behind a small mahogany and brass desk. Her tone was lazy.

"I *am* sorry, Major Orvenalix, but the governor left *explicit* instructions that he was *not* to be disturbed until *further* notice."

"I see. Well. Fine. You give the good governor this message for me, then. Tell him that as of," he glanced at the wrist chronometer set into the chiton of his left truarm, "three minutes ago, three especially equipped patrol submersibles of the Replerian Domestic Commerce and Customs Protection Association were dispatched by me at maximum cruising speed for the Imperial AAnn Enclave, where they will attempt to carry out the release of two human and one Tolian prisoner. Should the AAnn Commander refuse to comply with this request, the commander of the three vessels has been empowered to secure their release by force . . . Tell him this straight and tell him this now, or you'll find yourself tomorrow in the awkward and much less relaxing position of scraping willoweed off the hulls of shrimp trawlers over in Faertown."

To her credit, the professional smile remained frozen

on the girl's face. The difference now was that the ice showed.

"I will give him the message, Major." She stood.

"And I might suggest a more regulated intake of oxygen. Your present rate of consumption intrigues me only as a xenobiological curiosity. Save it for those it may affect."

She fled from range of the pickup.

You deserve to have your antennae knotted, you old reprobate! That was unnecessary.

The message was designed to produce results. It did. Governor Washburn was on the screen almost immediately, fumbling with the clasps of his blouse. His appearance was generally rumpled and unkempt. Well, that was too bad. This was one siesta the planetary major-domo would have to forego.

Now, however, he was wide awake—and angry.

"Deity, Major! Primal urges. Obscenity! What is all this about? If you wished to begin an interstellar war in my jurisdiction, you might at least inform me in advance."

"I think you can discount the possibility of any extra-Replerian conflict, Governor."

"You bet your mandibles we can!" the executive roared. "I'm countermanding those orders now! I want those subs back in port and docked quietly by sundown! I want their captains and crews restricted to quarters until they can be properly instructed about keeping their mouths shut concerning this whole fiasco. There may still be time to keep this out of the faxpax."

"I'm afraid I'll be compelled to neglect those instructions, Governor. But this will be kept as quiet as possible. The three submersibles are under order to observe strict cast silence until something has been resolved—one way or the other."

"I see." Washburn did. He could recognize a fact when it crawled all over his face. This ability put him a cut above politicians on more "civilized" worlds, who'd lost the talent. "Perhaps some good will come of this, any-how. Running a backwards, nowhere world like Repler is thankless enough. At least I'll have the pleasure—if we survive—of seeing you demoted to the point where you'll no longer be an irritation to me."

"All things are possible, Governor," Orvenalix said soothingly. "But for now, I suggest you compose yourself as well as you're able. It's not unlikely that we'll be hearing from the Commander of the AAnn base. When he does contact you, I'd suggest moving away from the speaker and lowering the volume somewhat. He will likely not be inclined to sweet reasonableness. I have the utmost confidence in your ability to handle the conversation which will ensue."

Later, neither could remember who cut the other off first.

"Move away, female!" hissed Parquit. "I'll have no blood spilled here without consent." Reluctantly, Kitten backed up to stand between Mal and Porsupah.

The guard returned silently to his station. Kingsley walked over to Rose, grinning. "Looking feisty as ever, isn't she, Dom?"

Rose whispered. "Be quiet, you fool. There's trouble for you here."

"Nonsense! She's the prisoner. Wasn't she put off to see me, though?" He chuckled.

"You have a grudge against this male?" asked Parquit. The question was purely rhetorical.

Her voice was even, without a hint of the emotion boiling beneath it. "He spent a small time, recently, doing unwanted, ungentlemanly things to me, Excellency. But I endeavor to always remain ladylike. I promise to make his death as quick as possible."

"Did you do as she claims?" said Parquit interestedly. He turned to face Kingsley. "Is that essentially true?"

Kingsley was no interpreter of AAnn intonation, but he was suddenly on guard. "Not exactly, I . . ."

". . . lie a lot," the Commander added. He examined

the youngster closely. Kingsley shifted uncertainly under the close observation.

"You don't appear to be armed."

"I'm not. Your people took my weapons as soon as I landed."

"As was only appropriate. It would be required now anyway. Such things would impair the engagement."

"Engagement? What engagement?"

"Well, it seems the young lady made a vow. Under AAnn social convention, I should not attempt to prevent her fulfilling it. As my having her for dinner would certainly do. And despite your species' noted predilection for personal combat, one which I am told approaches our own, I have never had the opportunity to observe such an action. I've seen transceived casts of simulations, but never one in person. It should prove entertaining. I am in dire need of such, these days."

"Now look here, Excellency, I'm a guest. Surely—"

"Death-vows take precedence over common, let alone forced, hospitality."

"But I'm not an AAnn! I'm not subject to your social conventions."

"Then why do you and your superior claim sanctuary? For yourself—you do not even understand your own reasoning. Pagh!"

"Excellence," Rose began. The Commander turned sharply, as if anticipating the sentence to follow. He gestured at Kingsley.

"This one means so much to you?" Parquit was watching the drugger closely.

"It's not that, really, but—"

"You bastard!" Kingsley shouted. "You rotten, putrid . . . !" He took a step towards the older man, halted when the guard's rifle came up menacingly.

"My, everyone wishes to kill everyone else," Parquit mused. "I'm not unfamiliar with humanx history. If you humans hadn't encountered the thranx when you did, it's conceivable you would have both been sufficiently weak for us to defeat you. A black day when that meeting first took place. Otherwise we would now be in a position to pursue our natural destiny of galaxy-wide domination at a more natural pace."

"Don't hold your breath," said Mal.

Parquit turned to face the freighter-captain. "Periodic minor conflict is necessary in order to correctly ascertain an opponent's strength before waging war, man. We made an improper evaluation last time. We will not make the same error again."

"Okay, I retract the request. Hold your breath."

The Commander ignored him, turned to Kitten. "So, young female. Is the center of my office agreeable to you?"

"Just give me an arm's length." She smiled ferociously.

Rose made a last try. "This *does* violate accepted standards of politeness, Excellency."

When Parquit had concluded the AAnn laughter-equivalent, he spoke again. "See? A good idea! I am amused already. To hear *you* complain of a violation of politeness. To hear *you* cite accepted standards. How many standards of civilization have you violated? How many beings owe the visit of the Thiever-of-Thoughts to you? The Mindburner? Or He-Who-Walks-Blacksand? Do not speak to me of politeness! . . . . You! Are you afraid of this female? You substantially outmass her."

"No, your Excellency. Save your insults for this . . . this maggot. I'll fight her."

"Then be to it! I give you," he checked his own time-piece, "ten time-parts. No one will interfere."

Kitten shrugged out of the elaborate confection of crepe and silk. She crumpled the delicate material into a wad, handed it to Porsupah. Moving away to one side of her companions, she stood in very unregulation under-garments.

"Must you fight indecently, too?" said Porsupah.

"That's funny coming from you, you lecherous musk-rat! This isn't going to be pretty, and I could barely walk in that thing. Give me a kiss for luck. And stop playing with your whiskers. It makes me nervous to see you nervous." Porsupah dropped both hands awkwardly to his sides.

Mal knelt until his head was on a level with the smaller Tolian's. "He outweighs her by a good 30 kilos and he doesn't look slow. You think she can handle him?"

"I don't know. She does."

Kingsley found Rose and the AAnn Commander staring at him interestedly. After all the talk, the silence in the under-room weighed heavily on him.

He took a step towards Kitten. Another. "Listen," he said, smiling nervously. "If you want an apology or whatever, I'm willing to go through the whole bit. We all seem to be in the same ship here." He held out a hand.

"You really feel that way?" She relaxed. "Well, I suppose I'd gain merit by forgiving. Once, anyway. As you say, we do seem to have the same unpromising future."

Kingsley let out a deep breath. "I was hoping you'd feel that way." He stepped forward abruptly, his left leg coming up in a vicious *hsi* kick, using the tibia like a knife-edge, aiming for her temple.

Her right arm shot up as she dropped, deflecting the kick over her head. At the same time, her left arm drove forward from her hip, knuckles first. Her awkward position caused her to miss the solar plexus, hitting him slightly low.

Kingsley whoofed loudly and stumbled backwards, one hand going to his stomach.

Porsupah whispered to Mal, "Kitten comes out ahead on the first exchange of greetings."

Kingsley moved forward, trying an unsubtle right chop. She didn't even bother to block it, but spun to her left, jumping and twisting in one motion. Her heel hit him on the side of the jaw. He crumpled to the stone flooring, scattering sand, and had enough left to roll to his feet. He came up spitting blood and white splinters and there was nothing civilized left in his expression.

His rush was completely unchecked, animal-like. She hit him sharply on the side of the neck. It slowed but didn't stop him. His head hit her hard in the midsection and they tumbled into a complex, flowerlike table arrangement to her right. Rose had to scramble to get out of the way.

Despite the destruction, Parquit was enjoying himself hugely. Personal combat was one of the highest arts of the AAnn. This exotic spectacle was one few among even the highest nobles could afford to have staged.

Kingsley staggered dazedly to his feet, trying to clear his head. Kitten lay stunned on the sandy floor. Mal took a step forward but had to halt when the guard's rifle came up.

Staggering drunkenly, Kingsley stumbled over to the inert body and raised a heel over her groin. At the same time both long legs locked at different angles around Kingsley's free leg and pressured. Flailing his arms, he crashed to the hard floor, landing heavily on his side. He rolled to his knees, attempting to rise, just in time to meet a flying kick that made pulp of the left side of his face, the cheekbone giving way completely.

Kitten stood, holding her midsection, which throbbed painfully from the solid butt it had taken. She'd had her satisfaction. But Kingsley, somehow, got to his feet. He feigned collapse, then charged furiously—not at her, but at the guard, trying for the gun.

This guard was one of the Commander's personal attendants. He was neither lazy, slow, nor overly involved in the proceedings.

Kingsley rested a good two strides from the guard, who hadn't moved. There were two small black holes in his perfect skull, one in front, a slightly larger one directly in the back, where the energy bolt had sprayed out.

A strange drumming sound caused Kitten to turn, panting, from the ugly corpse. Parquit was thumping his tail on the floor behind him.

"Well executed, female, very well indeed! And with little damage to yourself. You are formidable, yes, formidable."

"My tummy's killing me, but if you'd like to have a go-round yourself, Excellency . . ."

"I am honored, but I fear my time for personal combat is past its prime. Nor do I feel the need of putting myself in jeopardy, even from a small female."

"I offer protest," said Rose. He was watching two attendants remove the body. "I have few enough friends left on this planet." Actually, he was more worried about word of the circumstances surrounding Kingsley's death getting back to his father. He had enough who were sworn to kill him.

"Why bother, since you will be leaving so soon?" said Parquit.

"I'm aware you bear no love for me, Commander. Must they be informed of such things?" He indicated the little group.

"I reiterate, why bother? They are not going to contact anyone anyplace for some time, if ever. I no longer intend to act in a manner merely pleasing to you."

"Going to risk an interstellar incident over us?" said Porsupah. "Strange priorities you have, Commander."

"I hardly think your disappearance would engender more than sincere regret among your friends and associates, since you are here quite illegally. And perhaps some mild anger on the part of the being who'll be responsible for replacing you in the ranks of the Church."

"I seem to have heard something similar somewhere before," Mal whispered to Kitten.

"Oh, shut up, ox!" She winced. "Nova, that abomination had a hard head!"

Chimes rang somewhere from within the Commander's spacious desk. He pulled out an earphone-speaker setup, appeared to listen intently for several minutes.

"I hear. Yes. For how long? Have you transcribed it? Good. I want it on record. Send it out to the transport as soon as it comes round in orbit again." He replaced the apparatus in the desk.

"It would seem, beings, that someone else is not concerned about off-planet ramifications."

"What do you mean?" asked Porsupah.

"There are three vessels of the local constabulary lying close offshore my harbor. They are very much aware of your presence here and appear quite insistent about having you back. Their attitude is decidedly unfriendly. I've never known the Major to act so belligerently. You must mean a lot to him. Or the information you've obtained."

"What do you propose to do about it?" said Kitten.

"Orvenalix is no fool. He must be conversant with the kind of defensive popgun I am permitted here. No doubt those ships are equipped with that in mind. However, we have a few surprises not included in the agreements. I should prefer to avoid a running battle where some of the installation may be damaged and my personnel subjected to an inglorious death. . . . Therefore, in the interests of preserving peace and avoiding unnecessary destruction, I'll offer your would-be saviors a chance to back off and motor away to wherever they came from."

"Why should they do that?" asked Kitten. Suspicions were congealing in her mind that were not attractive.

Parquit stared at her shrewdly. "I believe you have some idea. Your gladiatorial talents, if nothing else, have identified you as what this disreputable specimen insists you to be. Namely, trained agents in the service of the Emperor's enemies. I suspect you have some idea of what is taking place here. You've been here for over a day now, operating unsuspected. I have great respect for your abilities. I don't know precisely how much you've learned, because we've no way as yet of deciphering the vidcast you sent out this morning. That's one thing I hope to persuade you to reveal, later, at my leisure. I am not confident that it was damped out sufficiently early. The presence of those three vessels is partial proof of that."

"I wouldn't attempt to deny that," said Kitten.

"That is a beginning." Parquit showed teeth. "The fact that they were able to slip inside our defenses without triggering any alarm shows they are either far better equipped than that type of vessel normally is, or that our defensive preparations here have been woefully inadequate."

"Probably both," offered Mal. "If you're referring to that animated blob of caulking putty—yeah, we've seen it." Porsupah tried to restrain Mal but the captain shook him off. "No, I'm tired of games. It hasn't done me any too good so far. Let's be direct for a change."

"You two will be the death of me yet!" the Tolian exclaimed.

If Parquit was surprised by Mal's disclosure, he didn't show it.

"It is more likely that I will be. Come with me, then. I had not planned to attempt this at this time, nor have my technicians. There are last-minute preparations to supervise. You will be able to observe from the top of the Harbor Tower. Watch closely and take note of what transpires. Possibly you may be able to convince your Major that further attempts to save you will prove unefficacious. A simple demonstration should suffice."

The Commander came around from behind his desk. "You see, we have delved deeply into the creature, its physiology, its motivations and response. It has been on an extensive training program for some time now. The results have been mostly positive. This will hurry but not disrupt things. It is a dumb animal, true, but it has proven capable of responding to training, to command."

"We watched some of your 'training,' " said Kitten.

"Really?" This time Parquit showed some surprise. "You will tell me how that was managed some time." Clearly no one at the base had made a connection between a sudden epidemic of nye falling asleep on post and the presence of the three aliens. Which was just as well, even if it didn't seem useful just now. No point in revealing more than was necessary. And they might have occasion to use the same stunt again—if they could recover their pistols.

Of course, if someone got the idea of analyzing the contents of the ammunition . . .

"I fail to see," said Kitten, "how coercing the creature from point A to point B and back again is going to frighten away three armed ships. No matter how intimidating the thing is masswise."

"Our program has been far more ambitious than that, female. Clearly you did not see very much. As you will soon observe."

They were standing in the Tower. The three subs were barely visible, lying on the surface offshore. The three mammals had been offered the use of a mounted magnifier by Parquit, adjustable to human-Tolian eyesight. Tube launchers were visible on the ships, just above the waterline.

Something in the way of an escape attempt might have been tried, since the technics in the Tower were all occupied. Only the two guards the Commander had ordered to watch them every minute prevented it.

Kitten was holding an awkwardly shaped transceiver mike. The Commander's voice sounded from a speaker set in its handle, as well as from speakers around the room.

"It is time now, female. You may speak to your 'rescuers.' I suggest a brief warning. Remind that the final decision to engage in hostilities is theirs. If they still exhibit obstinacy, I will take action. Controller, open the channel."

The transceiver operator made slight adjustments to two dials, gave Kitten an unmistakable go-ahead sign.

". . . supah and Lieutenant Kai-sung. Please acknowledge our. . . ."

Kitten spoke into the mike. "Listen, whoever you are. This is Lieutenant Kai-sung."

"Lieutenant? Are you all right?"

"Present company and location excluded, just fine. My companions likewise. The Rectory received my 'cast?"

"A substantial portion, Lieutenant. Enough—before it was damped out to the point where amphi couldn't do any good. We got the newsy parts, anyway. What's all this about some kind of 'alien monster'?"

"There is one, it is alien, and it most definitely is monstrous. Your friendly local snakes have apparently trained it to—well, I'm not sure what. But the Commander here seems pretty confident about its ability to handle you."

"We've got energy screens and gelisite torpedoes that'll kill devil-fish on concussion alone at three-hundred meters, Lieutenant. We intend to have you out of there."

"Your final wordings, human?" That was Parquit's voice, breaking in.

"An accurate evaluation, snake. Now be so good as to produce the two Lieutenants and their civilian companion immediately or . . . . . HOLY. . . . !"

There was a confused scrabbling sound at the other end of the linkup.

"What's happening around them?" said Mal, eyes glued to the single magnifier. Porsupah edged him out of the way.

The sea around the three ships seemed to be boiling. A puff of white smoke issued from one of the subs, followed by similar puffs from the others. Muffled explosions followed. Water geysered heavenward in several places close by two of the vessels. The ocean heaved convulsively.

The blue-green water under the ships seemed to turn gray, then black as ink. Two massive glistening pseudopods, the limbs of some impossible amorphous sea-deity, rose out of the water on either side of the two, arching and meeting overhead. Even without the aid of the magnifier, both Mal and Kitten could see puffs of red-yellow exploding against the horror. They were carried off by the wind as though they were smoke and not the places where armor-piercing missiles impinged and shattered. Energy screens flared and died, coils overloaded. The two pseudopods formed an obscene cathedral over the crazily rocking ships, hung frozen for an instant.

Then it came down.

The waters swirled, angry and disturbed, above the spot where the two manned vessels had floated seconds before. The third was already jetting full throttle for the horizon. "Damn. Damn, damn." Kitten dug her nails against the unresisting metal of the speaker-mike, scraping the shiny tube. Porsupah remained glued to the magnifier, unable to tear his eyes from the site of the disaster. Already there was nothing to indicate that an unimaginable blasphemy had come and gone. The two submersibles did not reappear.

"Fast." That was the freighter-captain's sole comment. You've seen stranger things on other planets, more impressive, more awesome. Haven't you, Captain? Haven't you?

"That was necessary," came Parquit's voice over the speaker.

"I understand," said Kitten, "you son-of-a-bitch! Those men didn't have a chance. You knew damn well they wouldn't have a chance."

"I did not know for certain. As I said, the procedure was not yet perfected. The probability, however, was high. Despite the insufficient number and type of tests we ran. Our expectations were more than fulfilled."

"Goddamn you slimy, cold-blooded . . . !"

"Something's happening." It was Porsupah's voice. He was still staring through the magnifier. The boiling of the sea had resumed, much closer to shore. Grinding and creaking sounds suddenly poured through several speakers. The personnel in the Tower were not reacting as though this were normal procedure.

"Nova!" breathed Mal tightly, "I think . . ."

Metal moaned from one speaker, a long, basso aaahhhhh. There was a tremendous wrenching sound and the building snapped like a viol string. Except for those techs well seated at their consoles, everyone was thrown heavily to the floor. Several respectable explosions followed, shaking the structure violently.

Hammurabi had regained his feet first and was already

wrestling with one of the guards. The other one, still stunned from the fall, was groggily trying to aim his rifle so as not to hit his partner. Porsupah laid him out with a fast round kick behind the left aural opening.

None of the technics or operators seemed inclined to dispute the humans' ownership of the two energy rifles. Instead, they worked frenziedly at controls and switches. Completely ignoring the threatening aliens in their midst, they argued among themselves and with the equally frantic voices which babbled from numerous speaker grills.

"I can't follow all this," said Kitten as they backed towards the portal.

"Something's scared them," whispered Mal. "Badly. Something's running awry and they're scared. For a change, I concur with an AAnn situation evaluation. I'm scared too."

Another explosion shook the building. It was weaker and they kept their feet this time, slowly backing towards the doorway.

"Awry seems kind of a homogenized word for it," said Kitten, pointing.

Down on the beach, still visible through the transparent walls, a mass the color of space rose fifty meters into the china-blue sky. It towered above the control center and the tallest trees. The sun flashed silver on the malevolent bulk for the first time, as though strands of some bright metal ran in streaks just under the outer skin. Pieces of masonry and duralloy beaming, twisted and dangling like string, fell from the smooth sides. The thing moved purposefully from side to side, swaying slightly.

Most of it was hidden from view.

Its intelligence was no longer a matter for discussion.

Mal and Kitten carried the energy rifles. Being AAnn-size, they bulked a bit too large for Porsupah to handle comfortably. The Tolian did borrow a dart pistol from one of the guards. He led them down the stairs, again shunning the elevator, his hypersensitive hearing and sense of smell a better detection package than any artificial sensors.

Tortured screams from stone and metal followed them as they raced through turns and down corridors. The occasional AAnn they encountered was too stunned to contest their free passage and too scared to do anything about it anyway.

Still, now and then an armed guard or tech would realize they weren't where they ought to be and try to do something about it. The result was a series of brief running battles through the maze of structures. The first time she'd fired the unfamiliar weapon, Kitten had taken a bolt close enough to singe her left side painfully. Mal limped slightly on his right leg, where a shard from an explosive shell had penetrated. It was slight, but because he couldn't pause, the tiny trickle of blood from beneath the rough bandaging was continuous.

The monster was tearing the island down around their ears, and incongruously enough all Mal could think about for several minutes was that his companion was really splendidly constructed. Not merely athletic, but damned attractive. A burst of heat warmed his face. There was a short scream from a far corner where a guard had dropped. Kitten turned to look over her shoulder.

"Well done, anthropoid! You almost caught that one. I'm getting tired of nursemaiding you."

Well, at least it put his mind back on business.

"Any idea of how far we are from the harbor?" Mal yelled to Porsupah.

"Not yet. The thing seems to have moved inland with ease. So it's not restricted to the aquasphere. For all we know, it may be flexible enough to surround the entire island." The Tolian jumped over an AAnn in scientist's smock. The reptile's head had been split by a collapsed lighting fixture. Another crash sounded from behind them and a shudder ran down the hallway they were running along.

"That could have been the Tower going over," shouted Mal. "The thing's systematic enough to do that."

"Peot was right after all," said Kitten. "This thing's

as nasty as he described it. Wonder how the good Commander is making out?"

"Let's wonder about it over brandy and pastry . . . and an honest-to-gee steak . . . at your Rectory," said Mal. "And concentrate on practicalities now." He slowed up.

There was a double door at the end of the corridor. Damp gray sky and green ocean were visible through the glassite material. Porsupah ran up to it, stopped, and hurried back. His comment was perfunctory.

"Automatics are out. It's shut tight."

"Emergency circuits closed," added Mal. He raised the energy rifle. Four blasts knocked the right side of the armored doorway sufficiently askew for them to slip through. They went fast and gingerly, avoiding the hot edges.

The tiny harbor lay just ahead, down a slight slope. It was drizzling slightly, large warm drops. Visibility of the cove was poor, but sufficient.

It was a mess.

"Systematic's the word," murmured Mal. "It cut off all retreat first thing."

Docks and piers had been smashed straight down into the sand and water. Metal pilings and groinings were twisted like wire. Scraps of hoverafts and regular ships, as well as two or three hydrofoils and at least one helicopter-type were visible—including the pulverized remains of their own. The least damaged of the assorted vessels was one that had been torn neatly in half, like a piece of foil.

Dull explosions continued to sound behind them, spiced with an occasional faint reptilian scream. The slight slope and high trees prevented visual observation, a state of affairs none in the small group had any desire to rectify.

The humid mist was settling fast, but several islands were still visible. Except for the relatively empty equatorial seas, one was rarely out of sight of land on Repler.

They ran rapidly the rest of the way to the beach. Not

so much to reach it as to get as far as possible from the thing behind them. On close inspection the wreckage was even less encouraging. The destruction had been careful and thorough. Nothing was left that could float anything larger than half a man.

Even to a group as hardened as the two officers and Hammurabi, the carelessly dismembered bodies of the few AAnn soldiers and harbor personnel were unnerving. There wasn't an intact corpse visible. Here and there one could discern an arm, part of a torso, a leathertine boot with the leg still in it.

Some of the grisly debris had clearly been torn, while other pieces were sheared off as neatly as with a surgical laser.

Kitten looked back over her shoulder.

"I think I'll take my chances with the devil-fish. Maybe we can make it to that nearer island."

Porsupah was peering hard into the wet mist. "That may not be necessary. There is what appears to be a still-intact craft of some sort floating free out there. It must have broken loose when the monster first attacked and drifted away unnoticed."

"So long as it floats," said Mal, stepping into the gentle surf.

"Don't be absurd," chided Porsupah. "Excuse me." The diminutive officer dove into the water and shot past Mal like a furred torpedo, his webbed feet frothing the sea behind him.

"Waiting makes me nervous, that's all," said Mal.

"Yes," Kitten muttered, staring back at the trees. At any moment she expected to see black hell pouring towards them over the palms. "We've got to get away to alert the Rectory, not to mention GalCenter on Terra and Hivehom. This is rather more than a local problem." She paused. "I wonder how Peot is coming with his electronic jigsaw?"

"I don't care about the Rectory, I don't particularly care about the pen-pushers at GalCenter, and I especially don't care about what that revived mummy expects to do about this thing. I expect he's outclassed. What I do care about is that for the first time in ten years I've got a bank account that's more than just healthy, and by hell and damn, I've every intention of sticking around to spend it!"

"Your mind is rotten with credit pollution!" she sneered in disgust.

"You question my motives without knowing a damn thing, and—"

A cough and rumble turned their attention to the choppy water. The sound settled into a steady, low grumble. A moment later a boat appeared out of the mist, Porsupah at the left side of the peculiar double helm. It was only a small open powerboat, but it looked able to hold them all comfortably.

"Sorry it's not a raft," said Pors, "but it appears to be near full fuel-wise and not terribly difficult to operate. It should suffice to get us elsewhere—our primary concern at the moment, I suspect."

"There might be an automated way-station nearby," suggested Kitten, "where we can either pick up something a little faster or else transmit cityside."

"Our scaly friends might pick up a distress signal this close by," said Mal thoughtfully.

"If there are any left. Please, let's argue about it elsewhere and elsewhen, hmmm?"

They boarded the tiny craft. At a respectable speed only a million kilometers or so too slow, they headed out of the cove. Only fog swallowed them up.

The Vom paused in its work and considered the destruction it had wrought. It was full-fleshed, unhungry, sated on life-force, for the first time in memory. It could detect a last pocket of high-quality force on the island. It was buried in a strong chamber deep within the island itself. Content as it was, the Vom decided, after some thought, not to trouble this last group just now.

It relaxed, flowed out to a comfortable configuration, and listened. The Guardian still retained its ancient ability to blur its whereabouts. Strain as it might, the Vom had not yet rebuilt to the point where it could penetrate that mindweb. Leaving the search for the Enemy, it let its perception roam, out, free, open, for the first time since awakening, testing its revitalized neural complex.

Tiny bits of life-force impinged here, there, on its fluid consciousness. Were recorded and stored for future sorting and analysis. Great clusters of lesser intelligences flowed in the seas about the island. Not as exciting, but still suitable for assimilation and fueling.

To the north, however, there was a really respectable body of strong life-force, by far the greatest within the Vom's range of detection. It would be enough to stimulate the Vom to full, pulsating awareness. To a state of elemental power. Perhaps the Guardian would also realize this, and go there to defend. Perhaps it would not, electing to put off a confrontation still longer. Either way, it was a destination, a reason for moving. The Vom considered. It decided.

It went.

Philip was at the landing to greet them as they pulled into Wetplace. He was fairly dancing with impatience and concern as they went through the brief but necessary tying-down procedure. They'd borrowed an emergency raft from the sailor's station they'd found. Humid fog was as thick here as it had been on the open sea. Limpid drops rolled sinuously around Kitten's thighs as she stepped out of the raft. The black tower loomed indistinctly in the feather-soft drizzle.

"Kitten, Captain Hammurabi! How pleasurable to see you again! I was worried. And I have such things to tell you."

"And I have a story or two for *you*, lad!" said Mal. Together they headed for the tower.

As they entered the now-familiar elevator, Mal recounted quickly most of what had occurred since their departing. The young engineer was quiet throughout, listening attentively. In fact, by the time Mal finished the youngster seemed downright grim.

"It all fits," he said.

"Glad to hear it," Mal replied. "What fits?"

"With what Peot said."

"And what has he said?" asked Kitten.

"That the creature's power and strength grows in minutes and hours, not days. That it soon may be strong enough to resist anything Peot and the Machine can throw at it. In which case the only alternative to catastrophe on a galaxy-wide scale will be planetary sterilization."

"Whew! You said that calmly enough. Does he realize how much chance we'd have of getting Council-Chancellor approval for that?" Kitten said.

"He'd be included under such a program too, of course," Mal added.

"The concept of death in all its manifestations and aspects is one he's more than familiar with. He doubts the actuality would be more than merely anticlimactic. The possibility does not concern him. As for the other, he has some inkling of how slowly even the best non-totalitarian bureaucracy moves. He only suggests what he believes may work."

"Cheery prognosis from a potential savior," Kitten murmured.

"Still, everything is future tense. Where's your friend?"

"Pors? He's taken another ship and gone into the city to help the Major organize things at the Rectory. And to give a first-hand report. Does Peot think the monster will continue the kind of destruction we observed at the Enclave?"

"Not for a while, it seems . . ."

"Haw!" Mal snorted.

". . . at least until it has located and reckoned with Peot himself. It knows of the Tar-Aiym's presence on Repler, and . . ."

"Tar-Aiym?" interrupted Kitten. "I know that word. Peot claims to be a Tar-Aiym?" But Philip ignored her.

". . . until the Guardian is destroyed, the Vom knows it will always be in danger. It is a highly logical organism and will always bow to priorities. Finding and eliminating

Peot is first. Destruction of puny humanx resistance falls
considerably lower on the list."

"And if it lo   es our resurrected madman, naturally
it will come directly here."

"I should suppose so."

"Naturally Chatham has not been told of this."

"Naturally not."

Kitten sighed. "Well, I hope it takes its time. I'm not
sure I could take another sight of that thing without a
few days to blot it out of my mind."

Governor Washburn was very upset. He'd been forced
out of his beloved daily schedule. The Governor was a
most punctual person. This awkward diversion had already forced him to miss at least one address to a local
assemblage of parents of school-age children—voters all.
Not to mention the unveiling of the new seafood processing plant on Isle de Rais.

He'd accepted the chair offered by Orvenalix only to
hop out of it almost immediately and commence pacing
in the small office like a target in a shooting gallery.
Porsupah was an interested spectator.

"The thing is bloody preposterous! Alien monsters indeed! That's work for infantile minds. And for that you
draw me from my official duties! For—"

"I've seen the thing, Governor," said Porsupah quietly.
"It is far from insubstantial."

"So I've been told." Washburn waved a hand diffident-
ly. "Understand me, Lieutenant. It's not your powers of
observation I question. Merely the preciseness of your
description. An understandable penchant for exaggeration
induced by excitable circumstances . . ."

"It is not impossible that certain details have been
slightly exaggerated. The creature *may* have left a survi-
vor or two."

"Surely now, the weaponry we stock, even though designed for dealing with devil-fish and subsand crawlers
and the like, is sufficient to handle your 'monster.' "

"A point by way of information, your Governorship,"

countered Porsupah. "Two well-equipped submersibles from this city, fitted out with precisely that sort of equipment and manned by able men thoroughly familiar with it, were destroyed by this creature as though they were no more than dreamsmoke. I saw it. I observed gelite torpedoes and armor-piercing projectiles utilized against it. They might as well have tried to annihilate it with feathers. And the crew of the submersible that escaped does not desire a second encounter."

The Governor had another ready reply, but this time Orvenalix broke in. He waved a sheaf of faxed reports at the fuming executive.

"Perchance, has the Governor found the time to scan any of these reportings. Which have been flowing in with distressing frequency for the past two days now?"

Washburn cocked an eye at the sheets.

"I receive innumerable reports daily. Which are these?"

Orvenalix thumbed through the sheets, his pincers moving easily from one to the next.

"A minor consortium of four fishing vessels returned to the same place where per deuce-week, for the past year and a half, they have caught between four and five thousand kilos of edible seafood. Their take this last time barely was worth weighing in . . . The jet skiff *Lady Laughing* with a family of four on board outbound from Repler Harbor disappeared while headed south-southeast at latitu. . . . well, that doesn't matter. They've not been sighted or heard from since . . . Two trawling submersibles disappear in a fog off Isle Ellison . . . undersea garden of Hon. Yaphet McKnight Luttu, retired, is devastated in a single night . . . shoal of migrating stone-skippers hurl themselves ashore at Isle Royal and suffocate . . . dozens of similar sightings, reports, remarks from reliable, frightened sources, Governor. At first the tone was one of curiosity. Not now. Word gets around. Fear shows."

"On a planet as recently settled and relatively unexplored as Repler, disasters and strange occurrences take place daily, by the bushelful," the Governor replied.

"Mind, I'm not saying that your monster might not be responsible for one or two . . ."

Thranx numbered among their virtues phenomenal patience. Under exceptional, rare circumstances, it could be lost.

"Governor, semantic evasion of a problem will never eliminate it! In fact, if I may delicately point out, if you do not squarely confront this situation, it will confront *you!*"

"I do not understand, Major."

"I'll try and make it as simple as possible, your Governorship," Orvenalix pushed a laminated sheet of irradiated plastic across the desk. Tiny yellow dots glowed within the three-dimensional map.

"All disaster reports and sightings have been plotted on this chart. Both confirmed and suspected. Excluding those obviously the product of hysteria, they form a rough, zig-zagging path from the AAnn Concession towards Repler City. Since our agents escaped from there, by the way, we haven't been able to raise a signal from it, vidcast, radio—nothing. Should the line continue at its current pace, Governor, whatever is at this end of it will be here in three days. At which point you will have the opportunity to debate a question that has become purely academic!"

Washburn considered the map, considered the stocky insect across from him, considered the befurred officer sitting placidly in a corner. He slumped slightly. A good deal of hot air disappeared along with the bravado.

"I see. Yes, well, you do make some strong points, Major. Strong. Perhaps . . . perhaps some few precautionary measures—nothing extreme or alarming to the populace, you understand—ought to be carried out?" He looked hopeful.

Orvenalix sighed.

"Yes Governor. With your permission I believe I can—"

"Yes, yes, Major! Very good, excellent! I can leave the matter in your hands, then?"

"Yes sir." Orvenalix made a point of glancing at his desk chronometer. "In fact, sir, if you hurry, I think you can still make the unveiling of that new processing plant. I've taken the liberty of having a skopter made ready for you. Second deck-level. The pilot is already warmed up. If you hurry, you should make it with minutes to polish your speech."

"Why that's very thoughtful of you, Major!" Washburn relaxed, beamed. "I'll remember it, you can be sure. And now, gentlebeings . . ."

Orvenalix and Porsupah stood as the Governor left the room. When the door had snapped shut behind the planet's chief executive, both eased back into their seats.

"It is not in my crop to be angry at the man. He is one of those who refuse to recognize the possibility of their own impotence."

Porsupah looked at his superior curiously. "Do you think you *can* do anything, Major?"

Orvenalix swiveled and depressed several studs on a panel set flush into the desk. The triangular head turned slightly, compound eyes faceting the light.

"No more than I think our good Governor will make his unveiling. That chronometer is set forty minutes slow. Two things, Lieutenant. Firstly, while I believed your report, I confess to having some hesitation . . ."

"But sir, we . . . !"

"Relax, Lieutenant, relax. Understand my position. Visitations by alien monstrosities are not common in our well-organized universe. But then I received these . . ." He pushed a sheaf of reports across the table, over the map. "Following all those disaster claims, I decided to try and obtain visual corroboration. I ordered a pair of aircraft to imago the AAnn station, agreement or not. Such proof would also provide backing for any action I felt required to take—with or without his Governorship's permission. But it's better this way . . . Apparently some of the automatic weapons there are still in operation, because the two planes were fired upon. However, imagos and frozepix of the island were obtained. The devastation is incredible. Not a structure left standing, half the vegetation flattened, great gaping holes in the ground—utter chaos ...

The second thing is this. On returning, the two pilots were ordered to criss-cross the undersea route the creature is believed to be taking. Even if the thing stuck to deep water, it was hoped they might get a glimpse of it ... Only one plane returned. The pilot was completely catatonic. When he didn't respond, the controllers took over and landed the plane on automatics. The healer's can't do a thing for him. That's where he is now, in the Rectory hospital. I'm told he may never recover ... Something burned out his brain, Lieutenant. Too much input. Cerebral overload."

The speaker set into the desk at the Major's right crackled, formed words.

"Your straight-line call is now being put through, sir. Channels have been cleared. There will be a normal delay." Something beeped and the voice went away.

"Priority call?" queried Porsupah, interested.

"The nearest task force of respectable size, Lieutenant, is based on Tundra V. Further off than I'd like, but there's no reason for anything closer. And I'm not going to fool around asking for a cruiser from here, a korvette there. This requires action at the fleet level, and I intend that we shall have it!"

"A task force? But our resurrected advisor claims that any physical attack on our part will only provoke the monster to action."

"I've heard of this other. Be that as it may," said Orvenalix softly, "what else am I to do? Should I fail to defend my nest post I would be forever barred from it. I am nest-mother here by proxy. I will not sit idly by while this thing approaches and not prepare to meet it. Warning or not." There was a second beep, high-pitched, from the speaker.

Speaker and vidscreen cleared together. An elderly thranx, with curved-in antennae and chiton aged a tyrolean purple, gazed out at them. There was no hint of age in his voice, though. Although it was hazy from being bounced through at least a dozen relay stations.

"Ashvenarya here."

"Orvenalix, Major, commanding Rectory, Repler III. How are you, Admiral?"

"Let you know after you explain this nonsense about a class one emergency in your spatial vicinity requiring task-force response."

"I doubt if you'd believe it if you saw it, Admiral. Though I haven't and I do."

"So far you haven't convinced me of much, Major."

"Class one requires no explanation, sir. Even priority transfer can leak."

There was a brief pause at the other end.

"All right, Major. You're proper and correct. I'll have a cruiser and a squadron of stingships dispatched . . ."

"Negative, Admiral. Full task force, with every battlewagon you can muster. I said class one, I mean class one. Full task force, or it might as well be a complimentary card expressing best wishes for my health. Stingships haven't the firepower."

"That's the first time I've ever heard anyone argue with stingships' firepower. *That* I can use as justification. I hope you're not just knotting your antennae, Major."

"I'm perfectly sane."

"Yes. Well, the ships will be on their way to you in one hour, HH standard. And I also hope, Major, that you can back up this request to the task-force commander, or you'll be back at central student HQ doing logic terminations."

"I think I can do that, sir."

"I hope so, because I'll be commanding it." The connection snapped off.

"Sir," came another voice from the speaker, "Tundra V has broken communication. Shall I attempt to restore . . . ?"

"Thank you operator, no. Communication ended." He turned to face Porsupah. "Do you pray, Tolian?"

"Occasional meditation. I haven't the inclination for prayer."

"Then it might be an idea to find someone who does, because I can't suspend belief long enough to, either. And I like to be covered all ways."

"I've never heard a class one call before, sir." In spite of himself, Porsupah was a little awed.

"Class three's a threat to the Commonwealth. Class two a threat to the Church. Class one is a threat to the race."

"Any particular race?"

"Ought to read the Book, Lieutenant. The race of reason, of course."

The AAnn did not sweat, so the engineer's exhaustion was not particularly visible, except to another AAnn. "The transmitters still work, Excellence, Oasis knows how. And we have some emergency power."

"Thank you, Engineer First." The Commander limped slightly. His left leg had been badly bruised by a falling beam as he and the others had scrambled for the safety of the maximum security shelter buried in the center of the island.

The shelter had been built to take thermonuclear attack and anything else short of direct hit by a SCCAM shell. It had—apparently—protected them from the overwhelming fury of the monster. Perhaps thirty had survived. Thirty, out of the complex's entire complement. Thirty, plus one.

"You sure did have something you wanted kept secret, didn't you?" said Dominic Rose. The old man's talent for surviving had preserved him once more. When the destruction began, he'd stuck close to the Commander, reasoning correctly that the most important being on the island would head straight for the safest place. In a fair fight he'd have done just the opposite, knowing the AAnn. Parquit noticed he still held the slim, deadly metal case in one hand.

" 'Pears your brain-boys didn't calculate too well."

At another moment, drug or not, Parquit might have turned and with great pleasure ripped the human from throat to groin. As it was, he had neither the mood nor the inclination.

"To say we have underestimated the creature and its abilities would be an understatement of sufficient magnitude to make the Lord of all Nests shudder in his cave. We knew some of the thing's talents, yes, but little of its potential. And we believed its intelligence that of a high-order domesticated animal. We were wrong. Wrong everywhere. I confess to puzzlement as to why it does not continue on and destroy us as well. I have not the faith in that shelter some did."

"Seemed like a pretty secure sheltering to me," Rose said.

Parquit spared him a contemptuous glance, waved at the destruction all around. "For a manifestation of the normal universe, yes. Do you really believe mere metal and alloy saved your miserable life? I think it not. The monster left for reasons of its own. For which I am grateful. It gives us a chance."

He stepped gingerly over a flat length of metal that had been one of the foundation beams supporting a transparent roof. It was flattened like straw.

Parquit reached the remains of control. The Tower was completely gone, but some of the equipment in the lower portions had survived. He leaned over the engineer fourth working there. "Well, manipulator, what say you to a link-up?"

"If our orbiting station can handle the first connection and boost what's left of our signal sufficiently, I say yes, Excellence."

"And what does the orbiter say?"

"He says maybe."

"Do this thing, and I will lay first sand in your lodge with my own hands. And feed your first-born from the Emperor's preserves."

"It will be done, Excellence!"

The entity Parquit was so anxious to talk to, with the

ruins of his command still smoking about him, was named Douwrass N, Prince-of-the-Circle, the Emperor's Long Fang for the fourteenth quadrant of the Empire.

The request he made had fewer light-years to travel than that of a certain officer of the Church, but was essentially the same. For example, preservation took precedence over protection.

Prince-of-the-Circle agreed. He also questioned, for he had stronger reason than Ashvenarya.

"Your life is balanced in this, Parquit RAM. Not that that is of consequence."

"Naturally, Highness," said Parquit.

"But mine also will go under the Emperor's paw for consideration. That *is* of consequence. Yet I cannot argue with your need. I have access to the original reports of discovery of the creature and have been following your special project with some little interest. I regret its demise and that there are none responsible left to chastise properly among the so-called scientists."

"Do not blame the Passed, Highness. They were outclassed. We all were."

"Perhaps. One thing worries me, though, Commander. It is not to be anticipated that the humanx will react with welcomes and hosannas to the appearance of an AAnn battle fleet in one of their frontier systems. Not to mention a subsequent request for said fleet to use nuclear engines on the territory."

"Logical," Parquit replied. He winced. The pain in his left leg was worse. "Yet I believe they'd eventually be thankful. Not that we can expect a lower species to act in a civilized fashion. That is not the important thing. What I must impress upon you, Highness, is that the destruction of this creature supercedes everything else. There is a belief that it is somehow capable of traversing interstellar and possibly even intergalactic space. It grows daily in power. It must be destroyed now, here, before it can manifest abilities we cannot begin to comprehend . . . You may have noticed in the reports how it ignores the fury of a full laser with seemingly no ill effects. It is apparently also immune now to enormous electrical impulses and various other destructive energies."

"It was right that you contacted me," said the Prince. "Instructions will be relayed to the Eighth battle fleet to proceed at maximum displacement to Repler. I place my good hand, the Baron Riidi WW, in command. An attempt will be made by shuttle to remove you and the other survivors from the station."

"We are grateful, Highness."

"It is not a matter of gratefulness," the Prince replied sternly. "You and the others are all who remain who have observed the creature first hand. I expect it to be destroyed on the planet. Yet I must consider all possibilities, including the impossible. If feasible, your knowledge should be saved."

"It is so recognized, Highness. It is not to be inferred that I slavishly offer thanks. I shall be grateful because I should be most amused to hear the humanx not only agree to, but request, bombardment by ships of the Emperor of one of their own planets."

"I had not considered so," said the Prince. "The Axis of the Universe is Irony. Clean killing, Commander."

"Clean killing, Highness."

The Vom had arrived in the waters outside Repler City. It floated near the surface like a thick oil slick, roiling, folding in and out upon itself, feeding on the small lives of the bottom and the larger silver swimmers. In the several hours since it had made a cursory inspection of the water-front, more out of curiosity than purpose, it had been fired on by a multitude of exotic weaponry of different types and theoretically murderous capabilities. Peot's fears had not been realized, and in some ways it was worse because of that. The monster had ignored the efforts of the humanx defenders. It could take them when it wished and made the fact obvious. It was depressing.

The harborfront had been sealed off by police when the creature had appeared. The majority of the citizenry was aware only that something unusual was taking place at the harbor. A minor disturbance, perhaps a devil-fish attack. Nothing to get excited about. Go about your business, citizens.

It could not be concealed for long, however, that there was no devil-fish smashing insanely into boats and rafts and that the nuisance was in fact anything but minor. At that point Orvenalix, peaceforcer Mailloux, and the Governor would have the additional burden of a general panic on their hands.

Although it was a frightening thing to observe the monster's complete indifference to repeated assault, Orvenalix was prepared for it. Porsupah told him such would likely be the result.

What did disturb him was a related incident with more sinister implications.

While the creature was prowling half-submerged about the docks, a single shuttle was launched on its way skyward. The craft had managed to gain only a few hundred meters when it had abruptly wavered, veered crazily, and crashed into the shallow water north of the shuttleport. All inquiries from the port controller had been greeted with deathly silence.

When the full report was presented, Orvenalix ordered all shuttles grounded and those in orbit to remain there. This despite the howls and threats of merchants and citizens alike. Sure, a crash was unusual, but hardly unique. But if he'd merely lost control of his ship, the shuttle pilot should have been shouting non-stop for aid, instructions and suggestions. Or at least cursing respectably. There'd been not a squeak. The implication was obvious.

The Vom's second attempt at mental control after eons had proven as exhilarating as the first. Some slight hesitation in special cells, some difficulty in these first attempts would have been excusable. There had been none. The Vom was confident now. With a little more strength, it felt capable of assuming control of every intelligent mind on the planet.

But that would be unwise. No point unless—no, *until* it conquered a single other mind. One not of this planet. It was a reckoning long overdue, although the Vom would never interpret it in such terms.

Nor were its thoughts operating on a simplistic level anymore. Soon it would reach the point where it would not have to worry about anything at all.

But for now it could not pierce the Guardian's veil.

Something different should be tried. Possibly piecemeal destruction of this population center, while wasteful, could provoke the Guardian to some response. The Vom began to consider how it might go about destroying the city.

"Everything that can be done has been done," said Peot, staring at his ancient resting place. Mal, Kitten, and Philip stood around the towering alien.

"The Vom is now contemplating the reduction of selected portions of your central metropolitan center. This will be done in hope of forcing me to respond. It will not take place, as I plan to reveal myself to it momentarily. I regret that I have no way of predicting the eventual outcome, nor even the length of the conflict. The Machine assays anywhere from 60 to 40% chance of success. Every minute, the odds increase in the monster's favor." The alien shrugged in very human-like fashion, although it may have meant something else entirely. Or perhaps nothing at all.

"To those of your kind who still place hope in the imagined power of your tiny ships . . ." Mal jerked as he realized that the alien had been reading his thoughts again, " . . . I can only hope they are prepared to implement my final suggestion, should my own attempts end in failure. The Vom has already matured to the point where most energies are no longer a threat to it. Only by striking directly at its mind is there a chance. All, of course, is conjecture. Things may have changed. Yes, things may have changed . . . After all, the Vom itself is an indication of that."

"That's the first time I've heard you display anything remotely like sarcasm," said Kitten.

"You may be right. Final-sealing on my capsule must be concluded from outside. Young Philip has the instructions and knows what last needs be done. He has been invaluable."

"I've been called lots of things, but never that," grinned the youngster.

Peot entered the capsule, turning in the single couch-like affair to face outwards. The same straps and tubing and holds they had seen on his body when the container first opened were reattached. A few shining new devices and link-ups of familiar materials and unfamiliar construct had been added.

With Philip's help the alien began re-emplanting tubes and lines into its own body. Finished, the youth stepped back. The massive door began to swing slowly, ponderously shut. There was no click or snap. At that point Philip moved about the scaffolding which clung web-like to the capsule. He did things to hidden switches and controls, each recessed into its own concealing panel.

He climbed down from the spidery framework.

"Is that all?" asked Kitten.

The young engineer nodded. "A small light has been installed—up there." He pointed to the top of the capsule. A tiny, clear glow shone brightly, sharp against the dark metal.

"It's white now. When he makes contact with the Vom —joins battle, if you will—the light should go to yellow. If he wins it will begin to flash red."

"And if he loses?" asked Mal.

"Then the light will go out."

"I hope it's fast," the ship-captain grunted. "Being tied down like this is costing me a small fortune commission-wise. And I can't leave because that crazy over-bug has grounded all shuttles until this idiocy is resolved."

"If friend Peot doesn't win," Kitten shot back, "you'll lose a damn sight more than commissions!"

"I just don't like sitting." The massive hands clasped, unclasped. Knuckles popped like wood.

"Swell. I've got an idea. It might help."

"Anything that'll speed this up one way or another, I'm game."

"Ha! I'll hold you to that! First thing, we've got to find a decent ship. I'm sure Kingsley's got something better tied up than that toy we drifted in on. Then we go back to the reptiles' enclave."

"What the hell do you want to go back there for?"

"I've fond memories of the place . . ."

"Bulls . . ."

" . . . and I want to look for something. Backing out?"

"Oh, Deity!" The captain turned away.

"Philip? You're more than welcome."

"No thanks." He was staring at the silent capsule. "If you can do without me I think I'd best stay around here. In case *he* needs me."

"Alright awready. Do we talk or go?" Mal asked irritably.

"Keep your plane oriented. We go."

"Would it be too much to ask what we're going *for?*"

"Tell you when we get there."

"In that case, I propose a temporary delay."

"For?"

"Dinner for two."

"Why Captain! How startlingly romantic of you! I thought you swore true to your cardmeter."

"Romantic, hell. My lower abdomen confesses to feeling decidedly cavernous. The offer to share was meant as a courtesy. No affection implied."

"Charmingly put. Always face Armageddon on a full stomach. Okay, let's eat."

Sealed once more within the capsule which was as familiar to him as his own body, Peot cautiously opened channels to the Machine, kilometers overhead. The computer responded to the linkup with satisfaction. It had not felt comfortable with the Guardian out of phase, although it had bowed to the necessity.

Arranging functions to comply with the reintegrated Guardian, it prepared channels, girded circuits, primed connections. Circuits in the Machine were ultimately compact. Information passed and changes were made by changes in the number of electrons in the shells of certain atoms. An unimaginable amount of highly concentrated energy, generated by a method as yet glimpsed only in theory by mathematicians of a few existing races, was placed at standby.

Borders defining organic from inorganic levels collapsed, blended, became hypothetical. Only the Guardian Machine remained. A decision, so: The haze surrounding Peot's consciousness, concealing, protecting him, vanished. The universe jumped into focus: fine-grained, high-resolution focus. The Guardian reached out. No longer would a policy of concealment serve. The thing must be done: now.

The Guardian impinged lightning-like on an ocean of alien thought, instantly charting mounts and abysses, analyzed.

Sized up.

Leaving a reserve and a small portion of its consciousness to protect its physical self, the Vom reacted a microsecond later. It was not properly positioned for maximum response. It was, however, no longer a time for probes and feints.

A sledge-hammer force struck the Vom, smashing cells, burning out channels, screaming along unprepared neural highways like sunfire. The vast heaviness recoiled, shook, recovered.

Struck back.

Within the Guardian Machine a few linkages were shut down, organic or inorganic. A few circuits burnt out, organic or inorganic. Overload. Repair procedures took over.

There was no time for subtlety.

Two pebbles on a shore contested for the same resting place in the sand. One thunderhead sought sky-domination over another. Now somewhere one saint ascended, only to be dragged back to earth; now the other. There was to be no instant resolution to the Old Contest. Both sides knew it, neither argued it.

There were—side effects. Energy was expended and brushed aside. It had to go somewhere. It did. Things happened.

The smaller of Repler's two moons slowed, stopped, began to rotate counter-clockwise.

On Parkman's Peninsula there was a great field of Dowar flowers. In the space of a heartbeat, they turned brown and died.

In the small village of Goodnight, a tiny herd refused to give milk. Seconds later a shoal of silvery *thrad* beached themselves in a frenzied rush from the sea.

In Formantown, three things dissolved: half a pier, two crystal altarpieces, and four marriages.

On the other side of the planet in the city of Gallagher, hundreds of cats broke into the peaceforcer station and killed a third of the local force before the alarmed cityfolk, the other peaceforcers, and the local veterinarians (there were three) could drive them out.

In Repler City, every inhabitant, from Orvenalix to the Governor to Porsupah, experienced several seconds of vertigo. This continued at irregular intervals. It had a disconcerting effect on the population.

In Haven, all fell into a deep sleep. All except a small monkey-like primate from Carson's World, name of Ev Taars. A mechanic, Taars continued to work for several minutes, unaware that his six-toed feet floated four millimeters off the ground.

On the other side of the universe, a tiny intelligence suddenly expired violently, screaming. Its companion observed and commenced thoughts that would change the destiny of a hundred worlds.

The operator of the single interspace weapon on board the customs' korvette panicked and would have started shooting. Fortunately, the tracker had enough presence of mind to cut power to the lethal laser. When the gunner saw what was following behind the ship he'd nearly taken a shot at, he fainted.

The AAnn battle fleet, sixty ships strong, moved with precision into synchronous orbit about Repler. There were few commercial vessels floating in the section of space Baron Riidi WW selected. Those that were there elected to move rapidly elsewhere. The intruders made no hostile gestures. Yet it was apparent to experienced merchantmen that the AAnn warships were not there for pleasure. Formation told them that, formation and the fact that this many AAnn vessels had not been seen together since the last humanx-AAnn conflict.

The special shuttle bearing the Baron and a select company of scientists and commandos entered atmosphere, dropping slowly towards the planet circling below. The inhospitableness of the globe was clearly illustrated by incredible bodies of water, thick masses of moist air, and tropical vegetation. The Baron felt unusual sympathy for the local commander. Under the best of circumstances this would not be a pleasant place to be stationed. Put conservatively, it was a hell-hole.

Yes, any questions of failure or incompetence here would have to take into account the horrible climatic conditions.

A Communicator Second entered the luxurious main cabin, saluted.

"Sir, the flagship gives word that the Governor of the humanx colony has attempted another communication."

"I believe I instructed Captain Elbraack to relay the standard message about indisposition of forces, technical difficulties, and the like."

"Your pardon, sir, but Captain Elbraack advises that he has been doing precisely that. He informs that the Governor declines to acknowledge all such attempts."

"Then what is he complaining about? We have a

standoff. I told the Captain that I do not wish to be
bothered until I have had time to evaluate the situation on the ground. I suggested one method of doing
this. Inform the Captain that if he feels he is incapable
of handling the situation without running to the communicator like a newborn hatchling at every small difficulty, I will be happy to replace him with someone
who feels otherwise."

"Yes, Baron." The communicator hastily backed out
of the room, forgetting to salute.

Riidi did not call the nye back. On some ships in the
Imperial Navy, forgetting to do proper obeisance to a
personage of Baronial rank would result in a short ses-
sion at the hands of the paingivers, or reduction in
class. The Baron was notorious among his equals for
disciplinary laxity. This and other idiosyncrasies should
have seen him ridden out of the Navy long ago. There
were, however, a number of ameliorating factors, not the
least of which was the fact that the Baron was brilliant.

Not particularly genius-brilliant, but natural-smart brilliant. He had the ability to absorb a great deal of information, reduce cogent facts to pithy solutions, examine
and evaluate all alternatives, and do the Right Thing.

He was a good reptile to have in a tight spot. This
made him valuable enough to survive most of the petty
jealousies which some claimed had held the AAnn back
more seriously than all the actions of enemy races.

The landing was made with practically no help from
the ground, since the Enclave's survivors hadn't been
able to scrounge much of the proper equipment from the
wreckage. Despite intensive battle training, the pilot
wasn't prepared for so much mist and moist fog. Moreover, the island was a tiny enough target in clear weather.
The landing was thus predictably rough, but Riidi said
nothing. He was content to have landed on dry land.
Although on this planet, he reflected, there really wasn't
any such.

The officer who greeted him had a haunted look about
the eyes. But his bearing was still straight, his tattered

uniform correctly aligned, and natural dignity subsituted for a lack of pomp and ceremony. He was flanked by two junior officers, each of whom had that same haunted, distant look. There was also a single elderly human.

Riidi was not surprised. The Commander had informed him via transceiver to expect the mammal.

Parquit saluted smartly. "Glory to the Emperor's line. His servant awaits you." The Baron returned the salute, muttered, "Glory." His salute was sloppy and brief. Already his eyes were taking in what was left of the Enclave. Taking in the twisted metal, the shattered foundations, not missing even the pulped vegetation, massive tree-trunks snapped off at the base.

"One creature did all this." It was not a question.

"One creature," said Parquit, staring at the Baron. The noble's gaze returned to the Commander.

"And you had nothing to stop it?"

"Baron, we tried everything, following the initial surprise. All our weaponry had no effect on it whatsoever. Nor did some small but powerful humanx devices."

"Ah! The locals have had belligerent contact with it also, then?"

"On a small scale, as far as I know. Yes. The contact was brief." Parquit made an effort to change the subject. "How soon can the nye be taken off? There are some in need of extensive medical care. I could have submitted them to a humanx infirmary center, but such was unthinkable, of course. The wounded concurred."

"Of course. What of your personnel elsewhere on the planet at the time of the attack?"

"There were not many. Away from the Enclave they were forced often to experience the local weather. A punishing duty for even a short while."

"I can well imagine." Riidi sniffed the moist, sticky air with distaste.

"The last returned this morning. They were recalled gradually, so as not to provoke awareness of anything unusual among the humanx populace. Such precautions are no longer necessary since you have arrived. The

Consul himself, of course, will remain in the capital until the situation has been clarified."

Riidi noticed the human smiling at him, paused.

"And what of this grinning primate, who finds the occasion so amusing?"

"A local. A drugger and trafficker in many things. Bloodhype, for one."

"I am that," said Rose, feeling it was time he said something. "Got a goodly sample of my wares with me, too." He held up the lethal case.

"What interest have you," asked Riidi, "with such as this?"

"Ploy and counter-ploy, sir. With the result that he has my word of safe conduct off-planet to a point of his choosing. Like all vermin with a talent for survival, he is basely intelligent."

"I think I understand, Commander. I prefer thinking of the situation that way, rather than trying to envision you making a voluntary agreement with such. Where is this monster now?"

"When it became clear we could not resist the creature, an ultra-high-frequency emergency signal was transceived to our scattered personnel. This drew them back to us. Until they arrived with their ships, we had no proper receiving equipment for local castings. Judging from what we have been able to intercept since then from the Rectory and receive from the Consulate, the creature appears to be lying just offshore the capital city itself."

"Which could complicate the procedure of bombardment," said the Baron.

Parquit glanced at Rose. "Yes, Baron. The prospect does not bother you, human?"

"Nothing to endear me to this clump of earth." The old drugger shrugged. "Unless . . . maybe I shouldn't leave here after all." He looked thoughtful.

Parquit was so surprised by this announcement that he momentarily forgot the Baron. "You have changed your mind, after all you have gone through to assure your safe leaving?"

"Naw. Just a crazy thought. From what I've been able to worm out, it just might be possible to communicate with the thing, somehow."

"What makes you believe that?"

"Well, it seems pretty clear to me that it can detect thoughts of other intelligent beings. It sure knew what you were up to. All your fancy equipment and all probably wasn't even necessary. Bet it would understand you if you just thought at it. Seems to be practically invulnerable. Sure, the thing turned on you once. Doesn't mean it's all-over evil. Might just have been defending itself, frightened, or uncertain, or who knows what? Properly approached in an unconfined situation, like now, it might prove docile enough to handle."

"Do you not realize," began Parquit, "that the monster deliberately carried out a complex program of deception? That it waited until it felt ready to break free?" The Commander made a sharp, angry gesture. "Is *this* the work of a potentially docile creature? I think not."

"Mebbee not. But the idea of controlling a thing as powerful as this has a heap of appeal. Even if the association was set up on an equal basis, say."

"An arrangement at best worse than uncertain," said Riidi in clipped tones. "Besides, the thing is not, as the Commander states, apparently inclined to friendly discourse. And we have no evidence of this unique invulnerability you speak of beyond the original records of the first expedition."

"But it is!" the drugger protested. "Ask your own people. You should've seen it, with lasers and torpedoes and all bouncing right off!"

"Yet we have no permanent confirmation," said Riidi, seeming to waver slightly. "I cannot risk recommending a single nye without more than verbal proof to present to my superiors. Not even that of my own subordinate." He looked pointedly at Parquit.

"Look, with half a chance I'd take it myself," said Rose. "Some day, but not today. But there *is* concrete proof. There was a special recorder going the whole time. I saw it activated and it never stopped until the thing broke in."

"You are observant," conceded Parquit. "Indeed, I set it myself. Yet it was smashed in the general destruction, I fear."

"You're crazy! It's back in the shelter, right where you left it. A big dumb-bell-shaped affair."

"You must be mistaken," said Parquit. "Yet your description is accurate enough."

"You must be blind. It's setting there still, I'll bet."

"Could you find it?" asked Riidi. "The Commander seems to believe it does not still exist."

"Sure I can get it."

"Do so, then, and I will see you receive proper recompense. The records themselves will be invaluable. Yet we cannot remain here much longer. You have," he glanced at a chronometer, "four time-parts." The Baron turned to face Parquit. "If the human is right, you will suffer for it."

"Baron, I . . ."

"We've got a bargain, then," said Rose. "I'll be back in two." He whirled and headed back into the ruins.

Parquit waited til the human was out of sight, then turned back to the fleet commander. "My thanks, Baron."

"Thanks are accepted, if not necessary. Not where the subject is mere vermin control. Your suggestion worked well. He is blinded by greed and thoughts of power."

"You had him thinking too fast to be reflective," said Parquit. "As to your own instructions, shall we return to the ship?"

"If all your people are boarded by now, as planned."

"Yes. I regret the need of treating such as *that* with such elaborate planning. Yet the drug he threatened us with requires the most delicate handling. Once released, we would have had no second chance. I am relieved to have it out of my sight."

"I understand," the Baron said. He turned and led the way back towards the shuttle, Parquit keeping pace at one side. "And now we come back to the problem itself. And the simple question of a possible interstellar conflict neither party would wish."

"I would suggest following the official conversation with the Governor with a private one involving the local military leader. He is sufficiently prosaic, enough to countenance the bombardment if convinced of its need."

"I wish it so," replied Riidi. "If this creature gains in power as rapidly as you imply, it should be destroyed as soon as possible. If it can be arranged, such action must be taken with the approval and agreement of the vermin authorities. If such is not forthcoming . . . well, the red sand blows where it will, Commander, where it will."

Rose heard the muffled growl of the AAnn shuttle when its engines caught. He turned and ran without thinking. After covering a few meters, he slowed and stopped. Such exertion was not good for a man of his age. Nor practical. So he watched quietly as the AAnn vessel made a perfect lift-off and rose on a pillar of yellow-red waxen fire. It disappeared into the comforting clouds.

He permitted himself a few choice cuss words. Actually, he was more unhappy at being outfoxed than being left behind. That lizard had set him up perfect and he, Rose, had been picked off clean and clear.

He brightened abruptly. If what the snake had said was true, then he wasn't completely marooned here. There should be some sleek Enclave hoverafts and maybe a foil-skipper or two tied up in the ruined harbor. The ones that those scattered diplomatic personnel had returned on. If just one held a fair amount of fuel, it wouldn't be impossible for him to make it back to the capital.

Once there—well, the same trick worked on different folks. The death he toted was very democratic. And there was another possibility, interesting in light of his prospects for the future. If the AAnn chanced across him again he'd be incinerated without thought—if he were lucky. With a complete record of his drug-running and other illegal activities, the humanx were unlikely to greet him with rosewater and lemonbeef. Nor would his colleagues in the underworld consider him a safe risk anymore. Even his friends would consider him too hot to help.

There remained that other choice. He'd only flippantly meant what he'd said about attempting a single-mind contact with the monster. Given his other chances, the idea took on a certain reckless appeal. Perhaps it *had* bolted off in a sudden snit. Maybe it *would* be amenable to some form of control or direction. Or if it were as intelligent as it seemed, an alliance? Rose spun thoughts inside-out, the reverse of small spiders. Such power! Ain't it worth a try for such a prize? Always do the unexpected, old man! You're running out of alternatives. The law of averages is ready to prosecute. Take the sun-risk, side-pockets, take it!

You're gonna die soon anyway. And there are plenty ready to give you a hand—down. Bootstraps, old man, bootstraps!

He realized the decision wasn't entirely sane. But it was made. So the creature was lying offshore the capital? That would take care of the usual commerce patrols. He would go there.

Perhaps all it took to make comprehensible contact with an evil-minded being was another evil-minded being.

He began walking towards the harbor. The laugh that bubbled up out of him was a little too high and went on a little too long.

There were a few standard hoverafts—and the big cargo waveskimmer. Deity knew what the AAnn, who hated water-contact, did with an open-decked craft. But it would take a beam or shell better than the lower lying, thinner-hulled rafts. And its tank was three-quarters full. It was a locally built craft and not an imported AAnn device, so the controls were familiar. The foredeck had been built up even higher to keep out any hint of spray. Even so, it would get cold up there.

The thing was built for long jaunts. He'd have a margin

of safety in the tanks that a raft couldn't afford. No point in making it to the city and stopping dead in the water. He'd like the option of further travel. It would be fast enough.

The Vom and the Guardian fought.

On certain levels molecules were badly battered. There was a change due and both sensed it. The Vom could not tell how or when, but it was still jubilant over the arrival of the AAnn fleet. For this was one way it had traveled between worlds, on the ships and backs and minds of other races, chained to the Vom-self. Chained.

Kitten piloted the hoveraft over a mild sea. Whitecaps sparkled like citrine in the early morning sun. The mist was burning upwards and it would be clear and bright soon.

If he weren't involved in an impossible series of events culminating in an absurd search, Mal might have enjoyed the sight. He wasn't hungry, nor tired, for the first time in some while. He longed wishfully for the routine and peace of a normal trading cruise, light-years from everything. He was just about fed up.

"Look, Kitten. I've been dragged through this once before. Government secrecy or no, dammit, this time I'd like to know what I'm getting into before it up and smacks me in the chops."

"Okay, we're looking for . . . you remember our late friend Rose?"

"I'm afraid so. What about him?"

"I never saw him without that case of bloodhype on the AAnns' island. He never put it down or let go of it for a second. I'd guess he slept chained to it." She was staring straight ahead, speaking softly. "I think it's safe to assume it'll still be with him."

"Sure . . . wherever the body is. You should pardon the sentiment, 'so what?' Are you so concerned about collecting evidence for a posthumous prosecution? If the case is still intact and unbroken, it'll stay put. The government can recover it anytime," he concluded.

"Don't you remember what Peot said?" she continued. "About the monster not being affected by energy weapons? What about biological ones?"

"You're kidding. The thing is utterly alien. And too big."

"As far as we know, bloodhype's nearly a universal drug. And as far as the thing's size is concerned, you know what a milligram of that powder can do. What about a few kilos? According to the reports, the monster ingests its food and expels practically nothing in the way of waste products. It's a super-efficient metabolic factory . . . Hitting or shooting the creature with the powder could have several effects. Open, it might be absorbed immediately. That would be ideal, of course, since the powder would go into the thing's digestive system rapidly. Or the powder might be ingested first, without the case."

"Or," interrupted Mal, "the monster might ignore it entirely. In that case the effort wouldn't be just useless, it'd be suicidal, because the thing's sure to notice the shooters. And if the powder were released at the wrong time, we'd be likely to get a pretty good whiff ourselves."

"I still think it's worth a try. Chances are we won't be able to dig the case out anyway."

"Agreed. But I'm beginning to see that no one's going to leave this planet until that thing is destroyed. And I've about as much confidence in the peaceforce at Repler City doing that as I do of finding that case."

"Then why let it upset you?" Kitten smiled.

Mal was staring hard out the glassite port. He moved to a swivel-mounted viewer, stared a moment longer. "I think we'll have to revise our guess about everyone in the Enclave being killed."

"Oh? What is it?"

"Unless this viewer is badly scratched, I believe our case, with friend Rose still attached, is coming to meet us. Yes, without doubt."

"Damn the man!" She actually stomped her foot. "How is it that such people are always the ones who manage to survive?"

"Carrion-eaters grow tough with age, Kitten. Hardly a new revelation. He'll pass us portside soon." He cut off and grabbed for a chair as Kitten threw the raft into a screaming turn. Clouds of spray flew meters high as the fans hit the water at an angle, threatening to turn them over.

"We'll catch him," she said grimly. "We're faster than he is. Where does he think he's heading, anyway? We'll be in city waters in five minutes. Doesn't he know he can be shot on sight?"

"He knows where he's heading. If he's still got that case of powder with him and if the wind's right, he could try and blackmail the Governor this time. Once it gets in the air there's no way to fight the stuff. You couldn't treat the whole population soon enough any more than you could get them all into pressure suits in time. The city couldn't take that kind of epidemic. Let me see if I can raise him on 'cast."

Mal made a few adjustments on the transceiver. "Wave-skimmer, waveskimmer. Hoveraft behind you. We are closing. Please respond, you bastard." No answer. "Doesn't the old idiot know the Vom is around here somewhere? There are easier ways of committing suicide."

No picture, no response. "You're in a maximum danger area, Rose! Wake up!"

Static; scratchy voice. "I know, Hammurabi." The on-board computer matched frequencies and the voice cleared. "I'm bright-eyed and bushy-tailed, to use an archaism better suited to your Tolian tagalong. Tain't dangerous for me! I know what I'm about."

"Crazy," Mal whispered to Kitten.

"Not by half, boy! I seem to keep running into you lately. Bad luck for both of us. Klashing Karmas. You alone?"

"Lieutenant Kai-sung is with me."

"Call me that once more," she murmured, "and I'll break your head."

"Listen, you touchy . . . !"

"My, my, dissension, dissension!" Rose's tone was mocking. "I am in desperate straits, I see clearly. Why not wise up and try a profitable, predictable life in subtle evasion of accepted convention, Hammurabi?"

"And be secure in my old age, like you? Huh-uh, Rose."

"Have you got the drug with you?" interrupted Kitten, unable to hold off any longer.

"My life-insurance? You must be joking."

"We want it," said Mal. "We want you, too, but I'd be willing to pass over that if you turn the stuff over."

"I've already had one offer pulled back on me. I don't think I'm ready to try the same again so soon. Let me think on it a mite. I've always been a gambler. I've still got a few chips left."

"Convince him! You're supposed to be the salesman!" Kitten whispered. "We're getting too close to the city." The computer indicated the shrinking distance between themselves and the island of Will's Landing, on which Repler City had been built.

"I've no time to argue with you, Rose. Turn about and hand the drug over and I'll see . . ."

"No good, Hammurabi. Sorry, lad. If this works out and you change your mind about me, I might give you a job as a taskmaster."

"Taskmaster?" Mal whispered to Kitten. "He *is* crazy!"

"See, lad, I know a good bit more about this monster than you think I know. I even know more than you think I know you know. I believe some sort of agreement wherein I supply, oh, locations of certain storehouses, general information, military advice and so forth might work out to mutual benefit. This thing has wants. I don't know how well it reads minds yet, or when."

"Listen, old man, you're asking for a quicker death than any you'd get from your own kind. There's more at stake here than your life. Or ours. Turn the drug over and forget any insane ideas you've got about trying to ally yourself with the alien. You won't even make a decent-sized snack."

"You haven't got another choice," Kitten added.

"How kind of you to be so solicitous of my health, little bird." He paused. "Your urgency intrigues me. You want the drug but are willing to let me go. What are you going to do, go into business for yourself?" he sneered.

"We think it might have some effect on the monster," she pleaded. Mal looked at her approvingly. This was a new act. It had appeal.

Rose only found it amusing. Or perhaps he found everything funny now. He laughed openly.

"You ascribe too much power even to jaster! Now if *you* were to personally guarantee my safety . . . off-planet transportation . . . immunity from prosecution . . . why, I might, just *might,* consider it."

"I . . . I can't. Not with *you.* With what you've done. I can't promise that for others."

"Ha! You see?"

"No, wait, wait!" Her face was taut. "Mal, see if you can raise the Rectory. There might be a channel open. I think the Major would consent to the bargain."

"You're really going to try and make a deal with that old scum? After what he had done to you? After what he was *going* to have done to you?"

"Don't make this any harder than it is, please!" She looked at him and this time it wasn't an act, no.

Mal adjusted the transceiver to tune in to any open Rectory frequency. "That's the first time you ever asked me a favor instead of threatening or blackmailing your way into it."

"Oh, shut up."

Expectedly, Orvenalix wasn't available. Kitten got him available.

"Well, Lieutenant, things are certainly interesting around here." He twitched his antennae in a motion indicating thranx sarcasm. "How does *your* garden grow?"

" *'Ple astwin nirer, hyl.'* Quite contrary, taking in certain cogent points." She explained the situation.

"I've linked up as you suggested," came Rose's voice clearly. The multiple hookup was crude, but would serve. "Tridee also. No tricks, now."

"You know who I am?" asked Orvenalix.

"My guardian angel? How could I help but know you, Major? You've cost me a lot, in the past."

"Would that it were more. I shall concur with the Lieutenant's recommendations in all respects."

"Swear by your hive-mother, the Queen, and your larval corridor."

"Done," said Orvenalix, after rattling off a long string of ancient thranx no one could understand. They apparently satisfied Rose, however.

Orvenalix betrayed none of the fury he must have felt. Restraining emotions as strong as that would drive many humans mad. Such emotional control was accepted matter-of-factly among the thranx.

"For all, uh, past discrepancies as well?"

"All that I have jurisdiction over. You'll have to take your chances on other worlds. I have only so much authority. You're stretching it now. Turn over the drug."

There was a long pause during which the only sound from Rose's end was that of the wind eddying across the pickup.

A sigh. "Oh, well, all right. It was a long-shot idea anyway. I think I was over-rationalizing for a while, there."

"He's slowing!" Kitten shouted, switching her gaze from the raft 'tector to the port.

"You honestly think that bloodhype will have any effect on that monster?" asked Mal.

She looked past him, at a spot on the far wall. "Maybe not. But I don't think anything else will either, except maybe what Peot can do. If that fails, you know the alternative. The drug has to be tried."

Rose slid over into the lee of one of the innumerable tiny islets that speckled Repler. They were so close to the city the towers of the central business district could be seen clearly.

"Have the case ready," instructed Mal over the comm. "And no tricks yourself. I'd as lief break your neck as make money."

"Impressive warning! Tricks, from *me?* Insults! I'm now an honest man, absolved of past sin. Didn't you hear? As clear of conscience and . . ."

"Pious, isn't he? Enjoys rubbing it in."

"Ready to convert, no doubt," said Kitten. "The man leaves a sour taste. To let him go free like this—that damn drug!"

"I'll try not to do anything crazy, like busting him one. Remember: Phrases of Import and Salvation, The Book, Chapter IX: 'To be angered by evil is to partake of it . . . stupid.' "

"You're a student?"

"I've read some of The Book. Who hasn't?"

They pulled alongside the waveskimmer. It rocked gently in the slight swell, engines idling. Mal could see Rose strapped into the pilot's seat on the high foredeck. Kitten cut their own engines and he glanced back at her. "Want to do the honors?"

"Every time I set eyes on that person my faith in humanity drops several notches. It's rock bottom now." She swiveled in her chair. "At least the case is intact. No drug, no pardon. You do it."

Mal grunted, took a step towards the door. When his foot came down, the floor wasn't there anymore.

The deck dropped away from under him, bounced up at a different angle. Mal found himself tumbling head over reason. The far wall turned into a ceiling, came up too fast. Dazed, he struggled to his knees while the ship played cocktail shaker around him. Several loud clangs sounded from the rear of the raft. Kitten screamed. He turned in her direction.

She was still strapped into the pilot's seat, silhouetted

against the gray sky. A jet-black curtain shot through with silver was shutting out the light. The blackness that finally overcame him was of a more familiar variety.

Down in the abyss of its vast consciousness, a miniscule portion of the Vom-mind noted the incident. It was recorded and filed for further attention. It could not be spared time for follow-up or evaluation. Not now. Worlds were at stake.

On some parts of Repler, iron changed unnoticed to gold. And on at least one island, to copper. Then back again. Fish of a hundred different varieties schooled, forming unnatural association.

A small, peaceful crustacean reeled under the impact of an intelligence boost of a hundred thousand times. It was immediately gobbled by a torpid bottom feeder.

The second moon, which continued to spin counter-clockwise, abruptly lowered its orbit a hundred kilometers.

Repler VI and VII were both gas giants. They began to break up, responding to titanic internal convulsions. Great clouds of ammonia and methane flew off like cotton into space.

On a large island, a snake-like reptile was trying to slither from one branch to one on another tree. Limbless body, straining. A force capable of destroying continents acted. Another pushed and lifted. A nanosecond of conflict. The pseudosnake leaped, missed. Fell and died. It was more important than an exploding gas giant or mass-scale transmutation. The killer knew it. The lifter knew it.

A rock spoke. The temperature of the sun rose, fell, rose again. There was a sudden high tide with no moon in the sky. Moral considerations aside, it was apparent that the Vom
    was winning.

With the resources of half a million years of accumulated knowledge and power, the Guardian-Machine fought back. But it had waited too long. Its power was finite. It could not grow as the Vom was growing. Too strong, too quickly. Miscalculation. The Guardian-Machine foresaw disaster.

The Vom was stronger now than it had been even when the Guardian was first activated, millenia ago. The stimulus of battle forced it to grow exponentially. It would forge another empire dedicated to, constructed for, one purpose. The perpetuation and greater glory of the Vom. There would be no mistakes this time. No under-estimation of an opponent. The Guardian must be rendered permanently inactive. This time the Vom would not abuse its life-resources. The small intelligences would be assimilated carefully, to insure continuation of a healthy ecosystem. No wanton consumption. Feeding would be judicious, entertainment and experiment well reasoned. It would . . .

Something struck the Vom elsewise. Something strange, new, unaccountable, and utterly undetected aforehand. It was raw strength, more powerful even than the Guardian-Machine, but not as mature, as sophisticated in the use of power. It was different and it showed. It fought unrelentingly, uncompromisingly, openly. It fought mathematically diverse and helically perverse.

Unemotionally the Vom retreated, countered, struck back. The counterattack rebounded. No victory; no defeat.

The stalemate was resumed.

A hundred parsecs away a quartz pebble (not very good quartz, but honest quartz) blazed momentarily with the light of a thousand suns. There were none around to appreciate it. The light died, but the pebble lived.

Stalemate.

"Well, what is it, Hanover?" Ashvenarya said gruffly. It would not have been proper nor seemly for a thranx to be upset this far from action, but the Admiral was tense nonetheless. Given the peculiarities of the situation, he felt it justified.

"We are within influence of the system, sir. The fleet is going off KK drive and . . ."

"I know that, lieutenant. The flagship went off it nearly thirty minutes ago and I should damn well hope the others followed suit. Get to your point."

"Sir, there appears to be another fleet already in orbit around the planet. Since we've received no official notification of another major force in this sector I thought . . ."

The admiral was already running for the lift, rubbing at his bad compound eye with silicon-treated tissue. The lieutenant had to move awkwardly, running every few steps. The old sector commander was moving on all four legs.

"You retain information like a machine, Hanover. Which is one of the reasons I keep you as aide. Egg knows there're few enough. You're quite correct. I ordered no other ships sent to Repler and there aren't any other Church or Comi nwealth forces close enough to be here before us. Whici leaves one alternative. Whoever mans those ships is neither human nor thranx. I admit that's not logical either, but then nothing about this situation has been so far."

The lift carried them to the bubble nexus suspended in the center of the battlewagon.

"Preliminary evaluation?" Ashvenarya barked as he floated smoothly down a rampway.

"The distance is still substantial, sir, and we have the sun full in front. Ship's predictors read thirty-nine confirmed, with at least twelve probables. Battle-fleet class, sir."

"Tunnels! Now I have this to worry on, too."

"I confess surprise, sir, that the commander of the local garrison did not try to warn you via interspace of this fleet's presence."

"Orvenalix is a capable officer, Lieutenant. I don't doubt he didn't because he couldn't. Or he might have tried and been jammed, coerced, shot . . . we swim in ignorance for now."

They entered a gravity lock, slipped slowly and easily into free-fall. It wasn't true free-fall, being rather a state in which artificial gravity was negated. Something like swimming through thin gelatin. The complex state, difficult to maintain, was generated only at the center of the ship, its battle headquarters and flight center. A military secret as fanatically guarded as the mechanism of the KK SCCAM weapons-system, the field would protect them from everything but complete power loss or direct hit.

"For another thing, lieutenant, he might have feared the AAnn would pick up and decode a message that might precipitate action."

"You suspect them then, sir?"

"They have a naval base of considerable size nearby. I know of few other races cohabiting this section of space that could mount a force of this size, even if they had the time to assemble them from across the Arm. Anyway, I would assume it to be our reptilian compatriots even were this a small force. With a fleet, I think the question becomes academic."

"Do you think they may already have . . . ?"

"No, no, lieutenant. Were that the case, we *would* have heard something."

Churchmen of many races, with thranx and human predominating, saluted smartly when the Admiral floated into the battle center. He returned them easily with a truhand while heading rapidly for his combat basket. The lieutenant took up his own post nearby.

The old Commander had run a thousand possibilities and alternatives through his mind while conversing with his young human aide. The thoughts itched. Incidentally, he reflected that Lieutenant Hanover might metamorphose into a fine commander someday. Despite the mask of fawning innocence he occasionally chose to wear, the lad was sharp as a sting. The mask was well-crafted, too. Another point in his favor. But he still needed honing and a lot of hard prodding in the imagination. He ought to receive plenty of both, this trip.

"Communications! I'd appreciate it if you'd try and raise the flagship of our unknown visitors."

At that moment a frail-looking thranx seated across the center, looking as much a part of his instrumentation as a computer terminal, turned slightly in his harness.

"By remarkable coincidence, sir, I have this very second acquired a signal which appears directed at us from the formation in question. I envision a confluence of objectives."

"Spare me the philosophy and put it through."

An elderly reptilian face, haughty and proud, white-scaled, appeared on the big screen over the commboard.

"His munificence," began the official herald, "the Baron Riidi WW, Ruler of Torsee Provinces, Executor of . . ."

"Spare me the titles this once," Ashvenarya broke in, "and put your commander on."

The face froze. "Proper diplomatic courtesy demands that . . ." The admonition was interrupted by a strong offscreen voice. It hissed surprisingly little for an AAnn.

"Never mind, herald." There was a brief flicker and another reptilian face appeared on the screen. It was sharp-featured, almost handsome, proud. The gaze was piercing. "Whom have I the pleasure of addressing?"

"Admiral Ashvenarya, Fourth Sector Commandant, Humanx Commonwealth, operating under United Church charter and I'll skip a few titles of my own. A little out of your regular bailiwick, aren't you, Baron?"

"And you too are here with so many ships for rest and relaxation on the pleasure-world below, Admiral?" The tone was mildly reproachful. "It remains that a threat to the entire galaxy lies on the planet below us."

"Would you be referring to a certain amorphous black monstrosity of unknown origins and, from what I am told, rather considerable powers?"

"Unless you know of another. As I guessed, our purpose here appears to be the same, then."

"Not quite, Baron. That's a humanx colony orbiting

below us, and my presence here is perfectly natural. Yours, I fear, remains open to certain questions."

The Baron affected an air of outrage. "No action of any sort was contemplated without the prior concurrence of the local authorities."

"I'd like to believe that, Baron. Indeed, I'd like to believe that. For many reasons."

"Not the least of which, Admiral, is that we are of no use to our respective races if we battle among ourselves, *fya?* If you will merely contact your commandant below —a Major of the Church name of Orvenalix, I believe— I've no doubt he will agree to the course of action I have in mind. I offer a joint council of war, not a declaration of one."

"I think we might struggle along without your help," the thranx admiral replied.

"Sir, the commander of the Imperial Enclave on Repler had the opportunity to observe this creature's strength at closer claw than was desired. This as his own station was being pulled down around his oculars. He would not agree with you. I myself inspected the ruins of his command. *I* do not agree with you. Were you to have seen the same, I venture to say you would not agree with you. In fact, I would hope that between the two of us we *may* be able to control the monster."

Ashvenarya considered. Briefly.

"Perhaps. Very well, I trust you—from microsecond to microsecond."

"My own extends no longer."

"Our ships will move into orbits confluent with yours. While I determine upon a course of action you will take no action on your own. This must be understood."

"Understood," replied the Baron placidly. "Only, please not to take overlong, Admiral, or our agreement will become strained . . . by time."

"It might prove that a joint action of some sort is required, much as the thought distresses me."

"I have little love for your kind, either, Admiral." Teeth flashed. "Under normal circumstances . . ."

"Which these are definitely, conclusively, not." Ashvenarya waved and the contact was broken.

Despite the violent attack levied by a new and completely unexpected opponent, the Vom found cause to rejoice. A second fleet! More strength to complement its own! It could now travel from planet to planet in almost respectable fashion.

For possibly the ten thousandth time it tried to analyze this new power arrayed against it. About the Guardian's mental attitude it had no qualms. The Guardian-Machine had been and would be an implacable opponent until one of the two ancient enemies was destroyed.

But what of this new factor? Could it mayhap be persuaded into a realignment of forces for mutual benefit? With a galaxy at stake, the Vom was willing to share. Or could it at least be convinced to withdraw from an ancient and private conflict, leaving the way clear for the Vom's victory?

The Vom reached out again and made contact. What it encountered on a non-combatant level was surprising. This second opponent had not even fully matured, had not mastered its own power! In its probing the Vom must take care not to stir latent abilities, hidden secrets, not to upset the balance of internal power. The potential here was frightening.

In fear the Vom nearly backed off. But after determining that the being could not read the sub-surface layers of Vom-thought, it returned to the contact, expanded it.

(curiously: dialogue on a Different plane)

WHO ARE YOU?

(picture contact nee verbal/concept sub-vocalization)

A TRANSPARENT ORCHID : SUNSPOTS ON LEAVES: STAMEN AND PETAL: SLOW FUSION

(rejoinder)

AND YOU, MONSTER?

(arrow-straight conceptualization)

GREAT VOID : VOIDNESS? : ANGRY VACUUM

: DARK EFFLUVIA : MALIGNANT MIASMA :
CANCER MUSING : OLEAGINOUS OLLAPO-
DRIDA

(pause)

WHY DO YOU FIGHT ME?

YOU ARE EVIL

(confusion/introspection/analysis)

EVIL? THERE IS NO EVIL

IT MAY BE SO. BUT THERE IS WHAT IS COM-
MONLY RATIONALIZED AS GOOD. YOU
ARE CLEARLY NOT-GOOD. A GOOD-NEGA-
TIVE. YOU TRY TO RATIONALIZE EVIL.
CHAOS!

(consideration/thought/tacking)

FIGHT ME NO MORE AND I WILL MAKE YOU
MASTER OF HALF THE GALAXY.

THE GALAXY HAS TOO MANY MASTERS AL-
READY. NO.

WHAT CAN I OFFER YOU?

YOUR DEATH.

(anger/arrogance/disbelief)

COMPLAISANT COMPLIANCE? SURRENDER?
ACQUIESCE? INTRODUCE NEGATIVES INTO
A SUPREME FUNCTIONARY NEGATIVITY?
NEVER!

SEE? YOU *MUST* DIE (strange voice)

I CANNOT DIE : I WILL NOT DIE : I DO NOT
KNOW HOW TO DIE

THEN I MUST HELP YOU TO LEARN

The Vom terminated contact. With all its shadings and
half-tones, the entire conversation had taken perhaps a
few seconds.

The strange opponent possessed a self-confidence that
conflicted with its lack of self-knowledge. Maybe, the
Vom considered, it was fighting on too personal a level.
Possibly an exterior demonstration would have some
moral effect.

Using its fully matured mind for the first time beyond the battle, the Vom reached out . . .

On board the humanx flagship *Zimbabwe,* instruments died with suddenness and finality. The eerie blue-green of the local emergency lighting flickered on a moment later.

There was little panic in the nexus. After all, this was the nerve-center of the fleet. The personnel were the class of each rating. So there was no hysteria.

Things went otherwise on some other ships.

"Communications, all ships report status. Hold position, hold fire. Commodore, damage report. All hands to battle stations."

The replies came thick and fast.

"Communications, sir. All intership comm units, including storage and backup facil . . ."

". . . no visible damage or shorting, sarge! It's crazy . . . !"

". . . ities on all ship channels inoperable. Emergency backup systematization totally inoperative, Admiral."

"That's impos . . . ! Status report!" Ashvenarya accepted the situation and changed in mid-sentence.

Again, quick reply.

"All communicators down to hand-units inoperable. Engineering reports central KK drive unit shut down for sub-light as well as supra-light capability at 0954.4 shiptime." The communicator's tone changed to one less officious. "That means the whole ship is in free-fall status, sir."

"Going to play havoc with the housekeeping. What else?"

An engineer was bent over a heavily instrumented console. He was checking dials and meters against a computer readout. A muscle twitched nervously in his neck.

"All exterior and numerous interior systematizations report dead, underpowered or inoperative, sir. Computer indicates conjunctive causation. With the exception of basic life support and non-offensively oriented interior emergency functions, the ship is effectively immobilized."

"Dead, you mean. *Kyash!*" Ashvenarya swiveled his basket to face the human Commodore. The *Zimbabwe* was, after all, his command.

"Do you think the shuttles and lifeboats will operate, Moorea?"

"They're all self-contained, of course, sir. But even assuming that whatever has affected the ship has spared them, the bay doors and release mechanisms are ship-powered, so . . ." Moorea shrugged helplessly. "We can utilize abandonment methods, true, but . . ."

"No, I'm not ready for that yet either, Commodore. I want no precipitous action here. KK storage cells don't just go stale like honeyfrye, nor do emergency battle power-backup systems for communications and weapons complexes die while their life-support counterparts continue to operate. We are the subjects of a selective attack procedure of unknown power and undeniable effectiveness! . . . Lieutenant Hanover!"

"Sir?"

"There ought to be several ways of contacting the other ships of the fleet. We're orbiting tight and close. Try mirrors, wave handkerchiefs. I'm not particular about how you do it. I've got to know if ours is an isolated case—it's not inconceivable that we are the victims of some local spatial phenomena—or if, as I suspect, everyone else has been hit the same."

"Aye, sir." Hanover left his basket and commenced pulling himself via hand and claw holds to the nearest lock. Since the gravity for the ship was supplied by KK storage power when the vessel was not in supralight space, the ship was in full free-fall. The lock had no purpose now.

"Oh, and Hanover!"

"Admiral?" Hanover exerted pressure on a bar near the lock, floated steady.

"See if you can help the dispensary personnel, Doctor Furman and Surgeon Lee and the others, get organized. They may need some extra help. Authorize whatever they need. Going from .91 gee to no-weight as abruptly as the rest of the ship probably did, there'll be a lot of men who lost more than just breakfast."

"Yes sir." The Lieutenant turned and pushed off, disappearing like a feather down the lock-tube.

"Well, Moorea?" The Admiral's antennae twined in frustration. "No crystals of wisdom to offer?"

"I didn't think the AAnn had anything like this, Ash."

"Don't bet that they do, Pat, don't bet that they do. I dearly hope that, if it's not a natural occurrence, the AAnn *are* responsible for this. The alternative scares the sugar out of me. And I haven't been that frightened, Pat, in a long, long time."

On board the heavy cruiser *Sanderling* not too many hundreds of kilometers away, his munificence Baron Riidi WW was expressing similar sentiments, in which Admiral Ashvenarya figured prominently.

Mal's head cleared with surprising speed soon after he opened his eyes. He stared upwards and was confronted with the badly bent roof of the hoveraft. Pushing against the hard *pecces* behind him, he struggled to a kneeling position. By leaning on the outcropping for support he managed to inch his way to his feet. He stood there, holding on until most of the dizziness had passed. At about that time he became aware that *pecces* was not a normal fixture in Replerian hoverafts.

Encrusted with shells and barnacle-like organisms, the sharp spine of the reef projected a good meter and a half through the floor.

There was a moan forward. It was followed by some weak, if highly imaginative, cursing in feminine tones.

"You all right?" he queried.

Kitten tried to swivel the pilot's chair, failed. The pivot ring was jammed against the supporting metal. She unstrapped herself, moving with slow, pained gestures, and staggered towards the foreport. It had shattered on impact. Cool seawater lapped gently against the bottom of the sprung doorway. A small crustacean was already inspecting this new addition to the reef.

Except for a slight list to the back and right, the raft was fairly level. Mal took a step forward, nearly toppled. He put out an arm to grab a bar projecting from the near wall and noticed idly that it was stained red in places. Looking down at himself he was surprised to discover that the red came from a broad but shallow gash across the right side of his chest. He'd lost a lot of skin but not much blood. He ripped material from his left sleeve to bind the wound. Fortunately, the bleeding had nearly stopped.

"See anything?"

"We're on a reef," she replied. "Rose's waveskimmer is jammed up in front of us. Part of it seems to be under our bow. Probably what's causing our listing. What's left of the skimmer, anyway. It's in much worse shape than we are—not that this is seaworthy, either. Looks like he took the brunt of the blow. Bottom's been ripped out."

"Any sign of the monster?"

"Looks like it's lying just under the surface of the water. Right about where the reef ends, which isn't far enough away for my liking. Funny how peaceful this all is. The reef runs out about another twelve meters past the skimmer and then seems to drop off sharply. From there on as far as I can see the water's black as ink, like you could walk on it."

She left the port and moved back to the doorway. Mal moved up behind her as she stepped gingerly from the raft. Bracing a hand against each side of the doorway, he saw that the *pecces* itself lay barely ankle deep, even protruding above the water in several places. The Vom claimed his attention almost immediately.

Mal felt as though he were standing in front of an armed SCCAM shell. "It may be intelligent enough, but it sure doesn't seem to notice us."

"We don't know how it perceives things," said Kitten as she picked her way over the uneven, slippery footing. "For all we can tell it might be paying all its attention to us. Waiting to see what the lab animals try next, I guess.

Since it could have killed us at will before I don't think it intends to. Yet." She turned. "You're higher than I am. Any sign of the old bastard?"

Mal leaned out, hooking an arm around the doorway. A brief spell of nausea, then the sea air cleared his head completely. Peering around the front of the uptilted raft, he could see the top of the waveskimmer easily. The bottom of the bigger ship had been shaved off as neatly as though with a laser. It lay tail up, part of its curved bow just under the nose of the hoveraft.

A recognizably human figure was strapped motionless in the foredeck pilot's seat.

"Looks like he wasn't thrown free. Seems to be light-out, though."

"Any sign of the case?"

"Sure is. It's still chained to his right wrist. Appears to be locked firm. All the jerking and wrenching around didn't tear it loose."

"Is he alive?"

"Can't tell. He's sure not preparing violent resistance."

"He'd better be alive. Otherwise it's liable to take us days to figure out how to open that thing. You can bet it's armed or full of acid or something. We haven't got days. What are you doing?"

Mal had carefully edged out around the edge of the doorway. It wasn't a long fall but the surface was sharp and inhospitable. The air cushion around the base of the raft was thoroughly shredded. There was, however, a ridge of metal running the circumference of the ship. The smooth sides of the craft made walking on the centimeters-wide strip difficult, but the captain's bulk belied his agility. He started edging towards the bow, pressed flat against the side of the craft.

From the bow it was only a short hop to the canted deck of the skimmer. He walked over to the motionless drugger, felt the thin wrist. The pulse was strong.

"He's alive, anyway! Can't say I'm as glad as you seem to be."

He moved to the side of the ship. Leaning down, he extended a hand the size of a battle helmet. Kitten paused, then walked over.

"Deck is slippery up here, too," he said. "That little walk was tricky, but faster than trying to improvise a ladder or rope. This is quicker yet."

He enclosed her right hand in his while her left grasped his wrist. She practically flew onto the deck.

"You're as physically complete as you look," she murmured.

"Apelike, you mean?"

"Let's not, now, hmmm?" She walked over to Rose and spent a couple of minutes examining him while Mal looked on. After a bit she flipped open a small compartment in the side of a belt and selected from a small packet one of several tiny ampules. It was no bigger than the nail of her little finger, but she handled it carefully.

There was a bare spot where the trousers had been ripped away. Gray hairs showed on the tanned leg. She jammed the ampule hard into the middle of the quadriceps.

"What did you shoot him with?" Mal asked.

"Dexatrinabuline. Emergency dosage. He'll come around and be hyperactive for about an hour, after which he'll sleep for another fifteen and then wake up good as new—unfortunately. It works fast."

"Sure does," said the drugger, sitting up. He glanced rapidly about the waveskimmer, then down at the wrecked hoveraft, finally out to sea. His eyes settled on the black reef that was the Vom.

"Nothing expansive," he said. "Just a little tap to inconvenience us. Maybe we . . ." He reached down and rubbed his thigh. "That was quite a jolt of whatever it was you gave me. Don't recognize it offhand but I've probably sold it."

"It wasn't done out of concern for your health," Kitten said grimly. "Now, how does one open that case of yours—without getting poisoned, burned, shattered, or otherwise 'inconvenienced'?"

"Now, why would you want to know that?"

Mal reached down and grabbed Rose's right shoulder. He could feel the bones and wiry muscles under the cloth. A slight pressure, so, and Rose winced.

"Okay, okay! No need to get tough. There's a solid gas-air pattern charge inside the shell that blows the case apart but doesn't affect the contents. You arm it by pressing this lock button, here . . ." he indicated a slot for a magnetic key, ". . . and then grip the handle. There's a trigger built into the handle underside. Once the keytab has been pressed and the trigger cocked, when pressure is removed . . . wham!"

"How long?" asked Kitten.

"When you press the keytab down, you turn your thumb to the right as far as the tab will go before letting up. That'll give you up to sixty seconds before the blast. More time than that wouldn't be practical."

"Not much time to get away," said Mal.

"It wasn't designed to be anything but a last-resort-type threat. Planning a little blackmail with it yourselves, mebbee?"

"If it can be placed against the creature," Kitten said, "chances are good that if detonated or absorbed the monster would take in enough to affect its system. It shouldn't be impossible. The thing can't be more than half a meter below the surface."

"There's a small lifeboat on the back of this skimmer. There was one on the raft, too, but it's been replaced by a hunk of reef. The draft should be shallow enough so that the Vom will ignore it."

Mal prodded the drugger's leg. "What do you think? Could the drug do anything?"

"Who can say? The Vom—that's its name, eh?—is an unknown quality. But this amount of bloodhype,"—he indicated the case—"is a unique gathering, too. Sure be an interesting experiment. Of course, if the monster does absorb the case and the drug, it might also absently ingest the boat and boatman."

"An admitted complication," said Kitten. "One that I

can't see a way around. We'll just have to chance it. Unhook the case from that wrist chain, please."

"You can't be serious, pretty-pretty! The idea's insane! I feel duty-bound to protect you from yourself. I don't believe I should let you have it." He clutched the precious container possessively.

"Unlock the chain," said Mal quietly, "or I'll simply detach the whole arm."

"You argue persuasively, Captain." Rose bent over and did something to the connecting links. There was a sharp click and the case was free.

Mal hefted it in one hand. "Very light, for so much death." He turned and walked towards the rear of the skimmer. "Give me a hand with the boat, Kitten."

"What makes you think you're going?"

"For openers, I can row faster, harder, and longer than you. I might have a chance of making it far enough back to the reef to escape. You wouldn't."

"What about your precious credit account, Captain? There's neither profit nor percentage in this for you."

"So I'm mentally erratic, like you say. Besides, Repler's always been a profitable stopover for the *Umbra*. I'd like to see the suckers live a while longer."

"I can accept your rationale," she replied. "But don't expect me to be ladylike about it."

"Kitten, I wouldn't expect you to be ladylike about anything." He turned to unfasten the braces holding the tiny boat. The blow that hit the back of his neck was very clean and carefully judged.

"Well struck!" applauded Rose. "I admire your work. Can I give you a hand with the boat?"

"The day I need to ask for your help I'll just sell my soul outright. Mortgage and all."

"As you wish. I will need yours, then."

She turned and straightened slowly, staring at the object in his hand.

"That's interesting," she said evenly. "You have a gun."

"Yes. It's not much of a gun, of course, but it'll handle

one person. I didn't think it would take the both of you. Not the way the Captain moves. So I decided to wait a bit in hopes of a better opportunity. I never expected you to be quite this obliging. Just goes to show. If you live right . . ."

The small boat rocked gently in the blue-green water.

"Where do you think you're going in this teacup?" she asked. Her eyes never left the muzzle of the tiny pistol.

"I'm going to try and skirt the edge of that thing. That should allow me to try out a crazy idea I might as well have a crack at. If it doesn't shift out, I ought to be able to slip into the city without being noticed. Current'll help with the rough work. At that point I'll have a number of options open. You'll excuse me if I don't elaborate. I don't think you'd be sympathetic. Right now, I'm arming this toy."

Laying the gun aside—not far enough aside—he set the keytab and tied down the trigger securely with a piece of cord.

"I can slip the knot on this fast enough if I have to. Gonna need both hands for steering. Anybody takes a potshot at me, either I'll release the trigger manually or shoot it loose. Either way the drug will be released into the atmosphere. As soon as I get close enough to the city, rest assured I'll do my best to stay upwind. You might as well stop staring at the gun. I'm not so feeble I wouldn't beat you to it."

He lowered the small air-compression motor into the shallow water.

"And now, my lovely-love, I bid you good-bye." The sea bubbled like soda-water around the stern of the little craft. It moved slowly off along the edge of the reef, careful not to stray over the Vom.

Kitten stared for a moment, sighed deeply, and walked back to where Mal was sitting on the deck. He was rubbing the back of his neck. He did not look happy.

"Well, I'm sorry, already! I told you not to expect me to be ladylike about it."

"Congratulations." He looked around suddenly. "Well, where's the case? And where's the old man?"

"Uh, considering that you didn't see anything, you've summarized the situation neatly." She pointed out to sea. The small boat was now a good many meters off, still chugging slowly along the reef edge. Soon it would round the first spit of the island and be lost to sight.

"Well now, how did you manage that?"

"He had a gun."

"He had a gun," Mal replied slowly. "Why didn't he pull it before now?"

She turned away. "He said he was waiting for a better chance."

"Well, he sure got one." Mal struggled to his feet and walked forward. He looked back at her and booted the instrument console something fierce. It did not improve its shape.

"That's not going to help anything, you know," she said.

"Maybe not, little girl, but it does wonders for my primitive, ignorant mind!" He booted it again.

"Oh, act your age, Captain! I . . ." She paused, looked past him.

"Well, don't stop now. What . . . ?"

He turned and stared in the same direction.

A considerable distance off, a small figure standing in a boat was flailing its arms frantically at the air. Towering on two sides of the figure, like the walls of a canyon, were two night-black nightmare shapes not quite as big as a pair of good-sized shuttlecraft. Their descent was graceful, almost ballet-like. Unconsciously, Mal had slipped an arm around Kitten's waist. This time she didn't move it.

"Was that a scream, there?" Her voice was even, but there was the slightest tremor to it. She was remembering an earlier time on another island.

"I think so. There! An explosion?"

"Maybe. Maybe . . ."

They waited anxiously. The halcyon sea recovered. The small boat was gone.

Needless to say, the small figure was too.

Kitten let out a long breath. "Well, I guess it wasn't a very good idea after all." She slipped gently out of his grasp and peered over the twisted railing of the skimmer.

"I think we ought to try and wade off the reef to the island proper. We can come back for blankets and supplies. It's bound to be warmer inland than out on these wrecks. Besides, they're liable to be pulled off the reef when the tide comes in. I don't fancy being dumped into the surf at 2 a.m." She slipped easily over the edge, hung by her fingers for a moment and dropped lightly into the shallow water. Her knees bent as she took the impact.

A tiny portion of the entity that was the Vom reacted to a foreign ingestion. A minute portion of the food did something odd to a few cells. The strangeness was communicated to the Vom-mind. The reaction extended. A group of cells were suddenly disoriented. At their center, neural deracination took place. Idly, then more attentively, finally in a state of real concern, the Vom sought to isolate the farrago. Some cells were by-passed and not affected. Others were . . . not *harmed,* but disoriented on an increasingly massive scale. They became incapable of performing their proper functions.

Synaptic connections were deliberately broken in an attempt to seal off the infection. The attempt failed. Had the difficulty been enzootic, the Vom might have controlled it. But it seemed to strike at random points, unpredictably. The difficulties this caused were not irreparable, but at the height of battle they were a disaster. A small portion of the Vom-mind was forced to shut down. The creature's power was noticeably weakened. The Guardian-Machine and the Other sensed it, pressed harder.

A whole quadrant of projection cells died before they could be shuttered down. The Vom quivered in pain, sending huge waves crashing across nearby islands, smashing through the brush and sweeping away small lives.

NOW (said the Guardian in a roar of triumph)

YES, NOW (came a quietly grim thought from the Other)

Hopelessly, desperately, the Vom fought back. Despite frantic repair and isolated control, the infection continued to spread. But the Vom's resources were immense. It was beginning to slow the disaster. It might yet contain the threat, survive, hold, rebuild, counterattack. It might . . .

A double-section of power-cells suddenly collapsed, unable to supply the awesome demands on their substance. An edge, a point, a limit had been reached and passed, and the Vom went over. Slowly, then with increasing speed.

It was a new sensation for the Vom. Sections of self died around it. The mind was partly but not wholly detached from the physical process, even as it fought back. When it felt realization that finality was about to occur, when death convulsions shook the ocean floor around it, it cried out a last appeal.

STOP! : CONCESSION! : I ABJURE POWER!

(the Other did not reply. the Guardian-Machine did)

THAT IS NOT OF YOUR NATURE : THE UNIVERSE DEMANDS YOUR PASSING

(Guardian-Machine and Other struck again)

Perceptions took on strange colorings for the Vom. Another new sensation. A last new sensation.

(a final observation. brilliant light boiling away consciousness as though the soul water was)

(then. . . . .)

DISSEMINATION

(long-thoughts were space-scattered)

DISSOLUTION

The great organic capsule broke into a thousand pieces. A thousand-million. And more.

(conclusion)

DISSIPATION

The trillion bits of no-vom broke down to the molecular level. Then the sub-molecular.

DEATH

(an empty conscious chaos lost the binding wire of thought. return to nothingness)

DONE! (said the Guardian, half in wonder, half in contentment)

It sought out the Other, said simply . . .

THANK YOU

NOT NECESSARY

(said the Guardian in reply . . .)

YOU PLANNED THIS : YOUR CONCEALMENT : YOUR TIMING OF ALL : YOUR MOMENT OF ENTRY : ALL PLANNED (statement of fact, not query)

YEA AND VERILY (then, curiously) WHAT WILL YOU DO NOW?

WHAT WOULD YOU SUPPOSE I WOULD DO?

(pause) I THINK YOU WILL DIE

THAT IS WHAT I SHALL DO : IT WILL TAKE A LITTLE TIME : ANY PART OF I-MACHINE CAN BE SHUT DOWN RAPIDLY ENOUGH : TO SHUT DOWN THE MACHINE-I WILL TAKE A LITTLE LONGER : I WILL SHOW YOU THINGS BEFORE THIS IS DONE

I THANK YOU FOR THAT AND THAT THANKS YOU CANNOT REJECT : I HAVE POWER : I MUST ACQUIRE WISDOM

THERE IS MUCH WISDOM ALONE IN THAT THOUGHT : SO IT SHALL BE

YOU NEVER FEARED DEFEAT

I WAS NOT CONSTRUCTED TO BE SO IN-CLINED : NOT TRAINED TO : NOT A RACIAL AFFECTATION : THE VOM'S FATE WAS IN-ELUCTABLE

Mal set Kitten down gently, then dropped out of the tree to stand next to her. She drew her hair behind her with one hand, used a small piece of elastic plastic to bind the long wet strands. He was staring at her.

"Please, spare me the cracks about 'drowned kittens,' will you?" she said.

"Don't worry," he replied, mopping at his face with a sleeve. He was equally drenched. "I'm too tired. Damn lucky thing that first wave was as small as it was. Some of those later ones could have piled us into the rocks. Did you see anything?"

"Only a glimpse here and there. Mostly I was too busy holding onto that branch."

"Quite a sight. One second it was thrashing around like a loose ship-drive, smashing *pecces* and throwing up great gouts of water and sea-bottom. Then it seemed to sort of shudder lightly. It just fell in on itself and dissolved like black sugar." He removed a soggy boot, dumped a trickle of water out of it.

She shrugged. "Funny. I'd kind of expected something a little more spectacular after that build-up. I don't think it made a sound the whole time we were watching it. A violent, quiet end to everything. I wonder if we'll ever find out where it came from?" She was shaking water from the bottom of her blouse.

"Almost everything," he said cryptically. He took a step closer and gently placed a palm between her shoulders. She had just enough time for one quick, startled look as he shoved hard sideways, at the same time sitting down on a water-soaked but serviceable log. She folded neatly across his knees.

Keeping his left arm firmly across the small of her back, he lifted his right leg and hooked it over her left thigh. The resultant pose was classic, if undignified.

Kitten made a firm, sudden shove upwards, frowned when no give was forthcoming. Bracing her hands on the damp ground she pushed harder. She might as well have been trying to push her way out of an armored hunting cage.

"All right, Captain Hammurabi. My sense of humor is

departing swiftly. If you wouldn't mind letting me up . . . ?"

"If you'll think back a moment," he went on easily, "you'll recall that just prior to agreeing to make a certain jaunt with you to a certain Enclave, with certain suicidal desires in mind, I made you a promise. You may remember the substance . . ." She struggled harder and much less scientifically now.

"Striking an officer of the Church can be ruled a capital offense!"

"I'll take that chance, Lieutenant. But I keep my word and my promises. It's good business practice. I'll risk a restraining term. This won't take long. I suggest you strive to consider the philosophical aspects of the situation. You're good at that."

The ship-captain's palm had the seeming consistency of solid duralloy. The Lieutenant's often violent protests for the next several minutes of measured activity were of a nature far removed from anything philosophical.

Mal sighed and looked over to where Kitten was leaning against a tree. He made an adjustment on the small communit he'd salvaged from the ruins of the waveskimmer. He'd modified it to throw off a long-range homing signal on a widely used distress frequency. It would continue to cast for about an hour before the powerful little battery would burn out.

"Will you sit down? I didn't hit you that hard." He smiled. That produced several minutes of withering silence. "Suit yourself. You deserved it. It's been said, Book III, Chapter 21, 'Maturity is not a function of age.' If you're bent on proving otherwise . . ."

Kitten looked down at her feet. She'd been scratching abstracts in the still-damp island soil.

"It is possible" she began hesitantly, "that a certain small amount of that . . . that . . ."

"Eleemosynary chastisement," Mal offered.

"Whatever you choose to call it." She strolled over. "A certain amount may, just may, have been justifiable."

"If I'd given you what you deserved," he said, "I'd still be at it. But I decided to be charitable. And besides, my arm was getting tired."

"I can imagine," said Kitten, smiling slightly. "This one, wasn't it?" She touched his right shoulder.

He looked at her curiously—until she leaned forward and bit him good and hard above the right bicep.

He tried gently to detach her. She wouldn't let loose. Hammurabi's grandfather had spent his childhood in the slums of Bajallsa Port, one of Terra's greatest and dirtiest shuttleports. The teachings he'd passed on to his grandson were effective and unconventional.

Mal leaned over and bit her back.

She broke away in surprise and shock, rubbing her injured shoulder.

"Damn you, Hammurabi! You're no gentleman!" She lunged at him, her right arm coming around in a side chop. He caught it in one hand, did the same when she tried to counter with the left. She tried to bring up a knee but he spun her around and pinned her tightly against the tree.

"You're hardly a lady, Kai-sung."

She kissed him. After a moment's hesitation, and after she laughed at him, he relaxed enough to kiss her back. But he didn't let go of her hands.

When Porsupah arrived with a harbor launch, his cogent evaluation of the situation caused Kitten to chase him three times around the island. The diminutive Tolian was still laughing as they pulled away from the reef-free side.

On board two very different flagships, both commanders and many crewmen (or crewnye) turned from a discussion of their sudden return of power to view a tiny nova. It had appeared just around the planetary horizon. An omphalos of thermonuclear fire, it outshone even Repler's sun for a few seconds before dimming out. In its brilliance, the small flare on the planet's surface went unnoticed.

Fully aware that a confession of impotence in the face of probable bellicosity was not conducive to advancing one's career, both commanders agreed to keep the whole incident as quiet as possible.

Both moons were down as Porsupah reeled along the docks that edged the section of Repler City favored by visiting non-humanx.

His reflections were colorful if not clear. For such a small mammal, his capacity for fermented spirits was remarkable enough to draw comment from the uninitiated. He'd been granted a month's leave, local time, and was concluding the third day of a spectacular drunk. It was unmilitary and unChurchlike. But after hearing details, Ashvenarya himself had given the three of them leave to commit anything short of murder, and maybe that too, if they were discreet about it.

He gleefully recalled Chatham's face when the old miser had seen the crater that had replaced his precious island. Their crazy alien ally had done everything in an expansive way, including committing suicide. What a fantastic succession of facial changes when Ashvenarya had authorized complete rebuilding at Church expense!

Kitten and her hirsute merchant captain were off on some far island committing things of their own. The Tolian was happy for both. Now, if only one of his own kind and opposite sex were available to help him properly enjoy a few mild indiscretions. What he wouldn't give for the sight of a well-combed tail! He sighed, then frowned. His superlative sight was supremely out of focus, but it reported enough to tell him he was among unfamiliar buildings. He'd apparently wandered far from the entertainment district and the full bars into a rundown section of ancient warehouses and storage sheds that might have been built when Repler was first colonized. Several bore condemned signs. One pathetically declared that a new pleasure-pier was to be constructed here. The jungle began a little distance away. He was on the far fringes of the city.

Well, fine! Hail the intrepid explorer! Now where were those damned supplies? He took the small container of powerful liquid from his belt and downed a sizable swallow. He, himself, would dedicate the new pier now and beat all the pompous, arrogant, frog-faced politicians to the privilege! He staggered towards the water, halted against a wooden wall when his balance threatened to horizontalize him.

A tall figure strode out from between two long, boarded-up warehouses. The face was hidden, but the rope-shape coiled around one shoulder moved slightly. Even in the dark and drunk, Porsupah couldn't mistake it. He rubbed his eyes blearily, which only made things worse.

The figure halted at the edge of an ancient boat landing. It did something to a concealed mechanism. Porsupah giggled, burped violently. Apparently he went unnoticed.

A monstrous bulk heaved itself out of the sea close by the pilings. It blotted out much of the night sky. A few lights shone from the cylindrical nose. The faintest lavender iridescence was visible far far down the main body, hundreds of meters long.

A brighter rectangle of light appeared in one side of the vessel. A small platform floated out. It approached the pier, riding a barely audible basso hum. The tall human stepped onto the platform, standing behind a huge hairy alien Porsupah could not identify. The vehicle returned to the main ship the way it had come, the square of light disappearing behind it.

Porsupah staggered away from the wall and stumbled back in the direction he'd arrived from. Three days, *wasya*, three days! Long enough to start seeing things, hey? Want to fall out of a tree someday? KK-drive ships did not come within a thousand kilometers of planetary surfaces. The direst penalties would befall any who survived the cataclysm of their own making.

KK-drive super-battleships especially did not do this. They double-especially did not make secretive stops to take on board single apprentice sanitation engineers. No, no, down with the booze, already, *schuzz?*

Wait a minute! Down with booze? What blasphemy was this? Sacrilege! And over a simple dream-dream?

The hell with it. Heading for brighter lights and a chaser, Porsupah broke into an uneven but rousingly risqué Tolian ballad.

Behind him, the great ship lifted silently toward the stars.